CW01647699

Deadly Lies

Ann Girdharry

First published April 2021
Second edition published July 2021

Chapter One

'Wake up, Ronnie. There's someone in the house.'

The terror in his wife's voice woke Ronnie like a drench of water. He jerked upright so fast he pulled a muscle in his lower back. Ronnie's automatic instinct was to reassure Joan it was probably nothing and he was about to do just that and to tell her he'd check it out when they both heard a noise coming from downstairs. It was a dragging sound. Something about it made Ronnie go cold.

His mind flew to the grandchildren. They were asleep in the room down the hallway.

'It could be Lisa or Emily,' he whispered.

Joan violently shook her head. 'They don't get up on their own. They would have called if they needed the bathroom.'

Ronnie glanced at the clock. It was 2 am. She was right and the sound downstairs wasn't child-sized.

'Lock yourself in the en suite and call the police,' he hissed. 'I'll check it out.'

Joan grabbed Ronnie's arm. He pushed her away gently but firmly.

'I know the girls are the priority, I promise I'll get them first.'

As he swung his legs over the edge of the bed, Ronnie felt a stab of pain in his back. Sure, he was out of shape and since retirement several years earlier he'd been steadily putting on weight. Back in the day he'd been an amateur boxer, and he'd be damned if he was going to be frightened in his own house by some bloody intruder. Perhaps one of the grandchildren really had wandered downstairs. Maybe it was nothing. But that wasn't what his instincts were telling him.

Ronnie padded to the door. He stopped and listened, straining every nerve.

It had been his wife's idea to have the grandchildren sleep over every other weekend. At first Ronnie had been reluctant. He'd never devoted much time to being a father, and being a grandfather felt awkward. Then as time wore on, Ronnie realised Joan was right – the grandchildren were fun. For sure he'd never get to like children's films but there was something special about cuddling up on the sofa with a bowl of treats and two excited little girls. At some point, Ronnie had started looking forward to the grandchildren's visits. He used to be a hard-nosed businessman. Now he browsed children's videos and bought kids' games – things he'd never done for his own daughter. He even got Emily and Lisa's bedroom decorated exactly the way they wanted it – with matching pink bedspreads and a pink plush carpet and a lilac monstrosity of a dresser.

Standing in the gloom, Ronnie couldn't hear a thing. He tiptoed along the landing to the grandchildren's room. A couple of night lights glowed at floor level. He'd put them in because Lisa, the youngest one, was scared of the dark. Scanning the beds where their shapes should be, his heart pounded. Ronnie ran to Emily's bed, flinging back the duvet, desperately hoping she was snuggled inside. Nothing. He scattered pillows and the cover of Lisa's bed, smelling the children's sweet scent from their nightly bubble bath. Empty.

Ronnie shouted and ran along the hallway. He almost fell down the stairs and regained his balance by grabbing at the banister. At the bottom, he jabbed for the light switch. The downstairs hallway was flooded in yellow, just in time to see a person in black heading out the door, with one child bundled under his arm and the other being dragged behind.

Ronnie bellowed with rage and charged towards the front door. 'You fucking bastard!'

'Emily!' Joan shouted.

She hurled a vase and it smashed against the wall. *Joan,* thought Ronnie, *she didn't hide in the bathroom, she's right behind me.*

Blood pumped in Ronnie's ears drowning out his jagged breaths. Now he was in the night air and the security lighting outside the house didn't flash on. Ronnie jumped the two steps to the ground, the gravel of the driveway digging into his feet. Outside the house, a vehicle stood with doors open. He saw the intruder toss Lisa onto the back seat and Emily was fighting against being pushed in.

'Granddad!'

The sound which then came out of Ronnie's mouth was raw with fury. He yanked at the passenger door and as the man turned to face him Ronnie swung out his signature right hook. There was a satisfying crunch as it clipped the intruder on the side of the head. Ronnie followed up with his left hand and felt his fist impact the man's belly. Air gushed out and the man doubled over.

'You bastard!' Ronnie screamed.

And that's when Ronnie felt a pain so intense he was paralysed. It shot across Ronnie's chest and down his left arm. Trying to draw back for another strike, instead Ronnie's limbs were powerless and the intruder slipped from his fingers. Ronnie landed on his knees and the man kicked him in the stomach.

As the pain tightened across his chest, Ronnie watched through a mist of red. Joan was at the vehicle, trying to drag Emily out. Then his wife screamed. Ronnie was on the ground and he did his best to crawl back to help. *Move* – he commanded himself, but the pain in his chest was too intense.

All he could do was clutch at his own body and struggle to draw breath.

The back tyres spun, scattering stones in his direction. There came the roar of the engine as the car, and his grandchildren, disappeared out the driveway. Ronnie landed on his face in the gravel.

Chapter Two

Detective Chief Inspector David Grant didn't usually respond to Superintendent Fox within seconds. In fact, he made it his business to wait a good few moments before answering her calls simply on the principle DCS Fox wanted everything done yesterday. Then again, Superintendent Angela Fox's calls rarely came at three o'clock in the morning. The two of them had a prickly professional relationship though they never let it get in the way of the real work.

'It's a child abduction, David,' was the first thing Fox said.

Hot sparks like electricity skittered across Grant's back. It snapped him awake. A child abduction. The case most senior officers dreaded because the stakes were so high. Grant excelled at tough cases and this one sounded like one of the toughest.

'I want you to handle it. I need my best on this one and it's going to take at least three hours for me to get back from this damn conference I was dragged to,' Fox said. 'And in those three hours… well, you know…'

Yes he did – anything and everything could happen. With an abduction, the minutes after the event were vital. It would be up to him to allocate resources properly. He must prioritise actions on the go. He would have to be razor sharp and pinpoint the perpetrator's weaknesses because the likelihood of finding victims declined rapidly, starting from the time of a kidnap.

Grant grabbed his clothes.

'I'll be back as soon as I can. Don't mess it up,' Fox snapped.

One minute she was hinting he was one of her best and the next Fox was biting his head off, it was typical of the Detective Chief Superintendent. Grant rolled his eyes.

He didn't waste a second. When his wife stirred, he shushed her. Grant had been a top detective for over twenty years and his wife was a true copper's wife. Likely she'd be back asleep within minutes.

Speeding across town the roads were deserted and Grant jumped the lights. Street lamps picked out dark houses and damp, deserted streets. Three o'clock in the morning was the graveyard hour – when drunks had gone home.

Fifteen minutes later, DCI David Grant arrived at a suburban street in the expensive end of town. Here, the houses were set back from the road, with front entrances big enough for several cars. He noted how most properties had burglar alarms and security features.

Slowing the car, Grant approached a uniformed officer. Crime scene tape blocked the entrance to the driveway and the police patrolman directed Grant into a next-door neighbour's entrance.

'The crime scene is next door, sir,' the officer said. 'Two children have been taken from the house. We've cordoned off the whole of the front. If you'd like to speak to the children's grandmother, Joan Hardman, she's waiting in the squad car. This is the grandparents' place and she was here at the time of the abduction. Her husband collapsed and he's been taken to hospital.'

It was a crisp update and better than most Grant got. 'Good work, officer.'

'One other thing, sir – the man who was taken to hospital, Ronnie Hardman – the paramedics said his condition was serious. They suspect a heart attack. His wife didn't want to go with him until she's spoken to whoever is in charge.'

'I'll get to her as soon as I can.'

A group of Scene of Crime Officers, which everyone called SOCOs, were getting suited up in the back of their van. Grant jogged over to them. 'What do you know so far? Can you give me a run down?'

The Crime Scene Manager stepped forward. 'I don't know much yet,' she said. 'Patrol did a good job keeping the drive contamination-free. It seems there were two grandchildren in the house and they were taken in a vehicle. There was a tussle outside the property between the abductor and the grandfather. We're just about to go in.'

'Keep me updated.'

From across the road, two of Grant's detective sergeants, Diane Collins and Tom Delaney, arrived at a run. The Crime Scene Manager gave DS Tom Delaney the once over. It was the reaction of most women when they came across Tom's dark good looks and rugby-player physique. DS Delaney, on the other hand, gave the forensics manager a courteous nod. He had been dragged out of bed by Grant and yet he looked as fresh as if it was eight o'clock in the morning. Ah, the advantages of youth, Grant thought. But his fifty-seven years gave him one thing Delaney did not yet have – decades of experience on the job.

'Sir,' Diane said. 'We got here as soon as we could.'

DS Diane Collins had three teenage sons. An experienced member of Grant's team, Diane had worked with him for over ten years. Her blonde hair was shoulder-length and neatly cut, and she wore a navy trouser suit. Delaney would have gone by her place to pick her up.

'We need to get moving,' Grant said. 'Delaney, I want you to liaise with forensics and keep up to date with the scene as it unfolds. I'll speak to the first witness. Oh yes, and we need to find out why the security alarm didn't go off.'

The ground squelched underneath Grant's shoes as he walked across the grass and he made a mental note – with soft ground like this they might get lucky with tyre marks or footprints.

'Get an officer to cordon off the area by the gate,' Grant shouted. 'Once they've finished inside the house, ask the SOCOs to check the ground for prints. From now on, I want all coming in or out to happen from the side. Got it?'

A uniformed officer scuttled off to carry out Grant's instructions.

The drive was full of flashing police lights. By the fence, neighbours clustered together, dressed in coats draped over their nightwear.

'Diane, speak to that lot and find out if they saw anything. I've been told this is the grandparents' house, so track down the parents and get them here.'

Ten minutes for the first responders to arrive, plus fifteen minutes for him to get here which meant the getaway vehicle could already be clear of the town. Grant hurried to speak to the grandmother.

She was hunched in the back of a police car. Clutching her mobile phone, Joan Hardman was staring straight ahead at the headrest and Grant introduced himself and slid in beside her.

She was slight and looked mid-sixties, and when she turned to face Grant, he could see she'd been crying.

'My grandchildren have been taken,' she said.

'And it's my job to find them. I need as much information as possible and as quickly as possible. Please tell me what happened.'

The authority in his voice calmed her which was exactly what he needed it to do. Though she was shaking, she nodded.

She told him she'd been woken by a noise. There were four of them in the house – Joan, her husband and the two grandchildren, Emily and Lisa, and it had sounded to her and her husband as if there was an intruder downstairs. Ronnie had gone to investigate. She had called the police and then crept onto the top landing where she heard Ronnie shouting. The intruder was already at the front door and he was dragging the children with him.

'You say it was a man. Did you recognise him?'

'He had something over his face and I couldn't see properly.'

'And then what happened, Mrs Hardman?'

'Please c-call me Joan. There was a car outside. My husband chased after the kidnapper and Ronnie punched the man and then Ronnie suddenly collapsed and fell to the ground. It was dark. I grabbed hold of Emily's arm. There was a tussle and I had hold of her one minute and the next I let go. I'll never forgive myself. I just wasn't strong enough.'

Grant ticked off the details. One intruder and no accomplice present which, of course, didn't mean one did not exist. The children did not seem to know their abductor. Joan and Ronnie appeared to have been taken by surprise though Grant knew from experience this could be an elaborate ploy because no one and nothing could be ruled out at this stage, not even an innocent-looking grandmother.

'You tried to intervene, Mrs Hardman. This is not your fault. How old are your grandchildren?'

'Emily is six, Lisa four. When I got there, Lisa had already been forced into the car.'

Joan described the vehicle as a family estate and a dark colour – possibly black or dark grey. She'd done well to get the details and Grant jotted it down. When Emily was wrenched away from her, Joan had lost her balance and fallen backwards. Then she ran after the car.

'I know it was stupid trying to catch it. It was only once the car got away I went back to Ronnie. He could hardly speak. Please find them. Please find my grandchildren.'

Her huge pleading eyes were fixed on him and Grant nodded. He needed to keep her focused for just a few moments more.

'When it went out of the drive, which direction did the car take?'

'It turned right.'

'And at the end of the road?'

'A right turn again.'

'Did you get a look at the registration?'

Grant held his breath. If she'd got something it would be a miracle.

'I tried but I can't see as well as I used to.'

'Like I said before, don't be hard on yourself, you did well to notice the colour and type. If you think of any other details please let me or one of my detectives know straightaway.'

'Of course. Can I go to my husband now?'

'I'll get a patrol officer to take you there.'

As Joan Hardman went to open the door, she winced.

'Is there something wrong with your arm?' Grant asked.

She pulled up her sleeve. Underneath was a red and purple mark on her forearm, roundish in shape. It looked suspiciously like a bite mark.

'When did you get this?'

'It must have been in the scuffle with the intruder. With the children taken and then Ronnie collapsing I forgot about it.'

'Did the person who took your grandchildren bite you?'

'I don't know. I remember we were both pulling at Emily and I was determined to keep hold of her but now I think about it, maybe you're right and perhaps that's why I let go of Emily's arm. I felt a sharp pain and I lost my grip. It must have been because he bit me.'

Grant was careful not to touch her. Bite marks were discredited as evidence in a courtroom because experts couldn't link them to dental records with any certainty. But it was possible traces of saliva might be present in the wound. And that was important because then they'd have a DNA sample from the abductor.

'Did the ambulance crew disinfect the wound?' he asked.

'It went clear out of my mind and I didn't tell them about it, so no. And Ronnie was their priority.'

Excellent. He would get it photographed and have swabs taken.

'I want to have your arm inspected and I'll get that kicked off as soon as possible. And we're going to need recent photographs of Emily and Lisa and information about what they were wearing.'

'I've got photographs on my phone, and the children were in their sleepover pyjamas. Ronnie spoils those girls silly and they've got special pyjamas. Emily's have yellow elephants on them and Lisa's have little p-pink fairies.'

Searching through her phone, she started crying. 'It's terrible. I can't think about it or I won't be able to hold it together. When my daughter hears she'll go to pieces. How am I going to tell Alice her children are gone?'

'My team are locating the children's parents,' Grant said. 'Leave that to me.'

Breaking the news would not be a pleasant task but the good thing about being the one to do it was Grant would have the opportunity of scrutinising the parents' reactions.

Joan Hardman bit her lip as she showed Grant a picture of two adorable blonde children. They were hugging each other and smiling and Emily had a front tooth missing.

'This was taken last week. We went out for t-tea and cake.'

There was a box of tissues on the front seat and he passed it to her. 'Once we've finished with your arm, you'll be free to go to your husband.'

A uniformed officer hustled over when Grant beckoned and Joan Hardman was led away. Grant turned his attention to the activity near the house.

'Right,' he said to himself. 'Let's see what the crime scene can tell us about the perp. Let's see what mistakes you've made, you bastard.'

Grant shouted for Delaney and his DS was soon at his side. Delaney swiped at the screen of his phone and Grant stared at the high-resolution photographs of the inside of the house.

'Well done,' Grant said. 'Quick work is exactly what we need. Give me the rundown.'

'Here's what you should know, boss.' Delaney pointed to the first photograph. 'This is the back door which goes out to the garden.'

'And?'

'It leads into the kitchen. It seems our perpetrator came in here and he went out the front. The important thing is, the back door wasn't forced.'

Grant grabbed the screen. 'You're sure?'

'Certain. The Crime Scene Manager and I are in agreement.'

'No sign of forced entry? That means the door wasn't locked or he had a key,' Grant said.

If it hadn't been locked had it been left open by accident? Or deliberately? And if the perpetrator had a key, how did they get it?

Grant called over his shoulder to a uniformed constable. 'Bring Mrs Hardman to me before she leaves for the hospital please. I need to speak to her again.'

Delaney swiped to a second photograph. 'This is the other important one.'

It was a red handprint smeared on a white wall.

'They found this at the bottom of the stairs.'

Grant squinted. 'From the size I'm guessing it's from Emily or Lisa. What did the SOCOs say?'

'They thought so too.'

'It's blood,' Grant said. Did it mean one of the children was injured? A potential injury to a kidnap victim was the last thing they needed, especially when the children were so young.

'The SOCOs confirm it's definitely blood. Whose is another matter.'

'Shit. I want to know as a priority if this blood comes from one of the children. Delaney, contact the hospital to find out if Ronnie was bleeding. Joan had a bite mark on her arm though I don't think it bled and she said she was bitten outside. Which means this print is either the perpetrator's blood, or Ronnie's, or from the children.'

Mrs Hardman didn't mention a weapon, so how had someone been injured?

'Mrs Hardman told me she threw a vase,' Grant said. 'Could someone have been cut by a shard? Check it out with the SOCOs. It smashed against the wall next to the front door after the abductor got out. Ask the SOCOs about the shatter pattern and see if there's a possibility it caused someone to bleed on the stairs.'

It seemed unlikely because the vase would have fallen after everyone passed the stairs, but Grant wanted the opinion of the experts.

'Good work, Delaney,' Grant said, and he meant it. Delaney had flagged up the two most significant elements of the crime scene. His DS's clear thinking had bought them valuable time and it was more proof of Delaney's talent. Delaney could go far.

Diane was coming back and she brought Joan Hardman with her.

'You want to know about the doors, Inspector Grant?' Joan said. 'Why? That's my husband's domain. Ronnie takes care of locking them and he checks front and back and the lounge patio windows every evening before he comes upstairs.'

'And did he do the same last night?'

'Of course. Ronnie doesn't leave things like that to chance.'

'It's very important. Do you know for certain he did? And what about a burglar alarm? I see you have one installed and it didn't go off.'

Joan hesitated. 'I didn't see him do his nightly check if that's what you mean yet I know my husband, and Ronnie was thorough and systematic. There's no way he would have forgotten to lock up, especially not with the grandchildren in the house. As for the alarm system, it went off once by accident and frightened the grandchildren so much they always ask Ronnie to disable it and h-he's such a softie with them...' Joan swallowed and dabbed at her eyes, '...he agrees. Every time they're here, against all reason, he turns it off.'

Grant made sure he gave no reaction because he was here for the facts, not to blame people. So, the alarm had been conveniently disabled. Who might know this and use it to their advantage?

Delaney was a few steps away talking on the phone.

'I just checked with the hospital and they say Ronnie Hardman had no bleeding,' Delaney said.

Grant was running through a checklist in his head. *One perpetrator, no forced entry, dark car heading into town, one victim possibly injured. The first priority is sending out a Child Rescue Alert and then-* He stopped because Delaney had a strange expression on his face, sort of fixed and strained. Grabbing Delaney's elbow, Grant pulled his DS out of hearing range.

'What's wrong?'

'There's bad news about Ronnie Hardman.' Delaney glanced back in the direction of Joan Hardman. 'Mr Hardman's injuries from the tussle were minor but it seems he had a heart attack when he accosted the intruder. Then he had a second major one in the ambulance. Mr Hardman didn't make it, boss. He died on arrival.'

Chapter Three

Those little blonde-haired brats are my golden ticket to success. It's a wonderful feeling having them under my control. They'll give me the leverage I need. Once I'm through with that family, they'll wish they'd never been born. I hum a little tune to myself and tap my fingers on the steering wheel.

The snatch almost went to plan, marred only by the intrusion of the bloody interfering grandparents. Who'd think two old people could be such a pain? I didn't expect them to weigh in like they did. In fact, they were a bloody nuisance, throwing shit and shouting, and the old man got in a couple of punches. He had some serious power behind his fist except not much stamina. Fancy him trying his luck. Still, he keeled over without me hardly trying. Stupid bastard.

And all the racket they made. I was lucky those houses are so far apart, otherwise it might have woken some nosey parker.

Once I was standing inside their room and looming over them, the kids were easy to control. The younger one grabbed onto some stupid stuffed toy and I snatched it from her. After I took a couple of slashes at it their imaginations started working overtime. The bigger one only half- believed me when I told her I'd cut her sister the same way if they didn't cooperate. To fully convince her, I put my knife to her arm. It was only a nick, nothing serious. Then they followed me down the stairs like lambs to the slaughter.

They're quiet in the back, lying in the footwell like I told them. It means I can concentrate on the driving – not going too fast and making sure I stick to the route I've planned. The idea is to not draw any attention. That's why I chose a dark-blue family car because it blends in.

Meticulous planning is something I'm good at. I know the location of the security cameras along the high street and I'm taking a route which bypasses most of them. If the cops catch me on the town surveillance, it either means they're lucky or it means they're better than I think they are. Anyway, with what I have planned, stupid information like that won't help the police. I'm far too clever.

I arrive at the lock-up site. This place used to be private storage units before it got abandoned. The company went bankrupt and the metal containers were left to rust. The tarmac is pitted with potholes and grass has taken over which makes it an ideal place for me.

When you scope out a job it's all about preparation. As I already told you, one of my tasks was to survey the area and that's how I know there's only one camera on the approach road and it's outside a fish and chip shop. I took care of it yesterday.

I chose the unit a long time ago and I've prepared it inside. The metallic door opens with a squeal and, yeah, I should have taken care of that too, only it's not important because there's no one around to hear. Once we're safely in, I open up the back.

The kids are shit scared. I think one of them has vomited. They're grabbing onto each other and I drag the oldest one out by her hair.

'You.' I point to the smaller one who's snivelling in the footwell. 'Get out. Make a noise and I'll kill you both.'

I can see from her face she believes me and her compliance makes me smirk. The older one is a different story. She's got a sullen expression, sort of defiant. It's the same look I spotted on her at the house and the reason I had to use the knife. Well, her poor attitude will be disappearing soon enough.

I'm feeling good. For the first time in ages I feel on top of the world. I've done it. I've got the family by the balls.

Emily took hold of Lisa's hand and she squeezed it. Lisa's hand was cold.

'I want Mummy,' Lisa said.

'Sshh. Don't let him hear you. He doesn't like us talking.'

'I'm scared.'

'I know you are, Lise, but we've got to be brave.'

The man said horrible things and he shouted. He wore a mask and underneath it, Emily knew he was nasty. At preschool, Emily had learned about strangers who take you. They were dangerous. If one of them got you, bad things could happen. And they were well and truly gotten.

'Mummy is going to find us,' Emily whispered.

Lisa whimpered. 'I want to go home.'

'Sssh. We just have to wait a little while and then we can go home. Mummy is going to find us.'

'How can she find us if she doesn't know where we are?' Lisa buried her face in Emily's shoulder and she was clutching on so tight it hurt.

'It's all right. Hold on to me, Lisa,' Emily said.

Emily promised herself she wouldn't cry. She would be strong and she would look after her little sister as best she could until help came.

Chapter Four

Grant broke the news of Ronnie's death to Joan Hardman himself, with as much compassion as he could. His words fell like a body blow and Joan staggered. When she righted herself, the colour had drained from her face and she seemed to have shrunk. DS Collins put her arm around Joan Hardman's shoulders and Grant called over one of the paramedics.

Joan closed her eyes. 'No, I don't need help. Forget about me. We have to concentrate on the children. That's what Ronnie would have wanted. Please, when is my daughter going to arrive?'

She stuck her chin out and Grant caught a glimpse of a steely determination. He admired her for being able to face the horror. He had met all sorts in his long career and Joan Hardman had a lot of guts.

Joan's decision not to go to the hospital had been the right one because it had given him a head start on the details. Though likely the decision would haunt her for the rest of her life because it meant Ronnie Hardman had died without a loved one by his side.

Grant felt sad for her but he could not let his sympathy get in the way. He must stay focused. That was what he was good at and it was the only way to help this family.

He was about to leave Joan Hardman when a taxi pulled up and out spilled a man and a woman. Grant could hear the woman panting as she ran towards them. From the terror on her face, Grant felt sure she was the children's mother. She was dressed in an emerald-green evening dress, with a coat draped around her shoulders. It fell into the dirt and she trampled over it then one of her high-heeled shoes came off and she almost fell.

Grant went to help.

'Oh god. My children.'

The woman clutched at him, her eyes desperate. Her voice came out like a croak, which sometimes happened when people were in shock. He could hardly understand a word she said.

Grant put his hand over hers. 'I'm Detective Chief Inspector Grant and I'm in charge of this investigation.'

The woman stared at him, her eyes two dark pools of fear.

Diane Collins picked up the woman's coat and Grant encouraged her to put it on.

The man, who was presumably the father, was wearing a dinner jacket. A waft of alcohol came Grant's way. The father's eyes were wide and bulging, as if he'd just had the fright of his life – which, of course, he had. Grant watched them both very carefully. Harsh though it might seem, family members always had to be in the frame.

'Inspector Grant, we got a call,' the man said. 'We were told Emily and Lisa have been taken.'

'I'm afraid that's true. And you are?'

'Jack and Alice Glover, Lisa and Emily's parents. My wife and I were out for the night and Joan and Ronnie were looking after the children…'

'Alice,' Joan Hardman said, and her voice broke.

'Mum!' Alice shrieked.

'It's so dreadful, I'm so sorry, my darling.'

'It's h-horrible.' Alice was embracing her mother when she seemed to suddenly sense there was more. She pulled back and stared at Joan. 'Mum, you're shaking. You've gone white. Is there any news? What's going on! Somebody tell me!'

Alice Glover grabbed at Grant again and she shook him by the shoulders. Grant let her.

'For God's sake tell me!'

'Oh Alice, it's your father…' Joan said.

Grant cleared his throat. 'There's no easy way to say this. I'm sorry to tell you there's been terrible news from the hospital. Ronnie Hardman has passed away. He suffered a major heart attack on his way to Himlands General.'

Alice's mouth dropped open then she tipped back her head. Out came a high-pitched scream of pain. It whipped through Grant, and nearby crime scene personnel stopped to stare in their direction before getting back to their tasks. Well, Grant thought, either that's genuine or she's one hell of a good actress.

'Alice,' Joan said in a firm voice. 'I want you to concentrate on Emily and Lisa. Are you listening to me? *They* are the priority.'

'Your mother is right,' Grant said.

Alice's head flopped down, her blonde hair hanging in a mess. She was struggling for breath and on the verge of hyperventilation. 'I can't, I can't… Please h-help me. Y-you've got to find them.'

'That's my job, ma'am,' Grant said and he used his voice to help anchor her. 'I need you to think very carefully because I've got important questions to ask, can you do that?'

'I'll try.'

'Good. And you, sir, look dressed for an occasion, was it something special?'

'A dinner party,' Jack said.

Alice gave her husband a scathing look. 'Yes we abandoned our children for a *party*. I hate those dinners anyway.'

'No you don't, darling.' Jack seemed to recover from the news about his father-in-law. 'The police will get them back. They'll find them, I promise you,' he said. 'Won't you, officer?'

False promises weren't in Grant's vocabulary.

'I need a list of people who were at the dinner party with you. I also need a list of anyone who might have a grudge against the family or anyone you can think of with a reason to take your children. Can you do that for me? And who knew the children would be here tonight?'

'It's a regular date every other weekend,' Jack said. 'I guess only us and Ronnie and Joan know about it.'

'Don't be stupid! It's not just us. What about the old au pair? Inspector, I sacked Sylvie. What if she was involved?' Alice said.

Jack took hold of his wife's hand and he patted it. 'Don't be silly, Sylvie was an ordinary girl. She's not capable of kidnapping.'

'You don't know that. You didn't see the look on her face when I asked her to leave.'

'I'm sorry,' Jack said. 'I think my wife's emotions are clouding her judgem–'

'Shut up! And don't talk about me like I'm not here. Sylvie isn't the type of girl we thought she was.'

'When did you last see her?' Grant asked.

'Three months ago, just after Christmas,' Jack said.

'I'm going to need Sylvie's name and contact details please.'

Jack squared up against Grant. They were about the same height and Jack was clearly used to getting his own way. 'You're wasting time. Some maniac has driven off with our children and you want to speak to the *au pair*? Are you crazy? She's got nothing to do with it.'

A wave of alcohol and aftershave came Grant's way. 'Let me be the judge of that.'

Against the weight of Grant's calm power, Jack backed down.

'We need to set up a centre of operations and I'm wondering if that might be possible at your house, sir?' Grant asked.

Alice swayed slightly. 'Why?'

There was no point mincing his words and he needed to be straight with Alice, however difficult it was for the mother of two abducted children to hear reality.

'We're treating this as a kidnapping and I'd prefer to have a permanent base at your house in case the abductor makes contact. It will be disruptive because we'll have to move in specialised technology and we need officers present twenty-four hours. Frankly, it's the best place to be if we want to move quickly in response to how this evolves and it means we can keep in continuous communication with you both.'

'Absolutely,' Jack said. 'Anything you need.'

'I'm sending out a Child Rescue Alert so as soon as people wake up and switch on this morning, they'll hear a news flash or see a ticker tape message at the bottom of their television screen. There will be a special police hotline and all information will be collected and sorted and come straight to me.'

'Th-thank you,' Jack said.

Police units, border control, council services and especially members of the public via television and radio – they were often the best means of tracking down missing children. Grant would be circulating photographs of Emily and Lisa and the vehicle details within minutes.

He put his hand on Joan Hardman's arm. 'Once again, my condolences.'

And Joan Hardman gave a small nod, which broke Grant's heart.

'Shall I go with Mum to the hospital, or should I stay here?' Alice asked. 'What if you get news? I don't know what to do. I don't know if I should be with Mum or… I don't want to be away if…'

'I'll be in contact every step of the way,' Grant said. 'If you want to see your father please don't be frightened because it's my job to keep you informed and that's something I take very seriously. I'll ask DS Collins to take you.'

He wanted Diane to see how events panned out at the hospital and to get a view on the family dynamics. Family members had to be in the frame of the enquiry. All his sergeants understood the rules of the game and Grant knew he could trust Diane to sniff out any trace of suspicion concerning the parents or even the Hardmans. Better than that, Diane's cosy image meant people didn't feel threatened and they tended to let their guard down. Many a suspect had been fooled by DS Diane Collins.

Daylight was filtering through the sky and soon the sun would be coming over the horizon. DCI Grant borrowed the SOCOs van as a temporary hub and crammed his team into the back of it. They were joined by Grant's third detective sergeant, DS Steve McGowan. McGowan brought a tray of takeaway drinks with enough for the SOCOs and it got him plenty of slaps on the back. It was a chilly early morning and everyone was grateful for a warm-up and a caffeine infusion, except Delaney who had a herbal tea.

'Sorry I'm late, guv,' McGowan said.

Grant scowled because he hated tardiness, especially on a case like this. But McGowan was a veteran and worth his place on the team. Steve McGowan wore his usual open neck shirt, scruffy jeans and leather jacket. He handed Delaney's cup over without a smirk, and without a jibe about vegetarians or herbal tea drinkers – of which Delaney was both. McGowan was known for his dry wit and he had a sarcastic comment for most people though not many for Delaney. Why not? Because although Steve McGowan was by far Delaney's senior, he had a respect for their newest recruit, especially since the team's last case. It had thrown up the suspicious death of Delaney's father and had put Delaney through the wringer.

The aroma of coffee filled the van. Diane, Delaney and McGowan sipped their drinks and Grant brought everyone up to speed. He ticked the major points off on his fingers.

'What I want to know is – did the perpetrator have a key to the kitchen door,' Grant said. 'Find out. Three sets of keys to the Hardman house have been accounted for and they belong to Joan, Ronnie Hardman and Alice, and each set is where it's expected to be. Jack has the Hardmans' front door key on his clip but he doesn't have the back door one. It's supposed to be hanging on a board at the Glover house. I've sent a constable to check. And if the kitchen door was left unlocked, which is an option, was it deliberate or an accident – keep that in mind.'

'Ronnie Hardman might have made a mistake,' Diane said. 'Maybe he thought he locked it but he didn't.'

'Joan told me Ronnie was scrupulous. But we keep that option open too.'

'Yeah, well Ronnie Hardman can't give us an update now, can he?' McGowan said.

'The cleaner is the only other person who has keys and she's been with the Hardmans for seven years.' Grant glanced at his watch. 'It's four o'clock. McGowan, get over there and wake her up. Find out if she's left her keys anywhere in the last six months. Find out if anyone has even touched them and if you sense anything, bring her down to the station for further questioning.'

'Right, guv.'

'Uniformed division have arrived and the constables will be kicking off a door-to-door in the area. Delaney, you'll be our point of contact on that. Our first priority with the public is identifying the vehicle and any witnesses to the abduction. Then any suspicious activity in the street in the last few weeks. On the door-to-door, make sure they check for discarded clothing or a weapon.'

'Yes, boss,' Delaney said.

This was the first time Delaney worked a kidnap case. Liaising on the door-to-door operation was a step up in responsibility for his youngest sergeant. They must cover as large an area as possible, efficiently, and in as short a time as possible. The good thing was most people would be home so when the constables went knocking they'd be able to nab people before they left for work. Grant often gave Delaney tasks which would stretch him. It was how he'd learned himself – by working with a senior officer who trusted him and tested him.

'Collins, once you've finished at the hospital, I want you to coordinate a trawl of surveillance cameras. Which way did he drive in and which way did he go out? Check with the council's CCTV and local businesses. We've a timing of between two and two thirty for the abduction.'

Once Superintendent Fox arrived, she'd handle keeping the press under control so he didn't need to worry about the media frenzy. Grant took sips of his scalding drink. Phone and financial records for Joan, Ronnie, Jack and Alice would be requested and scrutinised. He had already decided his own number one task would be to squeeze the parents to see what came out. Why? Because there was conflict between them and his instincts told him to find out why. After that, he wanted to speak to the au pair.

'We've got more information about the blood,' he said. 'As well as the handmark, there were two drops at the bottom of the stairs. We don't yet know if it matches one of the children but we've got to keep in mind it could be a serious wound.'

'Shit,' McGowan said.

Grant's thoughts exactly. A life-threatening wound on a young child was precisely what they didn't need. Grant held up another high-resolution photograph. 'Then there's this.'

It showed a teddy bear with the stuffing spilling out. The toy had been slashed.

'This was found in the children's bedroom and it was done with a sharp blade. My guess is the abductor did this to coerce Emily and Lisa to cooperate. Maybe he threatened this would happen to them if they didn't do as he said. And then someone did get injured.'

'I don't like it,' McGowan said. 'Why bring a knife? That's reckless. It could have resulted in loss of life.'

'He went through all this planning to get in without being noticed and then he risks a murder? That's plain odd,' Delaney said.

It was what Grant had been thinking and that's why his team was the best in the business – Delaney was more brilliant than he ever realised, McGowan was hard-nosed and seasoned, and Diane was a cunning detective who could smell a rat from a mile away.

'I don't get the feeling this is a standard kidnapping,' Grant said. 'I can't put my finger on exactly why but I'm getting odd vibes from the family. We're going to have to dig deep and I've a feeling we're going to need our colleague Ruby Silver on this one. I'm bringing her in.'

McGowan groaned.

Ruby Silver was a top criminal psychologist and Grant had arranged to meet her at the Glover house. Ruby was seconded to the Sussex police force thanks to Grant. He'd discovered Ruby on their serial killer case where her expertise had been the clincher. Her profiling of criminals was second to none.

'Not her again,' McGowan said. 'I don't think I can stomach more of her whiny advice.'

'Shut up, Steve,' Diane said.

McGowan hadn't taken to Ruby, which was a problem. McGowan was a traditionalist. He didn't like new ideas or new techniques and he didn't like the young dynamic Ruby Silver. If it came to a choice between them Grant would find it hard – McGowan with his tough-cop image and cynical attitude which cut straight to the bone, or Ruby with her spot-on expert advice? And there was a complication with McGowan. McGowan had come up on Grant's radar as a possible source of leaked information on their last case, when Assistant Chief Constable Treadgold had been aware of what Grant's team would do before they did it. Since Grant suspected Treadgold of corruption, it had been a serious breach, though Grant had no means to prove it. Since then, nailing ACC Treadgold had become one of Grant's personal aims.

Grant downed his drink and lobbed his cup in the bin. He had more important things to deal with.

'Like Diane said, shut it. Ruby is in and I need your best.'

'You've got it, guv.'

The backdoor entry was a red flag. Was this an inside job? Did someone close to the children have something to gain? And what about the blood? Did it mean their perpetrator was hot-headed? Because hot was always more risky to deal with than cold. And deep down Grant had a feeling the perp was a clever bastard.

'It's up to us to bring Emily and Lisa home. Let's get moving.'

Grant met the eyes of each member of his team and he saw the fire in them which matched his own. Children always brought out the passion. They practically fought each other to be first out of the van but Grant beat them to it.

Chapter Five

Ruby Silver was a light sleeper. When her telephone rang, she was immediately awake and when she saw it was a call from DCI Grant, her skin tingled. A new case – just what she was waiting for. She listened to the details, tweaking the curtain to peek outside. The sky was dark and the stars sparkled. Grant needed her on a child abduction case which made Ruby both excited and nervous.

Rolling the names of the missing children around her mind, she pulled on her jeans.

Grant sent a picture of the children and they were two adorable fair-haired girls. As a psychologist, serial killers were Ruby's speciality yet profiling worked for any type of perpetrator including child abductors. This would be the first investigation of its type for Ruby and she was eager to get to work.

She tied back her dark hair and splashed her face with water. Working with Grant was the biggest adventure of her life. She'd come a long way from being a kid dumped in a children's home. Ruby had lived through plenty of bad times until her passion for understanding the criminal mind had brought her to Himlands Heath. Her first meeting with Grant had changed her life. It had freed her from the bad secrets of her own past and it had put a serial killer, the one from her nightmares, behind bars.

Ruby felt she'd landed on her feet because Grant was the best mentor she could have wished for and him believing in her made Ruby believe in herself.

Cramming down a couple of cereal bars, she set up search parameters on her laptop and launched the program. Looking through past cases of abductions would help her find common patterns about the psychological make-up and traits of kidnappers.

Eerily quiet and grey, the streets were cold and her breath misted in the air. Some nicer weather had arrived for the days but the mornings were chilly and damp and they would be for a long time yet – that was early spring in England for you, and Ruby was glad she had invested in a warm coat.

The taxi seemed to take an age to arrive at her door.

'Drive as quickly as you can,' she told the driver. 'It's an emergency.'

Alice and Jack Glover lived in an area full of nice houses. Their property had a picture window at the front and a huge conservatory on the side which looked like a mini-version of a botanical garden. There were swathes of snowdrops and daffodils along the front path and a large well-tended garden. This was a family with a decent income although it seemed they didn't like to be flamboyant.

At the door, a uniformed constable checked Ruby's details.

'DCI Grant is expecting you,' the constable said.

Inside the house, Ruby could hear voices, including the chief's. She walked along the hallway passing a lovely, and probably very expensive, painting of a Sussex landscape. Grant was sitting in the lounge. At the back of the room, technicians were scrambling to set up computers and phone connections. She guessed the equipment must be standard in a kidnap case for if an abductor contacted the family and so incoming communications could be monitored.

The room looked like something out of a home décor magazine with a white stone fireplace and a cream carpet. Grant was in an armchair. He was facing three people who were sitting side by side on a sumptuous sofa – a blonde woman, then a man in the middle, and next a dark-haired woman. They were all a similar age, probably late thirties, so almost ten years older than Ruby. The children's mother was easy to spot because she looked as if she'd been smacked into by a bus. She was wearing a green evening dress which complemented her fair hair. The dress must have been elegant at some point but her make-up was horribly smeared and her hair and clothes were a mess. The last couple of hours must have been hell for Alice Glover and it wasn't over yet. The man in the middle must be the father.

'Hello Ruby,' Grant said. 'I'd like to introduce my colleague, Ruby Silver. She's a psychologist.'

The man got up to shake her hand. 'Jack Glover,' he said.

Jack had brown eyes which were full of pain. He faltered, so Ruby spoke for him.

'I'm here to assist DCI Grant.'

The dark-haired woman dabbed a tissue at her nose. 'You're very young. I didn't know the police employed psychologists.'

Ruby was used to being dismissed because of her age. She'd studied hard and she had a talent for criminal psychology but the real source of her expertise sprang from her upbringing. Which, of course, was something she never discussed. Only Grant and Tom Delaney knew the details.

'It's more common than you think,' Ruby said. 'Are you a friend of the family?'

'I'm Natalie and I live next door. Alice and I are friends.'

From how Natalie's leg was pressed up against Jack's, Ruby wondered if Natalie might be better friends with Jack than she was with Alice.

Grant leaned forward. 'I know this is a terrible time but, as I explained, the more information you can give me, the better chance we have of finding Lisa and Emily. Let's go through this one more time and I'd like to start with where you both were this evening.'

'We've already told you everything ,' Alice said. 'I can't repeat it all.'

'My wife's exhausted. Why do you keep asking questions? You should be out there tracking down this maniac!'

Ah, so Grant was piling on the pressure. Which meant he had his reasons for scrutinising the parents. Ruby sat down quietly. With his hair silvering at the temples and grey eyes, Grant looked polished in his grey suit, though he'd been dragged out of bed in the middle of the night. With victims, Grant had what Ruby called the golden touch, and she could see he'd already won the respect of the family because they were hanging on his every word. This was the man they were pinning their hopes on.

Grant spread his hands in an apologetic manner. 'Please, if it wasn't important I wouldn't ask. Let's go through it one more time.'

Natalie groaned and rested her head back against the sofa.

Jack started talking. He wasn't good looking though Ruby quickly realised she'd misjudged him because Jack was the sort of man who attracted women's attention. He had a deep voice and charisma and a lot of masculinity. She found herself staring at him. Jack told them how he and Alice had been at a dinner party hosted by a friend.

'Like I already told you, Inspector, they aren't our friends,' Alice said. 'I don't even know why we go there. Carmichael is a business associate.'

Picking up a piece of paper, Grant ran his finger down it so slowly it was like torture. Even Ruby wanted to jump up and snatch it out of his hand. The more the DCI stretched this out the more the tension ratcheted up. Ruby licked her lips. He was doing it deliberately – playing them to see if they made any slip-ups. Putting on the pressure to find out what or who would give. She'd seen him work like this before, cool and stealthy, and the DCI would keep squeezing until he was satisfied. There was a reason his nickname at the police station was the grey panther.

Jack clutched at his own knees. 'For God's sake, Inspector, shouldn't you be out there!'

'I see you've not put the host on your list of potential enemies.'

'Of course not,' Jack said, pursing his lips. 'He and I get on well. Carmichael puts a lot of business my way and I do the same for him. I don't want to have to assess all our friends as potential traitors, surely you're not asking us to do that? How horrible. It would be like saying we can't trust anyone.'

'But can we?' Alice said, narrowing her eyes.

'And you told me you were both at the dinner party for the whole evening.'

'Yes! How many times do we–'

'What sort of business are you in?' Grant asked.

Jack ran his fingers through his hair. 'I run Hardman Construction for Alice's father. We construct and renovate properties. My father-in-law built the company up from nothing.'

Jack was talking as if Grant was an idiot who needed things repeated several times – which was a mistake on Jack's part. Ruby could see Alice was barely coping, and with her children taken and her father deceased on the same night, no wonder.

Alice's green eyes were red-rimmed as she turned to Grant. 'My father was what everyone calls a self-made man. When Dad retired he put Jack in charge.' Alice started crying and Jack put his arm around her.

'Where did the two of you meet?' Grant asked.

'Why the hell is that relevant? If you must know, at work,' Jack said. 'I was a manager at Hardman Construction and back then Alice worked in the office.'

Ah, Ruby thought, so Jack married the boss's daughter. That was interesting.

'I see you don't have many enemies because you've only put three people on this list.'

'Like I said we can't scrutinise everyone we know – it would make us go crazy,' Jack said. 'I've probably pissed off a lot of people in the business and that's normal. Bidding and winning on a big building project is competitive and Hardman Construction has an edge which I work hard to keep. There's no one I know I'd think capable of abducting Lisa and Emily. Whoever it is that person's got to be someone who's plain mad.'

'Have either of you had any strange encounters or noticed people hanging around the house? Has anything out of the ordinary happened?'

'Nothing,' Jack said.

Alice shook her head.

'You told me your au pair left?'

'I asked her to leave,' Alice said. 'You asked about who we can trust and well, we trusted her and she betrayed us.'

'Don't make it more than it was, darling,' Jack said.

'Perhaps you could tell us what happened,' Grant said.

Alice made a half-hearted attempt to push her hair off her face. 'I'm not exaggerating. She betrayed my trust and she lied. Basically, I found out Sylvie Delacourt had been leaving the children unsupervised. It happened in the changing rooms at the swimming pool which I know for a fact because one of my friends rang to tell me and it freaked me out. I mean, it was chance my friend was there and saw it. I'd had my suspicions about Sylvie and I don't think it was the only time. I think Sylvie had a habit of sitting them down while she went to get a drink or a snack or went to the toilet, and not just at the pool at the shopping centre too and at the park. She was strictly not allowed to leave them on their own. They're too young. She promised me it wouldn't happen again and then it did.'

'I see,' Grant said. 'So you didn't feel she was reliable?'

'She was deceitful and she lied to me and I think she told the children not to tell me and I didn't like that either.'

Grant nodded. His questioning was almost over and Alice and Jack Glover would stay under scrutiny. He wasn't done with them yet not by a long way and he intended to post Ruby and Delaney at the house to keep an eye on them.

'Right. Though nothing happened during the episodes the children were alone?' Grant asked.

'No, but it could have done!' Alice said.

'The children weren't approached by anyone? They didn't mention anything specific to you?'

Alice shrieked and shot her husband a dirty look. 'See Jack! I told you it was dangerous.'

'Mrs Glover, I'm not suggesting something actually happened what I'm trying to find out is if anything did,' Grant said.

'The children didn't mention anything,' Jack said.

'Of course they didn't, she told them not to!'

'Please, Mrs Glover, we need to stay factual. It's the best way for me to get a clear picture.'

'You need to know Sylvie made it difficult when I asked her to leave because she tried to argue her side rather than accept responsibility.'

Jack shook his head. 'We can't point the finger. Sylvie was a twenty-something young woman, how can she be involved? She came all the way from Australia and being asked to move on was a shock. After working with us, Sylvie was hoping to continue working in England.'

Alice cut Jack a cold look. 'I told her there was no way in hell I'd give a reference and I doubt the au pair agency did either.'

'Going back to your list of enemies, who are these three people?' Grant said as he held the list in his hand.

'They're business competitors,' Jack said. 'It's all I could come up with. They could have something against me and Alice or against Ronnie. Basically Hardman Construction trumped them on big deals, which means we got contracts which they were bidding for and there have been some pretty hefty contracts we've won. I'm sure they were green with envy.'

'And you think it might give someone a motive to kidnap Lisa and Emily?'

'I didn't say that, why are you twisting my words? Like I said, I can't imagine anyone we know would take our children. It's the best we could come up with.'

They would check out Jack and Alice's alibi for the evening and the list, going through alibis and people's stories. Close to the family, he had the au pair and the cleaner and on the face of it, neither seemed very likely suspects.

'In the next few hours I'd like you both to take some time with Ruby. I want you to work with her to map the movements of the children in the past few months. I'd like to know who they've seen and where they went. And then there's the keys to Mr and Mrs Hardmans' house. Are you certain neither of you have mislaid your sets? You've not lent them nor lost them?'

'Of course not,' Alice said. 'Like I told you, Mum and Dad's keys are on my main key-ring. They go everywhere I go.'

Jack held up his keys and jiggled them. 'Like I already said, they're in my pocket or they're on the hook in the kitchen. Your officer already checked, didn't they? And it's hanging exactly where it should be.'

'Right. And I'm sorry but we'll need to thoroughly search the children's bedrooms,' Grant said.

'What for?' Jack asked.

'It's surprising what can turn up in a kidnap case and any small clue can be important. I know the children are very young but it's vital to be thorough.'

'Anything you need. Anything. May my wife have a rest now?'

'She can as soon as the technical team have set up your mobile phones. With your permission, we'll be monitoring your incoming calls and social media accounts. If the abductor contacts either of you by any other means you must notify me immediately.'

Grant knew the number one reason for failure to recover kidnap victims came down to families communicating with abductors without keeping police in the loop. With threats being made against loved ones, families could be tempted to deal direct – with disastrous consequences.

'We need to work together on this and you need to trust me. Ruby, please can you start working with Jack?'

Ruby licked her lips. Oh gosh, this was a tough case and the emotional pain in the household was almost unbearable. Alice looked close to a breakdown. She was shaking and having difficulty walking so that both Jack and Natalie had to help her to her feet. Alice was staring at DCI Grant and her eyes were full of torment. Ruby wondered how Grant could stay so focused.

'My babies.'

'Yes, Mrs Glover. I know this is a terrible time for you,' Grant said.

'Please.'

DCI Grant nodded slowly. His patience was remarkable and he certainly seemed to be giving Alice Glover a lot of scrutiny.

'P-please bring my babies home.' Alice Glover collapsed into her husband's arms.

Chapter Six

Joan and Ronnie's cleaner, Halina Badawi, lived in an apartment on the fifth floor of a social housing block. DS McGowan knew the area and he knew it wasn't a block with current drug-dealing residents. The problem with these places was they always teetered on the edge of crime. It only took one or two bad tenants to move in to make it an unpleasant place to live.

There was graffiti on the walls although no burnt cars out the front. McGowan took the stairs which were free of rubbish bags and didn't stink of urine so overall it was a good sign. The Badawis had a two-bedroom apartment with a balcony overlooking the back of the railway station. Even with the secondary glazing, it must be noisy.

When Mr Badawi answered the door he was wearing a sleeveless vest hanging over baggy pyjama trousers. Like any normal person, he kept the chain on while he checked out who it was. When he learned there was a problem with the Glover children Mr Badawi asked DS McGowan to wait in the lounge.

The room was clean and neat and a healthy flowering plant hung in the window. The place had a cosy looked-after feel and smelled faintly of coconut.

A few minutes later, Halina Badawi appeared wearing a floor-length kaftan and with her long hair knotted onto the top of her head. Halina and her husband looked to be in their fifties.

She made mint tea for the three of them while McGowan asked what they did for a living. They were both cleaners. Mrs Badawi worked for private clients and her husband was employed by a company which had contracts to clean offices. They had two daughters who were away at university. One of their daughters was studying law and the other engineering.

'They're much more clever than us,' Halina Badawi said with pride. 'They're going to get great jobs and have great careers not be cleaners.'

'There's nothing wrong with what we do,' Mr Badawi said.

'I know, dear.'

She put a mint tea on the table for McGowan.

'Thank you, Mrs Badawi. I need to ask you where you've both been in the last few hours.'

'Please call me Halina. We've been here, asleep.'

'Can anyone corroborate that? Did you have any contact with neighbours or friends?'

'Well, no. We went to bed around eleven and the next thing was you came knocking on our door.'

McGowan took out his notebook. 'And I need to ask about your employment with Mr and Mrs Hardman.'

'You told my husband you're here because of Mrs Hardman's grandchildren. Has something happened?'

McGowan made sure he was looking straight at the couple so he could gauge their reaction. 'Emily and Lisa have been abducted.'

Halina clutched at her throat. 'No!'

'I'm afraid so and I need you to keep all details of our discussion to yourselves. An alert has gone out to the public with the children's details and it's important you don't tell anyone about the Hardmans or your work there or about what we talk about today. Any information you can give me might be vital. Could we start by you telling me about your work for the Hardmans.'

'Of course – I clean bathrooms, kitchen, living room, study – I do the whole house once a week and I've worked for Joan for almost seven years. What do you want to know?'

'Do you see the grandchildren when you're there?'

'Never, though I hear about them often. I go there on a Thursday and I've been going there from before Emily was born so I get all the news and, of course, I clean their bedroom too with all their things in it.'

'Right. And you have a set of keys for the house?'

'I have front door and back door keys and that's because usually Joan isn't there when I arrive. Plus, I have to take out the trash and that goes out the kitchen door. And I prefer to take my equipment out through the garden not through the house.'

'And you keep your keys where?'

'I'll show you.'

Halina took McGowan into the kitchen and she opened the door of a cupboard. On the inside there were several rows of hooks, each with a set of keys on them. He counted fifteen in all.

'Some people I clean for let me in and out. These are the owners who don't.'

'Lots of people trust you.'

'Of course, why not? People want a clean house and I do a good job. Only I know which key is for which house and not even my husband knows. I haven't written it down anywhere because I keep it in my head.' Halina tapped her temple. 'That was my oldest daughter's idea in case we had a break-in.'

'That was smart of her. And have you ever had a burglary?'

'Never.'

'What about the keys to Mrs Hardman's house, have you ever misplaced them or left them anywhere? Think carefully, Mrs Badawi, and please don't think I'm accusing you, we simply need to work quickly to establish the facts and find the children. That's what we're interested in.'

'Of course, I understand.'

Halina thought for a few moments, then she shook her head. McGowan felt his hopes sinking.

'I'm certain that's not happened. They're in my bag to and from Joan's house and when I get back I always put them on the hook.' She went to tap Mrs Hardman's hanging keys and McGowan stopped her.

'Please don't touch them. You're certain you've never mislaid them nor given them to anyone else?'

'Definite.'

'I'll need to take these for testing,' he said. 'And you're sure no one else apart from you knows which key belongs to Mrs Hardman's house?'

Halina drummed her fingers on the counter. 'Only me. Except maybe my oldest daughter might have guessed. Because she's clever like that.'

Chapter Seven

Sylvie Delacourt wished she could go to the gym. It was her usual place for destressing and she really needed it. She was feeling so strung out after seeing the abduction of Emily and Lisa on the news and the early morning rush at work had been awful. She'd tipped a milkshake into a customer's lap and spilled a whole canister of chocolate powder on the floor. When she dropped a tray of glasses, the manager had confronted her and Sylvie spilled her story of having known the Glover children. At least it got her a bit of sympathy and the manager rolled his eyes and told her to take a couple of hours' break.

Sylvie needed to think straight. Should she contact the Glover family? What would she say to Alice? The woman hated her and yet the children were missing so shouldn't Sylvie at least call? And what about Jack?

The streets of Brighton were always busy. Walking amongst the crowds, Sylvie headed for the promenade. Along the seafront she could smell the salty air and the gulls called out over the water.

Sylvie hadn't wanted to leave Himlands Heath. She'd imagined herself staying with the Glovers for another six months which would have given her time to set up her website and sort out graphics and a proper advertising strategy for her new business. Jack Glover had promised to support her business idea and to lend her money to start it up. Of course, it all went down the pan when Alice made a fuss. Stupid woman. Alice had no ambition. All Alice had was looks which were fast fading and a body which hadn't got back into shape after two children. Why did Alice have to ruin everything?

With no waitressing experience, Sylvie had been lucky to be taken on at the coffee bar. She had even more luck when another waitress offered her a room. Sure, the lodging the two of them shared was poky and basic. Sylvie didn't care. It was cheap.

Going back to her room, she rummaged for her towel and costume. She couldn't go to a gym anymore because the running machine and the weights would be too strenuous and too risky. Instead, she'd go to the swimming pool. A few gentle lengths might help stop the turmoil because she really needed to calm down.

Her phone buzzed and when she looked at the screen she saw her big sister. It was Chloe sending photos again – several of Chloe in a bar with friends and one taken at Chloe's desk showing a huge pile of files. As Sylvie scanned, she felt tears prickling the back of her eyes. She was more emotional these days which must be down to her hormones. There was no way she could tell Chloe she'd got herself into a terrible mess. She knew what her big sister would say – she'd criticise and pick fault and get to act like the superior one again. Sylvie's parents would do the same – they'd point out how Sylvie was always the one to get it wrong and how her sister was just so perfect. No, it was impossible. This mess was something she must face alone.

After her swim, Sylvie took her time in the changing rooms and repeated the mantra she'd been telling herself the last few weeks – this was going to work out. The odds were stacked against her and yet she could turn it around and make it a success.

As she brushed her hair by the mirrors, a sudden wave of nausea gripped Sylvie and she had to hold on to the edge of the sink. She feared she might actually vomit on the spot.

'Are you all right?' a woman asked. The woman came to stand behind and waited until Sylvie looked at her in the mirror. It made Sylvie want to shout at her because all she wanted was to be left alone.

'Yes, I'm fine. I think I need a snack,' Sylvie said.

The woman's eyes searched hers and Sylvie couldn't help feeling the woman had guessed her secret. *Go away,* Sylvie thought, *I don't need your pity. I have a plan.*

Chapter Eight

Three hours into the abduction and Grant needed to get moving on questioning the au pair and the business contacts and he was heading out when Detective Chief Superintendent Angela Fox arrived. He heard her distinctive loud voice barking at the constable at the door. Then came footsteps marching along the hallway. He went out to meet Fox and took her along to the kitchen, closing the door behind them.

'Give me an update, Grant,' she said crisply.

To have arrived here so quickly, DCS Fox must have driven the three hours non-stop. Normally smart and efficient, or as Grant would describe her, uptight, Fox looked ragged. He hoped she already knew about Ronnie's death.

'Ma'am, I'm not sure if you're aware but there's been a tragedy involving Ronnie Hardman...'

'I know about the fatal heart attack. Please bring me up to speed, that's what I'm standing here waiting for.'

Grant considered if he should offer Fox a coffee or a chair and decided against it because she'd already asked him twice to update her. Making her ask a third time would be unwise though on a different day with a different case, he might have been tempted – it was like poking a stick at a grouchy dog to make it bark and sometimes he simply couldn't resist.

'We've a blood trace at the Hardman house. Joan Hardman was bitten by the abductor and we're checking for DNA traces in the wound. Nothing so far from town surveillance cameras. No obvious family enemies and, so far, we've had no contact from the abductor. Entry was not forced to the house so either the abductor had a key or the kitchen door was unlocked. And only a handful of people know the children's routine of staying with the grandparents.'

The superintendent ran her hand over her hair, though the gesture didn't do much to calm the unruly strands. 'You've kicked off the Child Rescue Alert? Photographs have been circulated to patrol and the public? And to transport police and the ports?'

Of course he had. 'Yes ma'am, an alert has gone out.'

'I want a total news blackout on this one until we know what we're up against.'

'Agreed. The house-to-house has started and we've got two witnesses to the getaway car – Joan Hardman and a neighbour. Jack Glover gave me a list of three names and he told me none of them are likely.'

'Everyone has enemies, you know that as well as I do. Where are we at on suspects?'

'The au pair and the cleaner are top of our persons of interest list. McGowan is with the cleaner and I've got confirmation of the au pair's details and I'm going there now.'

Fox was clenching her hands. They had a prickly relationship which was mostly because Fox was new and ambitious and she didn't want him to outshine her. In terms of age Grant was her senior and he always imagined Fox was worried he was after her job, which he wasn't, because he was a man of action and he hated politics and bureaucracy. He didn't go out of his way to rile DCS Fox though he didn't always keep her updated. Being kept in the dark was something which drove her mad and usually made her rant and shout.

'You've got a handle on it and fast action out of the gate was what we needed. I knew I could rely on you.'

Now that was a first. A personal appreciation. Grant wasn't sure why, but it made him feel suspicious.

'You're not going to like this…' Fox said.

His instincts kicked in. *Didn't he have enough to deal with tracking two little girls? What now?*

'…but I need to inform you Assistant Chief Constable Treadgold has taken an active interest in this case.'

Grant couldn't hide his surprise nor his anger. *The son-of-a-*.

ACC Treadgold had been breathing over Grant's shoulder ever since Grant accused Treadgold of corruption. The conflict between them started at a boy's funeral at which Grant had cracked and confronted the ACC. Grant didn't regret it. The only thing he regretted was not being able to prove Treadgold's guilt in causing the boy's death.

'It's part of Treadgold's remit on tracking performance on abduction cases.' Fox massaged her own neck, though she kept her eyes firmly on Grant. 'I told you you wouldn't like it.'

'If he interferes I swear to God I'll–'

Fox held up her hand. 'That's enough. Keep your eye on the ball and let me deal with ACC Treadgold. Reading between the lines one thing's clear – he's looking for an excuse to make trouble for you.'

Fox was aware of his suspicions regarding Treadgold. It seemed like Fox was on Grant's side for once and he could do with someone watching his back. After Treadgold's many years in the force and being bent for most of them, who knew how many allies Treadgold had in his pocket.

'You found no evidence against him Grant, which means we can't take action.'

Grant tried not to grit his teeth. 'I know.'

'Right, so I strongly suggest you don't give him any ammunition to use against you. This case had better be run by the book,' Fox said. 'And I noticed you've drafted in our psychology expert and Ms Silver seems to be quite at home in the Glover lounge. Were you going to bother running that one by me first? Or did you decide to promote yourself in my absence?'

Fox didn't miss a trick. 'Ma'am, I was just about to ask your permission.'

Grant pushed Treadgold from his mind. There was only one thing which mattered and that was Emily and Lisa and he'd be damned if he'd allow a b-tard like the Assistant Chief Constable to throw him off his stride.

He was halfway down the hallway when his phone buzzed. It was Delaney phoning to say they had a partial on the vehicle registration.

'We were lucky,' Delaney said. 'One of the neighbours has insomnia. He woke early as he usually does and went to read downstairs because he doesn't like to disturb his wife. He heard the getaway car and he got a glimpse. He said he knew from the speed it pulled away there was something wrong and he got the last three digits which were TMR.'

'Fantastic work. Once you've covered the Hardmans' street, leave the rest of the neighbourhood to the constables. Join Ruby here at the Glovers and begin a search of the children's bedrooms.'

Grant punched the air. At three hours in, it was a great hit. He just wished he could see Treadgold's face once he found out.

Chapter Nine

It was lucky for Grant that Sylvie Delacourt had left her details with the au pair agency. The agency told him Sylvie was hoping to find a position with another family and this was proving difficult given the reason for her dismissal. In the meantime, Sylvie had found work in a coffee shop in the seaside town of Brighton. One quick call and Grant knew she would be coming in to work for the second half of the morning.

Driving at the limit the whole way, it still took Grant an hour to arrive. The coffee shop had a nice view of the sea and the long shingle beach of Brighton. Grant took a few lungfuls of sea air. The clock was ticking and this trip had better be damn worth it. Time to find out what had really happened between Alice and Sylvie.

Ordering a hot drink, he took a seat at the window. The place was filled with a wonderful aroma of pastries. Sylvie was easy to identify because he could hear her Australian accent as she chatted to customers. An attractive young woman, Sylvie had a fair complexion, a smattering of freckles across her nose and long auburn hair styled into waves. She wore a chic knee-length dress.

Grant called Sylvie over.

'I'm Detective Chief Inspector Grant from Sussex Police. Please would you join me for a few minutes?'

'My boss told me you were coming,' Sylvie said. 'I saw the terrible news about Emily and Lisa, it's about them isn't it? I can't stop for long though because I'm working and I've already had time off this morning.'

Grant had come all this way because he wanted to see her reaction first-hand.

'To start with, I need to ask where you were between two o'clock and four o'clock this morning.'

She slid into a seat opposite Grant. 'Am I in trouble?'

'This is an informal interview because I need your help.'

'Oh gosh, if I knew anything about the kids I'd have called the hotline. Let me think – at two o'clock I was fast asleep. I woke up at seven and I started work at eight.'

'Do you live alone? Is there anyone who can corroborate this?'

'I've a flatmate except she was asleep and she doesn't even wake up when I take a shower so there's no point talking to her.'

It seemed Sylvie didn't have an alibi and at that time of the morning for most persons of interest the same was going to be true.

'Do you know anything which could help me find Emily and Lisa?'

'How would I?' Sylvie said, picking at a serviette. 'I haven't seen the children for months.'

'When exactly was the last time you saw them?'

Sylvie took out her phone and her hand was trembling as she swiped the screen. 'Let me check, I can tell you exactly – fifteen weeks ago. Alice got rid of me just after the New Year holidays and whatever she told you is a lie – I didn't leave the children alone. That was her excuse. She made it up so she could kick me out.'

'Why would she do that?'

'Alice is insecure and she imagines a lot of things. If you check with the agency you'll find I'm not the first au pair she's told to leave.'

It was true and another reason he was here. The agency told Grant Alice Glover had sacked three out of six girls in the last few years. Sylvie had been the third failed placement and it was why that particular Agency was no longer working with the Glover family. Which explained why the Glovers currently had no au pair.

Grant stirred his coffee. 'Yes, that's what the agency told me. That's a lot of insecurity on the part of Alice Glover. Care to fill me in?'

'She's the type of woman who gets jealous of younger women and I'm sure you can work out the rest yourself – a woman who's losing her looks and a husband who attracts attention…'

Grant raised an eyebrow. 'And?'

'Want me to spell it out? There was nothing going on between Jack and me except she thought there was.'

'Why would she think it then?'

'I've no idea, you'll have to ask her yourself.'

'I see,' Grant said. 'And what about Emily and Lisa. Can you tell me about the children? What are they like?'

'They're easy. Lisa is totally cute and adorable and she does as she's told. Emily has more of her own opinions though deep down once she's sussed you out she's basically easy too. I enjoyed my work.'

'Did they have a good relationship with the grandparents?'

'Oh yes Lisa and Emily love their sleepovers with Mr and Mrs Hardman.'

'Alice Glover suggested you were angry about the dismissal.'

'Of course I was because it was unfair and I'd been there for six months working like crazy for that family with hardly any time off. I've never met such a stupid, vain, suspicious woman as Alice Glover. If she can't stand younger women then why hire an au pair? Alice couldn't wait to get rid of me, slinging accusations left, right and centre when she's the one who isn't fit to be alone with her own children. I bet she didn't tell you about that, did she?'

'Perhaps you can fill me in.'

'Sure I can.' Sylvie leant forward. 'Lisa had to be rushed to hospital to have *seven inch-long spines* removed from her leg. Why? Because Alice left her alone in the stupid hothouse with the butt-ugly giant cactus. Alice was on the phone *in another room* and Lisa fell onto one of those prickly fuckers. She could easily have been much more seriously injured. And Alice has the nerve to call *me* irresponsible? She's the one who's a bad mother. That's not the only accident either. The outgoing au pair told me Lisa almost *drowned* in the bath when Alice was supposed to be looking after her.'

'I see,' Grant said.

'Yeah and not even Alice's friends know the real details because Jack and Alice keep it secret. Jack knows she's not a fit mother. They had a huge row about the cactus incident, both screaming at each other and hurling abuse.'

Was this the reason for the conflict between the Glovers? And could there be any link to the abduction?

'Did you have a reason to come to Brighton? It's a bit of a way from Himlands Heath isn't it? Though this is a nice place.' Grant glanced around at the décor of the café. It was very Brighton – with a hippy vibe.

'You're exaggerating aren't you because I'd say this is a bit of a dump.' Sylvie shrugged. 'At least it's a job and I was lucky to get it. As for why Brighton? Simply because I had more chance of work here. It's much larger than Himlands Heath. Besides, I like the sea.'

'Jack told me you have plans for setting up your own business.'

'Had – with no finance, no job and nowhere to live it all went on hold. Still, I have my dreams and I've got ideas and I haven't given up yet even if Alice got the knife in. If you must know I was thinking of setting up my own au pair agency.'

'That's a big idea.'

'And why not? I know I can do it, all I need is a loan to get started. I want to set it up online where families interview candidates via the internet and I'd ask girls to post video snippets to present themselves and the families can do the same. I'd start small and grow as I go. I think I could build a reputation and work my way in.'

Sylvie was getting fidgety and she kept glancing towards her boss behind the counter. Perhaps she was worried about being told off? Grant didn't think so. He'd already got permission to speak to Sylvie and the manager had been fine about it. No, Grant was betting there was something else on Sylvie's mind. She wanted to get away from him. The question was, why?

Sylvie had lived with the Glovers which meant she'd been an insider. What did Sylvie know? Perhaps there was a reason for Alice to feel insecure? But if there had been something between Sylvie and Jack, how could it be connected to the abduction?

Every detective had their own strategy for questioning persons of interest. Grant's favourite was squeezing people like a lemon except he knew going in hard would make Sylvie clam up. She was independent and strong-minded and she'd already denied a relationship with Jack. Besides, Sylvie wasn't underage, so that was her business.

'We're working on all possible angles,' Grant said. 'The more time passes, the greater the danger for Emily and Lisa. If anything comes to mind, anything at all which might help, please contact us straight away.' He passed Sylvie his card.

'I liked those children a lot. Sure, I was disappointed about how I was treated but like the rest of the country, I want to help find them. If I think of anything I'll call.'

*

On his way back, Grant contacted DCS Fox.

'A quick update for you ma'am. The au pair stays as a person of interest.'

'You're not striking her off the list?'

'No.'

He could hear Fox musing this over. 'Nothing to move her further into the frame?'

'Not yet, but I have my doubts which means I'm not ruling her out. Sylvie Delacourt is resourceful. She's come all the way from Australia. She was thrown out of the Glovers and without knowing anyone she's found herself a new job in a new town. The agency told me she came on a youth visa so she has no recourse to public funds and they said she refused financial support from her family.'

'She sounds like a strong-willed young woman. And?'

'I'd say the chances of her having a close relationship with Jack Glover are pretty high, based on Jack's behaviour as well as Sylvie's. It doesn't mean the two of them were necessarily intimate. Maybe they got on well and it may have been enough to give Alice grounds for suspicion.'

And if this was true, the big question for Grant was why would Sylvie feel the need to conceal it? It made Grant take notice and meant he'd come away with more questions than answers.

'We'll be running full checks on Ms Delacourt.'

'Understood.'

Grant rubbed the back of his neck. It would soon be ten o'clock. Eight hours since the children were taken and he was still fighting to find a chink in the perpetrator's armour.

Chapter Ten

Tom pulled out a chair at the kitchen table and sat opposite Ruby. There was a great view through to the side of the conservatory and if he closed one eye it made it look like they'd been transported to some exotic location. If only. Tom loved Himlands Heath except sometimes it was so bleak and damp. What he wouldn't give to be lying on a sun-drenched beach with Ruby by his side, as she asked him to pass the sun cream, or better still asked him to lather some on her...

He stretched his neck and rolled his shoulders. 'It's coming up to ten o'clock. The children have been missing for eight hours.'

They were taking a break from the tense atmosphere in the lounge.

Ruby tucked a dark twist of hair behind her ear. Tom tried not to stare at her lips as she sipped from her glass. Today she was solemn, though he knew Ruby could be fierce. It was all hidden underneath a cool exterior. He'd seen her on the climbing wall, and seen the passion flowing out of her, and he wondered if one day he'd ever be able to unlock that and have it coming towards him.

'It's whizzed past,' Ruby said. 'I almost feel like I just heard Grant's message and jumped out of bed. When do you think Fox will call a press conference?'

'Not yet. They'll wait to see if the abductor gets in contact. If there are no kidnapper's demands then Grant and the super will make a judgement call on whether to put the family in front of the media depending on how we're progressing with eye witnesses and such.'

'It feels different when it's children, doesn't it,' Ruby said.

'Yeah much worse – which is why, when I left them, the constables were working their butts off on the street with the door-to-door. We're relying on them to get that golden nugget of information and every single one of them is dying to be the one to find it. The partial registration is a breakthrough and the public are dead keen to help. Everyone was cooperating even when we dug them out of bed at the crack of dawn. It's always like that when it's kids. If there's important information out there we'll find it.'

'I hope so.'

He gave her a smile and Ruby gave Tom a small one back. It didn't feel right, with two children in danger, to feel happy. It was because he was working with Ruby. Their friendship was slowly progressing. They often had breakfast together at Ruby's place and Tom had invited her to the cinema and to the park and once to the seafront for a picnic. She hadn't yet been to his place and he was working on it.

Tom was a keen sportsman and rugby was his thing. Though running wasn't his favourite, he'd agreed to train with Ruby because it was her ambition to run in the Himlands Heath fun run. When she'd asked him to be her training partner he'd been delighted because it gave him the chance to see her outside work. They ran together two or three times a week during quieter periods. It was fantastic to have nice times together and Tom knew he couldn't rush it. Besides, nothing gave him the impression Ruby liked him beyond being friends. He was always looking for a glimmer to show she felt the same way about him as he felt about her and he hadn't seen it yet. Maybe he never would.

Tom knew he must be careful because Ruby had had a difficult life. And she didn't trust easily. He respected that and no way would he ever cross the boundaries and make her uncomfortable. It would be her move or it would be no move at all.

They sat in silence.

A few minutes later, when they went back with the family, Ruby finished off her work with Alice. They'd almost finalised mapping the children's movements. Ruby had a pattern of who had had contact with Emily and Lisa and Tom knew she'd also been observing Jack and Alice's behaviour.

Jack had taken himself off to his study, though he'd left the door open. Like his wife, Jack was running on overdrive.

Tom settled himself near to the lounge window and tried to relax. Conserving his energy for the long haul was something he'd learned from the DCI and it was essential for a case like this where they'd be getting minimal sleep.

It wasn't long before Joan Hardman came back from the hospital and she dragged herself into the lounge, looking terrible.

'My house is a crime scene,' she said, and she threw herself into a chair.

'I need you here, Mum,' Alice said with a gulp. 'You know there's plenty of space. Then if something bad… happens...'

'Nothing worse is going to happen,' Mrs Hardman said firmly. 'Still, it's a good idea and I'd like to be close.'

At the sound of voices, Jack wandered back in and the three family members slumped in different chairs. Mrs Hardman stared into space, whereas Alice had her eyes squeezed shut. Jack kept biting his nails.

'Detective Delaney,' Jack said. 'I feel so useless. I've got to do something. I've got to get out there and start looking. I can't wait here.'

'DCI Grant said not to do that,' Alice said.

'I don't care. Waiting is driving me mad.'

'It's best if you leave it to us, sir,' Tom said. 'We're doing everything we can.'

'But they're my children.' Jack sounded desperate and he got up and stumbled out of the room.

'Leave him,' Alice said. 'He'll get himself together.'

Joan Hardman snapped out of her daze. 'There's no shortage of money. I'll give anything that's needed. If there's a ransom, I want to pay it.'

'Let's cross that bridge if we come to it,' Tom said.

A case like this was a waiting game – waiting to see what evidence they dug up, waiting to see if demands were made. Had the abductor left a trail? Would they identify a suspect? And meanwhile the family would be dragged through hours of agony. Tom was about to suggest Alice and Mrs Hardman lie down when the doorbell rang. It was the next-door neighbour, Natalie. A uniformed officer accompanied Natalie to the lounge and she went to hug Joan.

'Please accept my condolences,' Natalie said. 'I'm so sorry you lost your husband.'

'He died trying to save them. Does it sound stupid when I say it gives me some comfort?' Joan said.

Alice was still in her evening dress. 'I can't take it in about Dad. Lisa and Emily are all I can think about. Is there something wrong with me?'

'It's perfectly normal, Mrs Glover,' Ruby said. 'You're in shock and you've got a great deal to cope with. It might be a good idea for you to take some rest because you're going to need your stamina for the time ahead.'

Tom didn't want to mention they might need stamina for the coming days rather than hours. The worst kidnap cases were the ones which took weeks to resolve.

Alice nodded and Natalie helped her up and guided her out of the room.

'My poor Alice,' Joan said. 'This is a nightmare. If Ronnie hadn't suffered a heart attack he would have punched that man's lights out and then my grandchildren would be safe.'

Joan Hardman seemed to have aged. She must have collected a change of clothes because she wore jogging trousers and sweatshirt rather than her night clothes as she had at the time of the abduction. She had platinum blonde hair, which was dyed, Tom presumed. At better times, she was probably striking looking, as Alice was and the children too.

Joan had gone back to staring out of the window.

'I wonder if you could tell me more about Hardman Construction and your husband,' Tom said. 'A bit more background would be helpful.'

'I'm not sure I've the energy.'

'There might be a clue somewhere which could lead us to the abductor. The more information we can gather, the greater our chances.'

'You're very persuasive, detective. Something tells me you're rather good at your job.'

When Joan started talking she had a faraway look in her eyes. She told Tom she'd met Ronnie forty years earlier when she worked as a secretary at Ronnie's fledgling company.

'Falling for the boss is a cliché, isn't it,' she said. 'Like something you see in films, and believe it or not it's what happened for me and Ronnie. I knew it the moment I saw him and we've been happily married ever since. I think it's why Ronnie warmed to Jack – because Alice met Jack in the same way as us. She was a secretary and she fell for Jack when he joined Hardman Construction as a new manager.'

Hardman Construction had grown from being Ronnie on his own, then to a handful of workers and now to a successful company employing over fifty people. It covered Sussex county and a portion of neighbouring Surrey. Jack was in charge of the business and Joan, Ronnie, Jack and Alice owned the company equally between them.

'Ronnie was a workaholic. Before he retired, Alice and I didn't see much of him outside vacation times. That's why it's touching seeing him play with Emily and Lisa because he was never so close to Alice. The truth is, he was a bit of a stranger to his own daughter.'

Ruby was working on her laptop. She glanced up. 'I wonder what Alice thinks of that.'

'She's never mentioned it. When she was younger she was always close to her Uncle Phil, that's Ronnie's brother, or she was until Ronnie and his brother fell out.'

'What happened?' Ruby asked.

'Ronnie's always been the hard worker. He got where he is by years of long gruelling hours not by luck and Philip, who's younger than Ronnie, didn't have the same drive. Anyway, Phil set up a retail business which got into financial difficulties and when he asked Ronnie for help it was Alice who persuaded Ronnie to lend her Uncle Phil money. Unfortunately it all went south. Phil went bankrupt and Ronnie lost the cash he'd ploughed in and it was a big load Phil had borrowed. And then to make it even worse, many years later the same thing happened to Phil's son, Harry. It was like a repeating nightmare. Harry set up in business and after a few years he got into debt and he asked Ronnie for help just like Phil did. Harry hoped Uncle Ronnie would bail him out, but this time, Ronnie refused. Poor Harry went bust and he ended up going to prison.'

'That's quite a story,' Ruby said. 'And you still all get on?'

'Are you kidding me? Ronnie and I haven't spoken to Phil or his son for years, though I think Alice keeps in contact with her Uncle Phil. The only family Ronnie was interested in was Emily and Lisa. He spoils those children silly. Ronnie bought ridiculous amounts of things for them and paid for riding and dance lessons and clothes galore.'

Tom made a mental note to find out Alice's point of view on that one. And to flag up Phil and Harry Hardman with DCI Grant.

Joan lowered her voice. 'There's something else I need to tell you and I know Jack doesn't want to mention it. Could we speak in the conservatory?'

After making drinks, Tom carried them through to the hot house. It was humid and full of giant plants – cactus and ferns and exotic ones Tom didn't know the names of. Some of the cactus were covered in bright orange flowers and others had huge spikes which he carefully manoeuvred around. Joan was installed on a wicker chair.

'It's very nice in here,' he said. 'Reminds me of Kew Gardens.'

'I know. It's Alice's little haven and she's very proud of it. Our gardener gets advice from one of the gardeners at Kew.'

It made sense the Glovers paid for it to be done for them. Tom couldn't imagine Alice actually getting her hands dirty. He passed over Joan's drink.

'You're very kind,' she said. 'Only I don't like to talk in front of Jack. You see, a few years ago there was a rather nasty case of embezzlement at Hardman Construction and I know he doesn't like to be reminded of it.'

Well, thought Tom, the skeletons were coming out of the cupboard.

'I see,' he said.

'Basically, Jack found out Ronnie's senior accountant was cooking the books. Ronnie was devastated. He'd trusted Daniel Pearson for years. In fact, Pearson was a very early employee of Ronnie's. Of course, Ronnie sacked Pearson though it left a nasty taste and a lot of bad feeling, as you can imagine.'

'And it was Jack who was the whistle-blower,' Tom said.

'Yes.'

'Did it go to court?'

'Ronnie didn't want to prosecute, though he could have. Daniel Pearson was sacked and he was discredited and my husband felt that was enough punishment. I heard Pearson had some bad luck and some health problems afterwards, though I don't know the details.'

'Thank you, Mrs Hardman. I'll make sure we check it out.'

Joan rested her head back. 'I'm sorry, I suddenly feel drained.'

'No need to apologise. Why don't I go and fetch a glass of water?'

Tom's mind was turning over the new information. On his way to the kitchen, Tom quickly sent a message to DCI Grant. The kitchen was at the end of the hallway and the house was quiet and Tom didn't bother to announce his entry. As he walked in, he saw Natalie with her back against the counter and Jack pressed up close to her. And when they heard Tom the two of them sprang apart.

Tom stopped where he was, standing in the doorway.

'It's not what you think,' Jack said.

Natalie left the kitchen without looking at Tom. He caught the citric scent of her perfume as she brushed past him and he stepped aside to let her through.

'I'm not here to judge,' Tom said. 'Our job is to find your daughters and bring them home safely.'

Jack ran his hands through his hair. 'Of course. I know that. It's just.... I don't want you to....'

Misjudge him? Think badly of him?

'Mention it to your wife?'

'Something like that.'

It was a delicate situation. Tom knew their first priority was maintaining a good working relationship with the family. By leaving Tom and Ruby with the Glovers, the chief had given them that big responsibility. Tom didn't intend to mess it up. However, if there was information which could help, it was also their job to uncover it. Tom took his time. He nodded slowly at Jack.

'Then perhaps you could fill me in a little more, sir. To help me understand a bit better?'

'Would you like a coffee?'

'No thanks but a herbal tea would be nice, if you've got one.'

'You're in luck. That's what Alice drinks.'

Jack busied himself at the counter, turning on the coffee machine and taking cups out of the cupboard. When the noise of the machine had died down, he started talking.

'Natalie's husband, Sanjay, is filing for divorce. Their marriage has been on the rocks for a while. Natalie hoped they could salvage it and they've been seeing a counsellor only it doesn't seem to have helped. Sanjay wants out.'

'Right. And this is relevant because?'

'Because Natalie is a friend and she's upset about Sanjay. And I'm upset. And in a weak moment I cracked when I shouldn't have done. She's like a sister to me and I shouldn't have taken advantage of her.'

What Tom had glimpsed wasn't something you did with your sister.

'You mean it hasn't happened before today?'

'Of course not, Natalie is our friend. What I was doing when you walked in was crazy. I'm in such a mess over Emily and Lisa. You don't know what it's like. And Ronnie too, I mean he's dead for god's sake.'

'I know it's hard.'

'I can't stand it! What's happening? Why isn't there any news?'

Tom took over the pouring of the hot water and the carrying of the drinks to the table because Jack didn't seem capable of managing it.

'Oh god, my children. You don't know what it's like.'

The man's hands were shaking and Tom put his hand over Jack's.

'It's torture. I think I'm going mad.'

'Try to keep calm. If you need to speak to a counsellor, I can get that arranged.'

'It'll be getting dark and what will happen then? Lisa is frightened of the dark.'

Then Jack Glover broke down and cried.

Chapter Eleven

The house was quiet. Natalie had gone home and Ruby sat with Tom in the kitchen. She could see he was disturbed by the incident between Jack and Natalie.

'I passed on the information about Uncle Phil and his son Harry and about the embezzlement at Hardman Construction, and about Natalie and Jack,' Tom said. 'Grant told me to sit tight and get started on the search.'

Ruby had her characteristic small frown. 'I'm ready when you are.'

Tom shook his head. 'With his children abducted and his father-in-law passing away, Jack Glover decides to grope his wife's best friend?'

'It doesn't say much for his character,' Ruby said.

'Human nature never ceases to be disappointing. That's something I've learned on the job.'

'Oh don't worry, I knew that already.'

'Er, yes I guess so, sorry I didn't mean to be insensitive about your family and all. Anyway, what's important is – does it have any bearing on the kidnap?'

Ruby looked out of the window. Though she was dying to take a look she hadn't yet been through to the conservatory because she wasn't here as a sightseer. She smiled at Tom. She hadn't meant to sound know-it-all. Maybe she should let Tom know she was starting to feel positive about human nature and a lot of that was down to him because his friendship was something new and good in her life. The thing was, it would sound silly and unprofessional and she and Tom had work to do. They should start on the children's bedrooms. No, she should wait for a better time to tell him. *You're stalling, Silver,* she said to herself. *You're scared to open up. You've spent too long living like a damn clam.*

She followed Tom up the stairs. Emily's bedroom was decked out in pale blue and lilacs, and Lisa's was decorated in pink.

'What are we looking for?' Ruby asked.

'Anything which seems odd or out of place, or something missing which you'd expect to be there. Perhaps something hidden from the parents. Looking will also give us an idea about the children. If we come into communication with them, what link can we make with them quickly? It's little details which can make a life or death difference. Let's start with Emily.'

Emily was into horses. There were horse posters and horse ornaments. They found riding gear and photographs of Emily at the stables.

They systematically searched the drawers of an enormous lilac dresser.

'There was a twin of this one at the Hardmans' house,' Tom said.

They checked through the books on the shelf. Emily liked clothes. Or perhaps it was Alice who liked to buy them, because the child had more pretty tops and skirts and dresses than any child could wear. It was at the bottom of a box stuffed full of horse magazines where Tom found the surprise.

'Come and look at this.'

It was made of red silk. Tom tipped the camisole top onto the floor. It was a slinky sexy item and out of place in a little girl's room. There was no mistaking it as women's lingerie of the seductive kind.

'What size would you say this was?' he asked.

Ruby tipped her head on one side. 'I'd guess a ten.'

'You think it would fit Alice?'

'I think she's a couple of sizes bigger than that.'

'That's what I thought, and Natalie must be larger too.'

Ruby could see Tom blushing. Given how women were always so attracted to him it was odd Tom was embarrassed. He found it hard to meet her eyes. Using a gloved hand, Tom tipped the camisole into an evidence bag.

'You think it's important?' she asked.

'Everything is important. It might be nothing and it might be something. Who does it belong to? And what is it doing here? Why did Emily hide it?'

They moved into Lisa's bedroom. Lisa's room was full of cuddly toys. A bunch of them were on the bed and others were arranged on a long shelf. Some of the animals had secret compartments and zippered pouches only they didn't find anything of interest tucked inside.

'It was Lisa's teddy bear which the intruder slashed,' Ruby said. 'She would have found it very disturbing. Children this age believe their toys are alive.'

'Really? So the abductor killed the teddy?'

'Mutilated it more like and I'm not joking. Lisa is four, so part of her knows it's not true it's alive except there's another part of her which believes it is. A child's imagination is one of their driving forces. And he didn't only kill the bear, he slashed its stomach open. Since Alice told us Lisa brought it to her grandparents, it's likely one of her favourites.'

'Right. That sounds serious.'

'And it was in the middle of the night when dreams can get mixed up with reality, which would have made it worse. It would have been terrifying for her.'

'Got it. You think there might have been something hidden inside?'

'Either that or, like Grant thought, he did it deliberately to frighten them.'

They didn't find anything more of interest and Ruby noticed how Tom was careful to put things back as they had found them.

'The parents will want to come here,' he explained, 'especially the mother, and I don't want her to feel it's been disturbed, that wouldn't be right. It's going to be a place of comfort for the parents.'

Underneath his professional veneer Tom really was a surprisingly sensitive soul. It made Ruby like him even more. *Come on, Silver, say something.* She bit her lip but her words dried up. *If you like him let him know. Aren't you ever going to give the poor guy a hint?*

'What's up?' Tom asked.

'Oh nothing, I was thinking about the camisole,' she lied. 'Should we show it to the parents?'

'Not yet. We need to check with Grant and it will be up to the boss.'

An ear-splitting scream cut through the air. Ruby's knees threatened to buckle and every hair on her arms stood on end. It was Alice. Deep in her gut Ruby knew it was the sound a mother makes when they find their child is-.

Tom sprinted for the stairs and Ruby clutched the furniture and then followed behind. *Oh god please no, don't let the children be–*

Alice was on the lounge floor curled up in a ball.

'What's happened?' Tom demanded.

Jack was trying to prise something from Alice's hands and the more he tried, the more she screamed.

'Get off her,' Joan said, 'leave her alone.'

Jack didn't.

'Please stop, sir,' Tom said and he took Jack's arm.

Jack seemed to come to his senses and Ruby was horrified to see he was in tears. Alice stopped screaming.

The constable who was usually on duty at the front door explained. 'I'm sorry, detective. I was opening the post in front of the parents like DCI Grant asked me to and then Mrs Glover started screaming.'

The constable was wearing protective gloves and she pointed to a brown envelope lying on the floor. 'It was sent by special delivery.'

Ruby stared at the envelope. What had been inside? Was it a body part Alice was clutching? Please no. Ruby swallowed and gently put her hand on Alice's back. 'It's all right, Mrs Glover.' Except it wasn't, was it.

'Please step back, sir,' Tom said. 'Leave your wife alone.'

Tom had to drag Jack away and Ruby got down on the carpet and spoke close to Alice's ear.

'Please Alice. We need to know what you got in the mail. Can you show me? I'm not going to take it away from you I promise.'

Alice's reaction had been instinctive and was beyond reasoning with. Ruby waited and slowly, Alice uncurled. Ruby was frightened in case it was blood or flesh. She held her breath as Alice opened her hand. She seemed to be clutching a piece of material. It was pale pink with pink fairies on it.

'Oh god it's Lisa's pyjamas,' Joan said.

Alice was breathing heavily and staring at the people around her as if they were her enemies.

'I'm not going to take it from you. We're here to help,' Ruby said. 'Please can you show me?'

Reluctantly Alice opened her hands to reveal more of the material. It didn't look like a whole pyjama. Rather, someone had hacked off a leg. It was terribly difficult for the mother to let go of it and Ruby understood why. It was as if Alice was clutching her own child. Ruby held out an open evidence bag and when Alice finally blinked and the crisis ebbed, she seemed to sag. With a shaking hand she dropped the pyjama in the bag. Ruby passed it to Tom.

'Thank you, Alice,' Ruby said. The pyjama leg did not seem to have blood on it.

'You're certain this is from Lisa?' Tom asked.

Alice nodded and she started moaning. Joan hugged her daughter as Alice rocked backwards and forwards and they all understood the question no one could answer for her – are my children dead?

Chapter Twelve

On his way back from Brighton, Grant got the news about the pyjama leg. Forensics would be examining every millimetre of it and of the envelope and the team would be tracking the delivery back to where and who it was sent from. For sure, the abductor would have been clever and covered their tracks but they might get lucky. Meanwhile, he wanted to speak to Alice Glover. The poor woman, he felt for her.

Grant helped Alice walk to the hot house. She was in bad shape. Grant cleared his throat. 'I'll let you know as soon as we've got results on the pyjama.'

Alice let her head loll back on the chair and she stared at him with lifeless eyes. 'Have you found my babies? Are they dead?'

Her hair was a mess. He suspected she had not bothered to remove her makeup nor shower since the abduction, neither of which were surprising. And now, after the pyjama, the poor woman was a wreck.

'Don't give up hope, Alice. Stay with me on this one – I need your help.'

She gave the briefest of nods.

'A few queries have come up which I need to run by you and some of them might sound a bit odd except please bear with me. First of all, I understand your father didn't spend much time with you when you were a child. When Ronnie got attached to Emily and Lisa it must have felt strange.'

'So what if it did? I wasn't jealous if that's what you mean.'

'As far as I understand it, when Ronnie's will is enacted you'll own a third of Hardman Construction.'

'It's meaningless. I can't sell or do anything without the agreement of the other directors. And Dad is in charge of everything.' Alice's voice trailed off. 'Or he was.'

'I've a couple of more delicate questions,' Grant said. 'Please don't read more into this than there is only I understand there were a couple of incidents when Lisa was injured?'

Grant had checked the records and as Sylvie told him, an ambulance had been called on two occasions. Once, when Lisa had almost drowned in the bath, and the second time, when she had been injured falling onto a cactus in the hothouse.

Alice sat up. 'Did Jack tell you,' she hissed. 'The bastard.'

'What happened?' Grant asked.

'They were accidents. I don't remember because I wasn't feeling well. The doctor had given me some tablets.' Alice wafted her hand in the air.

Grant already knew the details. After Lisa's birth, Alice had suffered from post-natal depression and her doctor had prescribed medication.

'You were on anti-depressants,' Grant said. 'They affect memory and recall and you told the doctor you had a memory blank.'

'Exactly. I just remember finding her... it was all a blur.'

Grant consulted his notebook. 'On your statement you said Lisa slipped under the water during bath time and you found her unresponsive. She was revived by paramedics.'

'I only left her for a few seconds! When I came back, she'd gone under and I panicked.'

'And she was twelve months old at the time.'

'I know it was too young to leave a child on her own but I'm sure I only left the room for a second, I swear it.'

'And the second incident was when Lisa had inch-long cactus spines embedded in her thigh after falling in the hothouse. The doctors removed seven spikes. She was eighteen months old and it was a serious injury.'

'I didn't even know she'd gone in there! Jack blamed me, which wasn't fair. He's always blaming me for everything but where was he! Why was it only my fault!'

'It says in the paramedic's records you were the one supervising the children that afternoon.'

'Jack lied. He was home too.'

'I believe it was Jack who heard Lisa scream and he called the ambulance,' Grant said. 'Jack told the social worker at the hospital he thought you weren't fit to look after Lisa. He later changed his mind although he insisted on employing an au pair.'

'What a fucking joke! Can't you see how Jack is trying to blame me for everything? And the au pair thing was his idea, sure, except it wasn't for me it was so he could ogle young girls and have them come half naked into our kitchen and give him an eyeful. Have you any idea what it's like having them live here? They wear practically nothing and parade around like they own the place and Jack encourages it behind my back. The au pairs aren't for me they're for him!'

Alice was shouting. Grant nodded and kept his voice calm. She really was close to the edge.

'I understand.' He took a drink of water. 'Can you tell me about your uncle, Philip Hardman, and his son Harry. I heard they've been asking you for money.'

'More lies. Jack's always hated Uncle Phil and you shouldn't listen to a word Jack says.'

'Have Philip Hardman or his son ever asked you for funds?'

'I knew it. Jack's such a shit stirrer. Uncle Phil and Harry have *never* asked me for money not one penny. When I was younger, and I went on trips out with Uncle Phil and cousin

Harry, it was Phil who paid for everything. He spent *time* with me, which as you've so rightly said my dad never did. It was thanks to Phil I did normal things like other kids – learn to ride a bike, go to the park, go to the cinema. That's worth more than money. You know, when I was little, sometimes I used to pretend Uncle Phil was my dad – how sad is that? And I did it because my own father was never there.' She was shouting again. 'Once at a school concert, Phil came and I told my friends he was my father, because my own father was too busy to turn up even when I was singing my first solo. Do you know how that felt?'

Grant could only imagine how Ronnie had hurt Alice.

She angrily yanked her hair back from her face. 'Yes, and I don't care how cheesy it sounds. Of course I put in a good word for Phil and for Harry when they tried to get financial backing from my tight-arsed father, why shouldn't I? And you know what? If they ever asked me for money I'd give it to them if I could.'

Her voice had gone up so much Alice was practically shrieking. 'Jack hates them. Why? Because they like me. Because they look after me. So don't believe a fucking word my lying husband tells you!'

Chapter Thirteen

Ruby had her own office at the police station. It was on the second floor, with no window and space for a desk and a chair and nothing much else. Visitors had to squeeze around the door to get in. Detective Chief Superintendent Fox had told Ruby she'd move her to a more appropriate space once one became available, if it ever did. Oddly enough, DCS Fox had taken a liking to Ruby. Why was this strange? Because Fox, pretty much across the board, took a dislike to most people. Perhaps Fox made an exception because Ruby had found the breakthrough on the serial killer case, or improved the station's conviction rates? *Well,* Ruby thought, *it didn't get me any favours with the room.*

Still, Ruby wasn't complaining. She loved having her own space. It was fitted with wall-to-wall whiteboards where she scribbled coded thoughts. Ruby gathered her files, squeezed around the door and headed for the team briefing.

As usual, Grant had managed to wrangle one of the best incident rooms. It was larger and positioned at the end of the corridor so less noisy. McGowan was already waiting.

'Not again,' McGowan said rudely. 'I was hoping we got rid of you.'

Unfortunately, McGowan wasn't joking. Ruby had done nothing to start the fight between them, except of course to exist, she thought wryly. Though she'd be damned if she bowed to bullying from him. It wasn't her fault McGowan was a traditional, insecure, son-of-a-.

She plonked her files on a desk. 'DCI Grant has asked for my input which means you'll have to put up with it. Get used to it because I'm here to stay.'

'Bloody hell.'

'I've earned my place. Anyone would think you felt threatened.'

The exchange stopped as Grant and Tom walked in. Grant swiftly took in her face and McGowan's.

'I won't tolerate tension. You both got that?' Grant said. 'We're focused on one thing and one thing only and that's Emily and Lisa. Everything else gets left at the door. Understood?'

'Yes, guv,' McGowan said.

'Everything all right, Ruby?' Grant asked.

'Fine, sir,' she said, as she connected her laptop to the system.

Besides, she could fight her own battles. When she first arrived it hadn't been like that but these days she didn't need McGowan's approval to exist.

*

Grant had caught the tone of the exchange. Goddam it, if McGowan made this into an issue, he would have to tackle it but really, now was not the time. He hoped McGowan was professional enough to be able to focus on the task and if he wasn't, well, no one was indispensable.

'We're ten hours into it so throw out your ideas and questions. We need to take this to the next stage.'

Ruby sent her slides to the big screen. They detailed the movements of the children. Who, what and when were mapped out – preschool every weekday morning, a dance lesson for Lisa on Tuesdays, a riding lesson for Emily on Thursdays, a birthday party Emily had been to the previous Saturday, an unexpected trip to the supermarket and so on.

'A team of detective constables has been assigned to speak with everyone the children have been in contact with,' Grant said. 'Did you see any suspicious patterns? Or did the parents mention anything we need to flag as a priority?'

'No, it was all routine stuff – no new faces or changes in schedule.'

'There's the red camisole we found in Emily's room and there's three new persons of interest – Phil Hardman, who is Ronnie's brother, Harry Hardman who is Phil's son and so Ronnie's nephew, and the man accused of embezzlement at Hardman Construction, Daniel Pearson,' Delaney said.

Grant wrote the names at the top of the board. 'Good work. Diane will join us soon. We weren't lucky with tyre marks outside the Hardmans' property. As for the forensics, the lab results have come back and the handprint is Emily's blood group. It's possible the abductor has the same blood group so it's not definitive she's the one injured. We won't get the DNA result for another twelve hours.'

'That's bad news,' Delaney said.

Grant slung his jacket over a chair and went to the front.

'What about the pyjama, sir?' Ruby asked.

They all looked at him and Grant understood the unspoken question.

'We're assuming the children are alive. There's no evidence to contradict it.'

'You were going in hard on the questioning of Alice and Jack Glover,' Ruby said. 'What was the reason, sir?'

'Not sure yet. It's why I wanted you and Delaney at the house. In case.' Grant chose not to elaborate, because he had nothing concrete to add and until he did he'd be keeping his suspicions about the parents to himself. 'McGowan, can you give everyone an update on the Badawi family?'

'I've checked out the cleaner and her husband. They allowed me to search their apartment and there were no signs of Lisa and Emily having been there. Mr Badawi is short and broad. Joan Hardman described the abductor as normal height and weight.'

'What about their alibis?' Grant asked.

'I couldn't get confirmation. Like most people, the Badawis were asleep. One of the downstairs neighbours came back from a night shift at two and there were no lights on at the Badawi's place and he told me he didn't see or hear any movements before he went to bed around three. All the other neighbours were in bed.'

Grant wrote Halina Badawi's name on the board.

'Also,' McGowan said, 'the Badawis don't drive and there was only one abductor and he was a driver. As for the back door key – the Badawis have two daughters and the oldest might have a connection with the house keys. I've interviews planned with both daughters and I'll be checking out their movements.'

'Keep on it until you can rule them out or you can rule them in,' Grant said. 'Next. I met with the ex-au pair. Sylvie Delacourt also has no alibi. She's angry because Alice Glover accused her of having an affair with Jack. Is that sufficient motive to kidnap two children?' Grant put a red question mark at the end of Sylvie's name. 'I don't think so.'

'I've been researching kidnappers,' Ruby said. 'Half the perpetrators turn out to be family members. Of the remaining half, about one third are taken by friends or long-term acquaintances, and one third by strangers or persons who have made a slight acquaintance in order to carry out the kidnapping.'

Grant tapped the pen on the board. 'With no ransom demand, we don't know what we're dealing with. Then we have a dark estate car and the digits TMR from its number plate. I'm hoping Diane will bring the results from the surveillance cameras.'

It was a mammoth operation – Grant was assessing and sifting through as he went – checking his own decisions and identifying new priorities.

'Then we've got the key. Jack Glover's was on the hook in his kitchen. We're no further forward with finding out about the back door entry.'

Grant had pinned up photographs of Lisa and Emily along with a timeline since their abduction. The stress and the pressure were on his shoulders.

'And there's been one more breakthrough from the door-to-door – a neighbour at the end of Joan Hardman's street has seen a woman hanging around,' Grant said. 'I met the witness and she's reliable – she's a retired science teacher. She's seen the same woman on three or four occasions over the last few months. She described her as twenties to thirties, wearing jeans and a dark coat, dark wavy hair, medium height and build.'

'What was the woman doing?' Ruby asked.

'Nothing much which was why our witness noticed. The woman walked along one side of the street and back along the other side. Then she stood for more than ten minutes on the phone. I'm making it a priority to identify this woman and bring her in for questioning.'

'Do we have a description of the Badawi daughters? Could they be a match?' Delaney asked.

Oh, Delaney was good.

'Do we McGowan?' Grant asked.

'Both Ms Badawis are in their early twenties. I'll check descriptions.'

'Get me a photograph of the neighbour, Natalie. Interviewing Phil Hardman, his son Harry and the accountant Daniel Pearson is the next step.'

Grant was interrupted by the arrival of Diane. She was out of breath.

'Sorry, sir, I just ran up here from the car park.'

'If you're in a rush it means you've got something important, doesn't it?' Delaney said.

'I might have, or I might be clutching at straws.'

'Someone pour Diane a coffee,' Grant said. 'Better still, I'll do it myself.'

'What have you got?' Grant put a hot mug down on Diane's desk.

'We found positive footage from a camera outside the cinema and it shows a dark blue estate car heading out of Himlands Heath just after the time of the abduction. I've got the full registration,' she said triumphantly.

Grant glanced at the clock. 'At just over twelve hours into the abduction, that's great work.'

'There's something else. There are two possible routes after the cinema and I was trying to find any businesses with surveillance on those roads. The council cameras don't cover beyond the high street.'

Diane went to the giant map on the wall. She indicated the roads going out of town to the south. 'There are only two other businesses with cameras, one here and one here, and neither of them had footage of the car. Then I found one more camera. It's on the edge of town and it had stopped working.'

She tapped the board. 'It's at a fish and chip shop at the roundabout heading towards the A23 to Brighton. The odd thing was, the owner told me his son looks after the surveillance camera and it's always in working order.'

'Cameras break down all the time,' McGowan said. 'Especially the home-fitted ones.'

'I know,' Diane said, 'except…'

'Ah, I recognise that look,' Grant said. 'You suspect it could have been tampered with, don't you? Tell me everything you're thinking.'

Diane drew a red ring around the location of the fish and chip shop.

'I met the father and the son. They've had one break-in and two attempts in the past year and the camera helped catch the first perpetrator. The father told me they can't afford to have it not working which is why the son checks it regularly. And he says his son is one hundred per cent reliable.'

'And you don't think the son could have slipped up?'

'Unlikely. He told me himself he checks it pretty much every day. I know the obvious is it stopped working and nobody noticed except I can't help thinking – what if the abductor took out the camera in advance so he wouldn't be spotted exiting this roundabout?'

'Show me,' Grant said.

'There are three possible exits and on this road,' Diane followed it with her finger, 'there's an old site which used to house storage units…'

'Are you certain you're not latching onto it because it's the only pointer we've got?' Grant asked. 'You're sure the fish and chip story checks out?'

They were valid questions. Child abduction cases piled on the pressure. The heat was on to get *something*.

Diane shook her head and her voice betrayed her excitement. 'Sir, I think it's worth a shot.'

Everyone stared at him.

Grant kept an icy cool. Diversion to a search took resources away from the house to house. It was always more attractive to be taking action rather than searching for leads. Yet false action was wasteful – and it was a trap he could not allow the investigation to fall into. Plus they had new suspects to question.

If the son had messed up and not wanted to tell the father, Grant knew Diane would have suspected. And the lock-ups would be a perfect hiding place.

The buck stopped with him. Grant nodded to himself and swooped up his jacket.

'We search the lock-ups. McGowan, get working on the Badawi girls. Silver, I want you back at the Glovers keeping tabs on the parents. Collins and Delaney, you're with me.'

Chapter Fourteen

Tom drove and he took Grant and Diane with him. The tension in the car had ratcheted up the scale and neither the boss nor Diane talked much. Were the girls still alive? What would they find at the lock-ups? Tom's hands were sweating on the wheel and a team of six constables followed behind them, without sirens, on Grant's orders.

The lock-ups were deserted. It was a disused site, surrounded by a chain link fence yet with the front gate removed. They drove in along a battered tarmac road. Tom counted twenty storage units in all. Organised along two separate roads, they were giant metal containers each bigger than your average double garage. Given the scale of them, they must have been used for business or industrial storage. The metal sides of the units were deep rust coloured and weeds broke up the tarmac, giving the place a desolate air. Diane told them the site had been bought by the local Council with a view to building start-up pods for new businesses.

It would be an ideal place to hide out. Tom couldn't help thinking it would be even more ideal for stashing a body. He pushed that thought away.

Each unit had giant metal doors with metal retaining bars. They'd brought crowbars and heavy cutting equipment. The council had acquired the site when the storage company went into liquidation and they'd given the police permission to enter. The council had informed Diane there were no items in the lock-ups or if there were, the council wasn't aware of it.

If there were any nasty surprises, they'd soon find out.

Grant gave the orders. 'We'll split into two teams. Collins you lead one and take Delaney with you and three of the constables. If you find anything or any traces of recent activity, be careful not to contaminate the scene. Our first priority is preservation of life, our second is evidence.'

'Yes, sir,' Diane said.

'Remember to listen at each container. If the children are here, they might try to signal,' Grant said. 'Once we start cutting in, no one will be able to hear a thing.'

The adrenalin was pulsing so strong, Tom felt like he wanted to rip open the units with his bare hands. Even Grant had started sweating and he had ordered paramedics to standby. In case.

*

Diane led her group. Tom knew the chief had given Diane a lead as a mark of his approval. Grant was good at recognising when people had done well. Sifting through hours of footage would have been like hell. This was Diane's win.

Diane's team grouped around her. 'We'll first check the perimeter of each unit,' Diane said. 'We're looking for footprints or tyre tracks or discarded items. Notice if weeds have been trampled or if there are any signs of recent activity. Once we've searched the outside of each one and listened, then we try to enter.'

Diane patted Tom on the shoulder. 'Let's you and me check the first one.'

At the first unit in the row Tom pressed his ear against the cold metal. He called the children's names and tapped on the sides all the while looking for signs of recent entry.

'Emily? Lisa? I'm a police officer.'

He heard other officers doing the same at the containers on Grant's side. Was it possible the abductor was holed up inside one of the units? Tom felt ready for anything.

'Nothing,' Diane said. 'Let's check the next one.'

The doors of the second storage were practically hanging open. They followed the protocol and called out and inspected the area for signs of activity. Again there was nothing.

On the next unit the doors were firmly closed with the metal retaining bars kept in place by two giant, rusted padlocks. They were no signs from the inside in response to them calling.

When they reached the fourth lock-up, Tom pointed. It had rusty bars which were held in place with two brand new giant locks.

Diane called to the rest of the team. 'Bring the equipment! One of you run and tell Grant we've got something.'

Tom's heart started beating harder. Pressing his mouth close, he called out. 'Emily and Lisa, I'm a police officer and I'm here to help you. Please signal if you're inside. Tap on the walls.'

There was silence. They toured the outside and did a double check of the entrance area and it was there Tom spotted something bright in the grass. He bent close, being careful not to touch. It was a child's pink hair elastic, the sort used to tie back a ponytail.

Diane put on gloves and marked the spot. 'We'll get this photographed in situ.' She glanced at Tom. 'I say we go straight for a front entry. Do you agree?'

She was double checking with him because cutting the locks might destroy DNA or fingerprint evidence though it was their quickest way into the container.

'Agreed. It'll take way too long to torch through the side,' he said. 'If the children are trapped we don't know what state they might be in. Besides, cutting the locks won't necessarily destroy DNA.'

Diane turned to the constables who were readying the cutting gear. 'I want everyone double gloved to preserve what evidence we can. Now get this thing open.'

'Looks like you could be spot on, Diane. Phone the station and get the forensics team here,' Grant ordered.

*

It took twenty long and tense minutes for them to get in. Grant could feel the tension mounting and he had to order everyone to step back. Something or nothing? A dead end or a thread he could unpick? Grant's heart was thumping.

When the door finally creaked open Grant could see the rear end of a dark blue estate car.

'It's the same registration as the getaway vehicle,' he said.

Meanwhile Tom had retrieved an evidence protection suit and coverings from the car and he had suited up.

'In you go, Delaney, and I want you to call out a running commentary,' Grant said.

Tom went in. 'The back doors of the car are open, boss. There's blood on the back seat and in the footwell. I'm opening up the front driver's door. I don't see any blood in the driver's seat nor in the front passenger area. Going around the back to open up the boot.'

Grant held his breath.

'Nothing. There's no sign of the children.'

'Shit,' Grant said.

'Checking the glove compartment now. Damn, it's empty.'

Grant swore under his breath. Any old receipts or papers would have been too much to hope for.

'There are no obvious items in the rest of the area. I'm walking around the perimeter. There's nothing here.'

Tom came back outside and took off his mask. 'It's empty, guv.'

The assembled group almost screamed in frustration and Tom was trying to force back his disappointment.

'Look carefully,' Grant said, nodding towards the open lock-up. 'There's space in there for a second vehicle. The way the first one is parked makes me think there was already another one in there when he drove in. You see the angle of the car? He manoeuvred it to get it in. He would only have done that if there was something else already inside. Otherwise he'd have driven straight in.'

'Oh god, sir, you're right,' Diane said.

'Stay focused, people. Finding the car is a break because it means we're on the right track. Now forensics can get at it and all we need is one hair with a match on the database and we've got our key suspect.'

'Yes, sir,' everyone chorused.

'This becomes our second focus point. I want the public questioned with this lock-up as a new epicentre. Someone must have seen something and we're relying on you to find it. Collins, take the constables and get a door-to-door started straightaway.'

Grant checked his watch. Emily and Lisa had been missing for over fourteen hours and they'd had no word from the kidnapper. Was it a kidnapping? Or were they dealing with something else? Grant's stomach grumbled, reminding him he'd not eaten since mid-morning. It made him think of Emily and Lisa and how frightened they would be. Were they hungry? Were they dumped in the cold? Collins started to organise the constables. There was no question of anyone going home to rest, and anyway no one wanted to.

*

Twenty minutes later, Grant had only just set foot in the police station when his phone pinged. It was DCS Fox summoning him.

Fox hardly waited for him to get through her door.

'I heard about your little escapade.'

Ah, he thought, *and she doesn't sound pleased*.

'It was a calculated decision, ma'am. Based on the evidence from the surveillance cameras there was a high likelihood the abductor had used the lock-ups.'

'A high likelihood? Is that what you call it and you didn't think it important to run your splurge of *precious time* past me first?'

Strictly speaking he wasn't obliged to do that. Yet he judged it more diplomatic to stay silent.

Fox was on a roll. 'Six constables, specialised equipment and three detectives on site. Vital resources taken from the coal face and for what? A hair ribbon?'

'It was a hair elastic, yes, and we found the getaway car. Forensics are–'

'Forensics are doing their job.' She spat the words out. 'Which is a hell of a lot more than you seem to be doing. The kidnapper had been and gone, Grant, long gone and I've got ACC Treadgold *and* the Chief Constable breathing down my neck. They want results. I want results. I want those children found. The whole goddam nation is watching.'

Well then, if she'd just let him get on with it instead of dragging him in here for a telling off. He stood to leave and her icy glare followed him to the door.

'We're fourteen hours in and we don't have a key suspect? Is that all you've got for me? Quit trailing behind the perpetrator like a goddam lame dog.'

That was a new one. Fox sure liked to roll out the insults. Grant hoped soon he'd be laughing about it. Except, right now, he didn't feel so confident about that.

Chapter Fifteen

As I drive out of Himlands Heath I congratulate myself on a job well done. My plans have been cooking around my head for so long they've a stroke of genius in them. Now I can head down to the coast with a smile on my face.

The sun has come out and I whistle a little tune. I've always loved the Sussex countryside with the rolling South Downs and green fields and hedgerows. I missed it so much during my prison sentence. When I became a free man again, you wouldn't believe it of a con like me but the sound of bird song was enough to make me sentimental.

I take my time going down to Brighton. Firstly, I make sure I stick to minor roads without much traffic. Then, I stop often in laybys and remote spots to pass an hour or so and listen to the radio. I've got all day to waste. On the motorway, the journey would take an hour but with this route and the method I'm using it will last most of the day. And that's the idea.

When one of the kids wants to pee I consider leaving them to do it in the van rather than take the risk of them being seen. There's no one around, yet you can never be one hundred per cent certain, can you? Then again, is there DNA in piss? I don't know and it might turn out to be a nuisance because I'd need to get the back cleaned and then what if a garage gets suspicious? I decide it's better to let one of them out at a time.

I find a quiet place and then the smaller one says she can't do it unless she has the big sister with her.

I have to stop myself from smacking her around the head.

Half an hour later and we're on our way again. No one saw us, I'm sure of it. I've never been so grateful for clusters of trees.

The tricky bit will be getting the kids inside the house once I arrive. Which is why I need to transfer them at night-time because there's far less chance of being spotted by a nosey parker when it's dark. Hence my dawdling.

On the outskirts of Brighton there's a big park. I already sussed it out to see if the police have a habit of passing by, which they don't, or if the various parking spots have attendants, which they haven't. The park is packed at weekends and then deserted during the week, except for early morning when it's full of dog walkers and joggers. I can't stand sports fanatics – as far as I'm concerned they're a bunch of losers. Anyway, weekday late afternoon is ideal for us to pass under the radar.

I take the turn into the park and drive to the remotest spot it can offer. I'll wait here until it's nightfall.

*

Several hours later and I'm getting impatient. I've tossed a packet of biscuits into the back which shut up the whimpering. Those kids are getting on my nerves. I can't wait to lock them up and forget them. No more snivelling, no more piss stops.

I'm painfully aware how all it would take is for one of the kids to start screaming or bang on the side of the van and the game would be up. I'm betting they wouldn't dare because I've scared them stupid. Though as time passes my nerves are fraying. After the biscuits, I taped their mouths as a precaution and I've bound their hands. The only thing they could do is bang and I don't think they've got it in them. Thing is, I don't trust that older one. What if she tried something? What if an innocent member of the public later remembered something odd which allowed the police to pick up my trail? I can't risk being noticed.

Every couple of hours I move parking place. In that way I manage to hold out until dusk, then I can't stand it any longer. I have to get them inside the house.

I picked out the property ages ago. You see, I've been planning this for years. First in my head and then in reality. The money makes all the difference. Without the previous payoff, I'd never have been able to afford the rent for such a nice property. The thing is, the few thousand pounds I got isn't enough. It was paltry given the length of sentence handed to me and I deserve much more for what I've suffered. And I'm going to make damn sure I get it.

It's a two-storey, mid-terrace house on a Brighton street in an area an estate agent would call a desirable neighbourhood.

The neighbour on one side is an elderly man and on the other there's a woman who leaves early and comes back late. I don't assess either of them as being vigilant.

On the opposite side of the street there's one neighbour who's a different story. She's got a disabled parking bay out front. When I first rented the house I put my van in it and she went berserk. She had the nerve to come and bang on my door. She shouted at me, her hair purple and standing on end in spikes. Bloody hell, who does she think she is? I had to stop from punching her in the face. *Keep it together,* I told myself, *think of the end game*. People like her should be shot.

I need to park right outside my place to pull it off. I've got a big canvas holdall I'm going to use to transport the brats. Clambering over the front seats, I grab the biggest kid and tell her to climb inside the bag.

'If you don't, I'll cut your sister.'

When she hesitates, I wave the knife in her sister's face. Bingo. She steps into the holdall and scrunches down small. As

I zip it closed, I catch sight of her mutinous look. Didn't I tell you she was trouble?

She doesn't weigh much. I heft the holdall inside the house and dump it with my accomplice. Then I go back for the smaller kid, and not long after we've got both handcuffed to a metal bunk bed in the second-floor bedroom. Both of them got a visit to the toilet, which I wouldn't have bothered with but my accomplice dealt with it, and now the bedroom door is locked.

I strut downstairs and chuck the rag I used on the kid into the bin. Time for a drink.

'Do you want one?' I ask my accomplice.

She goes to the bin and picks out the rag, holding it with her thumb and forefinger so it dangles. Blood has streaked it red against whatever the fuck colour it was in the first place. 'What's this?'

'I had to nick the kid's arm. Nothing serious. I wiped it. I didn't want it making a mess.'

'This cloth is filthy. She could get an infection.'

'Don't be stupid and so what if she does?'

She doesn't dare answer me back. Instead she drops the rag in the bin and comes to sit on the sofa, curling up like a kitten. That's what I like – compliance. I pour myself a generous slug of vodka and a smaller one for her.

'To success,' I say, and we clink glasses.

Chapter Sixteen

Maria found it hard to believe he'd done it. He'd succeeded in nabbing the children and he'd got away with it. Part of her had been hoping he would fail.

When Maria first heard his plan several months earlier, she'd thought him mad. He believed he was a genius and Maria thought he was eighty percent crazy and twenty per cent deluded.

She watched as he poured a celebration vodka for them both. *Chink.* Bashing his glass against hers, he downed his in one.

They both knew what was coming next. Maria tried not to rub her palms together because he hated that habit. He poured himself another drink. Taking a small packet out of his pocket, he dipped in his finger and rubbed the white powder around his gums. He knew she was watching, waiting for her turn. It was part of his game. Finally he grinned and patted the cushion next to him.

'Here you go, babe. Come and get your reward.'

Maria skittered over. She kept the nail on her pinkie finger long, buffing and filing it carefully every day. Specially for this purpose. She dipped it in and took a scoop of powder. Then she snorted.

Her nervous system buzzed with it, filling her with confidence and power. Using the powder made her feel anything was possible. It showed her how her life should be.

Free from misery. Free from restrictions. Closing her eyes, Maria rested her head back as stresses and failures and time itself passed her by.

*

As it wore off, her throat felt numb. She was used to the after effects. Cocaine was supposed to make you paranoid and maybe it was true because now he was writing out his list of rules again, his pencil scratching furiously across the page. The room stunk of booze and sweat and stale food because he refused to open any windows.

'I need to make sure we don't forget anything,' he said. 'I want you to memorise my instructions.'

Her chemical boost was fading fast and she tried to grab it back except it evaporated like early morning mist. Maria gave a nervous nod and shuffled to the edge of the sofa to read over his shoulder. She scanned a few lines – wearing a mask was obligatory for entering the children's room, trips out must be minimised, the lights had to go on at this time and then off at this time as if a normal person was living in the house and the list went on. He'd got his eye on the details, in fact, he was obsessed by them.

She hadn't told him how she was relieved about the masks to cover their faces. They had to wear them whenever they had contact with the children and she hoped it meant he intended to let the children go at the end. After all, he was making an effort to make sure Emily and Lisa wouldn't recognise their captors.

'Don't give them anything to eat tonight,' he said.

'Whatever you want.'

Maria tried a small smile and she felt relieved when he responded. He was the boss, as he liked to remind her. She had to do what he said including being the passport to the Glover family.

After he had filled one sheet of paper and polished off another glass of vodka, his chemical high had worn off and his mood plummeted. It was always like this – one minute he was acting like he'd won the jackpot and the next he was obsessive-compulsive about all the shit which could go wrong.

'Let's go through the plan again,' he said.

This was the millionth time they had done the recap and her skin started itching but she plastered a pleased expression on her face. It was best not to antagonise him. Clearing the table, Maria forced down a sigh. Not acting obedient would make it worse for her. The best thing was to play along.

He plodded through it – how the police would be monitoring phone calls and texts and how they needed a way to contact the family which the police wouldn't know about. Would Jack cooperate? It was the big unknown. She believed he would and the plan hinged on it. After all, Jack was the one with everything to lose.

By the time he'd gone through it twice she knew she wouldn't be able to stand it for much longer. Then he fell asleep on the sofa with his mouth hanging open. Thank God.

Maria busied herself sorting out the mess of pizza boxes and glasses because one moment he didn't care and the next he demanded the place be tidy. Dancing around his moods was exhausting. It was tempting to go upstairs because she would have liked to whisper to the children through the little gap under the door to tell them not to be frightened. Maybe she could even open the door? The key was in his pocket and she might be able to get it without waking him.

He was snoring and she leaned over him, undecided, scratching at her palms. With all her will power she tried to make herself reach out and hook a finger into his pocket only she couldn't make herself do it. It was too risky. For one thing, he'd got a temper and for another, she was terrified of losing her supply of powder. Dependency did that to you. He was the one with the money and the drugs which meant he'd got a hold over her.

She stuffed the rubbish into the bin. If they pulled this thing off he promised her freedom and enough cash to call her own shots. Maria shuffled to the double bed crammed into the room next door. She scrunched the duvet to her chest and rocked herself to calm the jitters. Closing her eyes, she dreamed of a better life.

*

Emily was cradling Lisa's head in her lap. The room was dark with a crack of light coming under the door. Lisa was afraid of the man in the mask, and the dark, which meant Emily's little sister had cried herself to sleep. They were hungry and all they had was a bottle of water. Emily had been terrified the man would hear Lisa crying and come. He didn't like crying. It made him shout. It made him angry. Lisa must have understood too because she'd tried her best to keep it muffled.

A chain tied them to the bunk bed and the metal cuff around Emily's wrist was making a red mark although it wasn't as bad as the mark on her other arm. The man had cut her with the knife he'd stabbed teddy with. He'd done it when she'd tried to pull away from him at Granddad's house.

Emily wished now she'd screamed for help only she'd been too scared. Her voice had shut down. She'd obeyed him when he told her not to make any noise or otherwise he'd hurt Lisa. Why had she done that? Had she been silly? How she wished she'd screamed and screamed and then Grandma and Granddad would have come sooner.

Dropping Lisa's hair band out of the car window had been a big risk. Emily had done it when the car slowed down and the man seemed distracted. She hoped Mummy and Daddy would find it.

The room was bare except the bed, the water bottle and a bucket. She and Lisa realised around the same time what the bucket was for and they hadn't wanted to talk about it. When Lisa used it, Emily had tried to turn away.

What Emily liked was the window. It was high up and too high for her to get to because of the chain, but she could see the sky. It was getting all twinkly with stars. She knew it was the same stars she saw from home because she could make out the shape of one she recognised – Orion it was called. She'd learned it from her stars book.

The idea of home made her feel wobbly. *No,* she told herself, *you must be strong for Lisa.* Mummy and Daddy would find them. Mummy would come. They just had to be brave and wait.

Emily pushed up her sleeve. Although it had stopped bleeding, the cut hurt and her forearm was puffier than the other one. She mustn't cry and when Lisa woke up Lisa mustn't see it or the sight of it would scare her even more.

Chapter Seventeen

When forensics contacted Grant to say the blood belonged to Emily, Grant felt sick. He was glad he'd not had time to eat.

He spent the night at his desk scanning the information coming in – financial and phone records and background information. He could not afford to make mistakes. He read every docket and scanned every entry so far on the HOLMES2 database.

Grant interviewed the three men on Jack's list and all of them told him the same story -- Hardman Construction was a competitor, and Jack Glover led the company in a different way than his father-in-law Ronnie Hardman. Jack's adversaries didn't like the way Jack conducted himself. Yet all three expressed their condolences at Ronnie's passing away and their disbelief and horror over the abduction of Emily and Lisa.

Why had Jack put these men forward? With sound reputations, decent incomes and stable families, none of them were candidates to organise the kidnapping of two small children. What was Jack Glover playing at? Was he deliberately sending Grant down a blind alley?

Grant took a cat nap at his desk mid-way through the night. It left him with a sore neck. At five o'clock in the morning, he took a fresh shirt from his emergency stock. As he buttoned it, he grimly noted the time. They had passed the twenty-four-hour marker.

True to form, Delaney arrived early and Grant was ready and waiting.

'I want you to sit in on the interviews with Philip and Harry Hardman,' Grant said. 'I've asked them to be here for six.' Grant rolled his neck.

'Okay, boss.'

Delaney sounded nervous. It reminded Grant how anxious he'd been, back in the day, when his senior officer asked him to step up during high profile cases. It was the best way to learn. He patted Delaney on the shoulder.

'Don't stress. You know the drill and you know the case and the family. If something comes to mind, ask it. We'll start with Philip.'

Philip Hardman and his son Harry arrived soon after. Grant cautioned them and explained he was conducting informal interviews.

'We're not under arrest then?' Philip Hardman said, smiling broadly at his own joke.

'Dad, stop messing around. Not with little Emily and Lisa missing,' Harry said.

'If you wouldn't mind waiting here, sir,' Grant said to Harry. 'We'll speak to you after your father.'

*

Philip Hardman resembled Ronnie, though he was a slighter build. His jacket was faded at the elbows and his shoes were scuffed. Ronnie's brother was clearly used to being the guy who got a laugh, only Grant was far from being in the mood for funny.

'As I said, this is an informal interview. I want to speak about the abduction of your nieces.'

'A terrible thing. And with Ronnie passing away too,' Philip shook his head. 'I'm sure you know there was no love lost between me and my big brother except the rancour was on his side not mine. It's dreadful, simply dreadful. How can I help?'

'I'd like to know about the fallout between you and Ronnie.'

'It's water under the bridge,' Philip said. 'I phoned Alice yesterday to say how sorry we were. She was in a terrible state. Has there been any news?'

'If you could answer my question please.'

'Er, yes, of course. It was only a bit of friction between brothers. It was stupid how we let things get bad between us though I suppose you must be used to families acting like idiots, eh Inspector?'

As Philip Hardman gave a false laugh, Grant could feel his patience wearing thin. Nothing of substance had come through from the Child Rescue Alert and if Philip Hardman couldn't answer straight questions Grant would be damned if he could be bothered to hold his temper. Grant poked a finger down his own collar, loosened it a notch, and fixed cold grey eyes onto Philip.

Philip Hardman got the message.

'Anyway to cut a long story short, I had my own business and I got into serious debt. Ronnie was doing great at that time and Hardman Construction was going strong. He leant me money with zero interest and the lot. Unfortunately, my business went down the pan and Ronnie's money went with it. He was furious.'

'You fell out over it?'

'You've got to understand my brother. By then Ronnie was a successful man and he was livid I'd failed and he was angry I'd dragged him into it. He couldn't understand how I'd, in his words, made such a balls up. I was bankrupt so there was no way I could pay him back and he couldn't forgive me. It was more a pride thing.'

Delaney cleared his throat. 'Joan Hardman told me you weren't on speaking terms after that.'

'I know it sounds ridiculous. We never mended the gap between us. Of course, now I regret it.

A fallout between brothers over money, was that all there was to it? Grant stared at Phil Hardman.

'Ronnie and I weren't speaking though I always kept in touch with Alice,' Philip said. 'She was born a year before Harry. I doubt anyone's told you how Ronnie wasn't exactly a model father. He spent more time at Hardman Construction than he did with his wife and child. When Alice was born it was me who brought Joan home from the hospital with the baby because Ronnie had a meeting he didn't want to cancel, so don't think it was all one sided with me asking and Ronnie giving. I stayed close to Alice when she was growing up – used to take her to the playground with Harry and to the cinema and spend time with her and things like that, which Ronnie never did. He barely knew his own daughter. Of course, my link with Alice faded a bit once she got older but I've always had a soft spot for my niece.'

'And Alice's children, do you know anything which could help us find them?'

'I wish I did. I really wish I did.'

After a glance at Delaney, Grant slammed his notebook closed. Shortly afterwards, he slammed the door of the interview room behind them. He felt a heavy bad mood descending on him.

'Pressure from all sides and the case isn't cracking yet,' Grant said.

Grant was plugged into the station gossip tree and he knew Treadgold was visiting Fox regularly. He could feel the man creeping up behind him, waiting for Grant to make a mistake. It was as if he hoped the outcome of the case would be a disaster. That Emily and Lisa would turn up dead and then he'd be able to blame Grant and hang him out to dry. The sick bastard.

'Everything all right, sir?'

'No it bloody well isn't.'

*

Tom nodded. Though Grant had ordered him home to rest for a few hours, Tom had barely slept. He trailed behind Grant to the second interview room, recognising the steely determination which had settled on his boss's face. He didn't envy the person who got themselves on the wrong side of Grant today.

Harry Hardman jumped when they entered the room. 'Gosh, you gave me a fright.'

Grant glowered. *No kid gloves this morning,* Tom thought.

'Do you know anything which can help me find the children?' Grant asked, fixing his stare on Harry.

The young man was startled. 'What? I'd have come to you if I did.'

Harry wore jeans and a baggy shirt over a thin frame. He had a sullen air about him, Tom thought.

'What can you tell me about the family rift?'

'There's not much to say. I mean Dad and Uncle Ronnie fell out years ago. It was over money Uncle Ronnie lent to Dad.'

'Please don't make me drag this out of you word by word. With two little girls missing and the clock ticking, I've much better things to do with my time. Like your father, I understand you had business troubles too and Ronnie Hardman refused to bail you out?'

'Yeah only that was ages ago.'

Grant cracked his knuckles and Harry hurriedly continued talking.

'I mean, it wasn't my fault. Me and two mates set up a burglar alarm installation company. It was legit and things went well. Then we expanded to include renovations on buildings. I thought Uncle Ronnie could help by sending contacts my way and all that but he was pretty reluctant about it. Anyway, things started to go south. We sort of overstretched ourselves and had to borrow heavily from the banks and I hoped Uncle Ronnie would lend me a hand and he didn't.'

'He wouldn't lend money or he wouldn't give you advice?'

'Neither. I was let down by my partners and they scarpered. And Uncle Ronnie was family and he let me down too.'

'I see.' Grant glanced at the file in front of him. 'It resulted in a custodial sentence.'

Harry's expression turned sulky. He nodded.

Tom had read the details. Harry received a short prison sentence for bankruptcy. A prison sentence for bankruptcy was unusual. It meant Harry's business affairs had not been above board. In the court notes, it said Harry borrowed money fraudulently and set up a second business to try to bail out the first. No wonder Ronnie hadn't wanted to get involved.

Harry's attitude came across as whining. The man thought Ronnie owed him something and should have been willing to step in. But why? He was Harry's uncle, he wasn't Harry's keeper.

'And neither of you nor your father have had much contact with Ronnie and Joan up until now?' Grant asked.

'Not them, no. We always kept contact with cousin Alice though,' Harry said, 'because when I needed help Alice put in a good word for me with her dad, or she tried to. She's the only one I got on with. Poor Alice. Uncle Ronnie always thought so much of himself but he was mean.'

Grant cleared his throat. 'Thank you for coming in, Mr Hardman. I'll be in touch if there's anything else.'

*

Back in the team cubbyhole, Grant turned to Delaney. 'Observations?'

'It was interesting how neither of them mentioned Jack. Alice was the one who had all their sympathy.'

'Yes. I'd say Jack Glover is getting a lot of negative attention.'

Just then, Grant's day took a turn even worse as DCS Fox paid a visit. She rarely came down to the team space, which they affectionately called the cubbyhole, though goodness knows what Fox called it.

She marched straight up to him.

'Progress?' she snapped.

'Jack's business associates and Philip and Harry Hardman have been interviewed. Harry Hardman is the most likely candidate. He seems to believe his uncle owed him. Thing is, a grudge against Ronnie isn't sufficient grounds for kidnap. It would be a huge step and frankly I don't see Harry as having the nerve for it. Even if he did, has he got the brains to pull it off? We'll see what the background checks pull up though I'm not hopeful.'

'Why do I feel this is going nowhere? The press are gnashing their teeth. And so am I. Anything on the pyjama?'

'Nothing so far, sorry ma'am.'

'Sorry ma'am my arse. We've passed the twenty-four-hour mark! Find them or I'm throwing you to the press and they can rip you to pieces themselves. Anything from the public response?'

'We've had a string of suspected sightings. No pattern and they're scattered across the UK. Constables are following up. I double-checked but there are none so far I've flagged as priority and McGowan has ruled out the Hamadi girls. They were both seen at their universities early morning and they're too far away to have been directly involved in the snatch. And both sisters have short hair so they're not a match for our mystery woman who was seen in Joan Hardman's street.'

Fox leant her knuckles on a desk giving a good resemblance, he thought, to an orangutan. 'Shit.'

He knew she was thinking the same he was. That the longer it dragged on the smaller the chance was of finding the girls.

'Shit exactly. Ms Silver is back at the Glover house and I'm sending Delaney over there now.'

Fox narrowed her eyes. 'You think there's more there, don't you.'

She knew him better than he realised.

'Just what we don't need,' Fox said. 'Questions about the family. If you've got something on them I want to hear it.'

'Nothing definite. But both parents are hiding something and I'd bet my life on it. I've one more person to interview – Daniel Pearson, the man accused of embezzling funds.'

'The clock is ticking, Grant.'

She really didn't need to tell him that.

'We're going flat out. Something's got to give soon and if it doesn't, we'll need to prepare the family to do a press appeal.'

A press appeal would be a harrowing ordeal for Alice and Jack though sometimes it brought information from the public which would not have come by any other means.

Fox was grinding her teeth and Grant wondered if she was about to repeat the lame dog comment. He really didn't need it. Time to make a speedy exit.

'Don't give up hope,' he said. 'I need to see the accountant as quickly as possible.'

'Then bloody well get over there.'

*

At the edge of his awareness, Grant registered the temperature had picked up, which was a sign real spring was on its way. It would soon be lambing time which was his favourite season because he liked to see new life coming back into the world. His pleasure from it likely came from the long list of murder cases he'd worked. It also explained how Grant enjoyed holding babies – a fact his wife never failed to remark on.

Grant drove like a fury. Daniel Pearson lived on the outskirts of Himlands Heath and down a narrow lane. Grant took in the details of the property. The roof of Pearson's cottage looked in need of repairs and so did the fencing. If Pearson had been embezzling funds from Hardman Construction, as Joan claimed, he certainly hadn't invested it in his house.

Pearson was slow to answer the door. Grant remembered Joan mentioned Pearson had health problems and he wondered what those might be. The door opened to reveal a man in his sixties, roughly the same age as Ronnie. Pearson was tall and thin, with wispy sandy-coloured hair. He was slightly stooped and his complexion seemed sallow.

'I'm Detective Chief Inspector Grant. May I come in?' He'd deliberately not called ahead.

'What for?'

'The Glover children, Lisa and Emily, have been abducted. You must have seen it on the news.'

The man's mouth fell open, then he pressed a hand to his stomach. 'Goodness, I don't know what to say. How terrible. Please come through and no, Inspector, I wasn't aware. I don't watch much television these days.'

Pearson took Grant through to a lounge which smelled faintly musty as if the cottage didn't get much fresh air. The low ceiling had wooden beams hanging with cobwebs and it could have looked quite charming if it had been kept fresher and in a better state.

Grant resisted the urge to swipe the armchair clean before he sat down. He'd had years to suppress those sorts of impulses.

'I'm here to talk about the Hardmans and the Glovers,' Grant said.

Pearson seemed surprised. 'Oh?'

'The family have indicated there's history between you. Would you care to fill me in?'

'Okay but wait… you're not thinking I could have anything to do with the children are you? That's preposterous.'

'Mr Pearson, I need to work quickly. If you could simply fill me in on your view of past events and whatever happened between you?'

'Yes of course, I mean, if Alice's children are missing then I'm very sorry. As for Jack Glover, I don't think you're going to believe what I tell you though I swear every word is true. That man is an abuser and a violator and he should have been in trouble for what he did but he got away with it because he's a liar and a cheat who happens to be married to Ronnie's daughter. Ronnie let that blind him to the truth.'

Grant's impatience stirred and he stamped it down as best he could. *Keep it cool. Get the details and trust your instincts. And don't miss a damn thing.* 'If you could start at the beginning, sir?'

'Sorry, I'm not very well.' Pearson indicated his stomach. 'I've had part of my intestines removed and now I've got a damned ostomy bag instead of a bowel. I guess you understand what that means. It keeps me alive but it's changed my life.'

'I see.'

'No you don't except it doesn't matter. I'd been with Ronnie since the beginning. He took me on when he first needed an accountant and I stayed with him while the business grew. We were friends or so I thought. Then along came Jack and he fell for Ronnie's daughter, or likely it was Alice who fell for Jack because that man's a real snake charmer. That's why it took me so long to work out what was going on. It started one day when I went into the main office and one of the young secretaries was crying. The office manager, Maude, was looking after her. When I asked what was wrong, this girl, who was half Jack's age, told me Jack had tried to kiss her.'

Grant felt a frisson of excitement as his instincts kicked in. This was important.

'Anyway, I dismissed it and that's something I'll never forgive myself for. Maude didn't believe it either or she thought the girl was exaggerating although Maude thought the sun shone out of Jack's arse so it made sense she didn't want to think badly of him. The young woman handed in her notice a few weeks after and I didn't think any more of it. Then a few months later, I walked into Jack's office and I could hardly believe my eyes because the piece of shit was trying to get his hand up a woman's skirt. Now, there was no denying it because I saw it. And I saw how upset and uncomfortable the woman was which told me this was not something she wanted nor had she invited.'

Grant's attention was razor sharp as he made hmming noises, encouraging Pearson to continue.

'We'd taken her on as a receptionist while our own was on maternity leave. This time I didn't let it go. I got Jack on his own and he started spewing out the lies – he minimised the whole thing and said she had led him on and when I spoke to the woman she clearly didn't want to lose the work and she didn't want to take it any further. Again, I was a fool because I didn't take it up with Ronnie. I thought warning Jack would be sufficient – that me witnessing his vile behaviour would be enough to stop him.'

'Did either of the young women go to the police?'

'Not as far as I know. Our own receptionist came back from maternity leave and the temp left. I thought I'd made it clear to Jack sexual harassment was not to be tolerated and then one day, and it was a few months afterwards, someone left an anonymous note on my desk. It was written on a scrap of paper and it was a person's name and it said I should speak to this person about important matters concerning Jack's behaviour. I don't mind telling you when I read it my blood went cold. I'm not making excuses but you've got to understand Jack was the golden boy – he was Ronnie's son-in-law, Alice was pregnant with their first child, everyone in the office thought he was the best thing since sliced bread.'

'What was the name on the note?'

Pearson gave a small burp. 'Apologies, my digestion is terrible. The name was Zofia Kaminski. She'd worked as an admin assistant at Hardman and when I went to see her what she told me made me physically sick. She told me Jack Glover had tried to rape her at the Christmas party.'

Oh god this could be it. This could be motive. 'That's a serious allegation.'

'You're telling me. I remember sitting in Zofia's kitchen and she folded her hands on the table and stared me straight in the face and I could see her lips trembling. Imagine the courage it must have taken for her to tell me. And to this day I've no idea who left the note. I'm no expert, Inspector, but I believed Zofia. And then even worse happened and you're going to think me naïve and I definitely was because I intended to tell Ronnie and I stupidly felt it right to inform Jack first about what I was going to do.'

'Go on.'

'It was an absolutely idiotic decision on my part. You've got to understand Ronnie was the big boss and everyone took directions from him. Hardman Construction belonged to him – it was his baby. I was sort of the unofficial second in line mostly because I'd been around the longest except when Jack got promoted he always tried to sideline me. And then there was Maude, the office manager, and she reported straight to Ronnie and like I said, she thought Jack was wonderful and wouldn't hear a word against him. I went to Jack first because I thought it was the right thing to do, the gentlemanly thing, if you like. What a fool I was. When I confronted Jack about the rape allegation he denied it of course, and Ronnie was away on a business trip. I told Jack I would be informing Ronnie as soon as he got back.'

'And what happened?'

'What do you think? Jack got to Ronnie first. Jack told Ronnie he'd discovered I was cooking the books and had been stealing money from Hardman Construction for years. Ronnie believed I'd betrayed him and he was furious. He suspended me on the spot and I can still remember the hurt and hatred on his face when he did it. Of course, I tried to defend myself and to tell Ronnie about the attempted rape and Jack. He wouldn't listen. Ronnie thought I was trying to discredit his son-in-law. He didn't want to know about Zofia, he didn't want to investigate amongst the women staff, Ronnie just wanted me out. And then this happened.' Pearson pointed to his stomach.

'You became ill?'

'I wasn't sick. Six years ago at the same time this was all going on, I had a break-in and the man had a knife and he got me in the belly. I spent the best part of twelve months in and out of hospital.'

'Was this the property where you had the break-in?'

'It was and I'd have liked to move out only this place is so cheap to run. I still have nightmares about confronting him. That was the second most stupid thing I've done in my life.'

'Burglars don't often wound their victims. You must have startled him.'

'That's what the officers said at the time. I got him in the corner with the poker and that's when I found out he was a vicious bastard. I'll never forget his smile when he put the knife in. It was like something out of a horror movie. 'You think you're better than me, but you're not,' he said to my face. The man was a maniac. How I wish I'd never tried to tackle him.'

'Hindsight is a wonderful thing,' Grant said.

'He was a known felon, a man called Riley. The police caught him and he got nine years for it. Not that it did me any good him going to prison. I had no job, I'd lost my reputation and Ronnie made sure to put the word around so no one would take me on. I lost my health and my dignity because now I have to walk around with a disgusting bag full of you-know-what which I have to empty every few hours. In fact, six years ago I pretty much lost everything.'

'And you never tried to put the record straight with Ronnie Hardman?'

'I tried several times and he refused to speak to me. In the end I gave up. Ronnie is a very stubborn man. That's the part which hurt the most – we'd worked together for over twenty years and then Ronnie took Jack's word over mine. I'm pretty certain Jack must have moved money around so it looked as if I'd been siphoning off funds. Ronnie never understood the money side. It would have been easy to make it look bad for me and Jack was clever.'

'You're saying Jack set you up.'

'I'm sure he did. To get the heat off himself. I never took a penny from the company and that's the honest truth.'

The lounge clock dinged the hour and in the quiet afterwards, Grant could hear Pearson's wheezy breathing.

'Do you have contact details for Zofia Kaminski?'

'I used to have. She sent me a card when I was in hospital. I think she moved to London after.'

Pearson got up and rummaged in a desk drawer, then he wrote down the details.

As Grant accepted the paper, he couldn't help thinking Daniel Pearson had a pretty strong motive for getting back at both Jack and Ronnie. Still, his health meant he couldn't be the abductor.

And then there was Zofia Kaminski, what would she have to say about it? Grant's copper's instinct was kicking off big time. At last. This was the break they needed. Grant knew he was on to something.

Chapter Eighteen

In the morning, Maria was allowed to give the children food. She carried the tray carefully. She had prepared toast and strawberry jam, which was Lisa's favourite, and there were scrambled eggs. Half an hour earlier Maria had deliberately made a monster breakfast for him with a pile of sausage and bacon. It had left him bloated on the sofa, and though he tutted when the tray went past, he didn't protest.

'Remember to put on your mask,' he said as he handed her the key. 'And don't stay longer than you need to.'

At the top of the stairs, she pulled the mask over her face. He had installed a double lock. It was one of his many precautions though this one seemed exaggerated. Surely he didn't expect a six-year-old and a four-year-old to break their way out?

Lisa was curled up in a ball on the floor, linked by a chain to her sister. Emily was sitting with her back to the bunk. The older girl had a wary look on her face. Orange juice slopped from the beakers as Maria set down their breakfast.

'Eat up.'

'I'm not hungry,' Emily said.

Very likely the mask was scary for them. It was a Halloween one, a black-and-white horror number. Maybe that's why Lisa refused to look up.

Maria wasn't allowed to interact with the children but she hesitated because Emily's face was flushed and her lips were too red. Well, he wasn't there to see was he? Bending down, she placed her hand on Emily's forehead. It was burning. Then she noticed the way Emily cradled her arm.

'Have you hurt yourself? May I take a look?' Maria's voice sounded muffled.

Gingerly, Maria reached out to roll up the child's sleeve. Emily didn't resist and when her arm was exposed they both stared. In the middle of her forearm was a deep cut, livid red with the sides of the wound gaping open. Maria had to stop herself from gasping for fear of scaring Emily. The child's arm was swollen all the way to her elbow.

'It hurts,' Emily said.

'It's nothing to be worried about,' Maria lied. 'Have your breakfast. It'll make you feel better.'

When Maria went back downstairs she could not hide her concern.

'What's the matter? Has one of them died?' he asked with a sneer.

'That's not funny. I thought you said the cut wasn't serious. What happened to her arm?'

He shrugged. 'Nothing.'

It had been stupid of him to take a knife though he never listened to her. It had been even more stupid of him to use a dirty rag on Emily.

'I think it's infected.'

'All we need is for the kids to last long enough to carry out the plan. That's all I'm interested in.'

His tone made her shudder because she understood he meant it. To him, the children were pawns in the game. Nothing more and nothing less. Maria thought back to her own little brother, Billy. Maria used to look after Billy when their mother went out. She had lost contact with Billy years earlier and Maria knew it was her drug usage which caused the rift between them. Once, when he was little, Billy had to be rushed to hospital. He had almost lost his life.

Maria licked her lips. 'At least we should put some antiseptic on it.'

'Some what?'

'Antiseptic.'

'Sure whatever, put some on if it will make you shut up.'

'I'll need to get some from the chemist.'

'What the f–'

He grabbed the sheets of paper and waved them in her face. His flash of anger was about breaking the rules. Rule number one –they went out as little as possible, rule number two – they did nothing to draw attention to themselves, rule number three – and on and on. This had been planned for months and he had stocked the cupboards with food and bottles of booze so they could survive as long as they needed to. No trip to the chemist had been accounted for.

'What do you think this is?' In his anger, he was scrunching his precious papers. 'Something to wipe your arse with?'

Maria noticed he had ripped one of the sheets which meant he'd have to write it out again. He wouldn't like that either.

'I've already got that bitch across the road to deal with. We can't let anyone notice us. Got it?'

The bitch across the road was the woman with the purple spikey hair. She was the one who had gone ballistic when he'd put his van in her parking bay. It had happened months earlier and they hadn't seen her since although he had never forgotten because it went against *the plan – keep a low profile*. And the woman across the road parked her car in its bay every day which ate him up because in normal circumstances he would have slashed the tyres by now.

He slammed his foot into the coffee table, shoving it halfway across the room.

Maria pressed her lips together to stop them trembling. Was she really sure? Was it worth making the fuss and riling him up? Her little brother Billy had cut himself on a razor when he was playing in the bathroom. It had been a Friday night and their mother had left Maria and Billy locked in the house. By the time their mother returned on Monday morning, Billy's arm was puffy and purple. He was covered in sweat and was slurring his words. The doctors had told them it was blood poisoning and Billy had almost died.

She screwed up her courage. 'My little brother had something similar and he had blood poisoning. She could get really sick and then what good will she be?'

'What makes you a bloody expert?'

'Well… for a ch-child her age blood poisoning can be deadly.'

She was making him angry and that was always dangerous. He threw himself onto the sofa and leaned back. He was watching her with a nasty smirk on his face. Then he started cleaning his teeth with a toothpick. She could see her words sinking in and making him worry. It could be the flaw in his wonderful plan. It seemed like hours before he flicked the pick away.

'It's not worth it. The less people see me the better and I've already done the maximum number of trips out I'm allowing myself. The kid will have to survive like she is.'

'And what if she doesn't?'

'Will you shut the fuck up!'

He glared at her, toxic and volatile.

'I c-could go.'

Grabbing her wrist, he yanked her on top of him. 'And what the hell makes you think I'd trust you?'

She dragged up a smile and fixed it on her face. 'Because you know you can.'

He pulled her close, pressing her against the bulge in his jeans and she could smell his stinking breath.

Grinding himself into her, he grinned. 'Just so long as you don't get any funny ideas.'

'Of course I won't. You're hurting me.'

'I'll do far worse if you cock this up.'

She nodded and her lips quivered and she couldn't make them stop. 'Tell me what to do.'

'Ok-ay. Go straight there and back and no interacting with anyone. You walk ordinary and you look ordinary and you keep your head down. Any sign of trouble and you come straight back, got it?' His eyes grazed down her front. 'Go and make yourself look nice first, and remember once you're out of here I'll be timing you every step of the way.'

*

In the morning, when they heard someone coming up the stairs, Lisa whimpered and curled up clutching her knees tight. Emily could feel her heart pounding as the key turned in the lock. Was it the man? What did he want? Was he going to hurt them?

Emily pushed herself up using one arm. The other one hurt too much to use it and she hugged it to her stomach.

It wasn't the man. It was the woman and she wore a mask like the previous day. The knot in Emily's stomach loosened a bit. Emily stared at the breakfast tray and didn't feel like eating, even though the night before she'd been starving. The woman's fingers were gentle as she pulled up Emily's sleeve and Emily could smell the woman's flowery shampoo.

Lisa didn't move until the woman had left and the two sisters didn't talk until the footsteps had gone away and they'd heard a door closing downstairs.

'It's jam on toast,' Emily said.

Lisa opened her eyes and came closer.

'Don't you want any?' Lisa asked.

'Not really, you can have it all if you want.'

When Emily tried to sip her orange juice it turned her stomach. She really did feel strange but at least it was a relief to know they didn't have to meet the man again. The woman was much nicer.

'Is Mummy coming to get us?' Lisa whispered.

'Of course she is,' Emily said, and she closed her eyes and listened as Lisa slurped her juice and scooped in scrambled eggs.

Her arm was throbbing and she could feel a thrumming in her head in the same rhythm as the one in her arm. *Dum-dum, dum-dum.* It made her feel dizzy and a bit sick like one time when Mummy told her she'd been in the sun for too long. Emily hoped it would go away soon.

Chapter Nineteen

When Maria left the house, the air felt fresh on her face. She'd showered and was wearing her favourite jacket with a flowery lining and a dress covered in poppies which brushed against her legs. Maria liked flowers because they somehow made her feel happier.

He'd not allowed her outside for days and it all seemed so ordinary out here – not full of drugs and booze and messed-up thoughts. Why not keep walking? Why not go to the train station and get away? *Where to* – the little voice said in her head. *Where can you go? You know he'll find you.*

And if, or rather when, he caught up with her, he would show no mercy. Surely her safest bet was to see it through? Wouldn't that be the best way and then she could get her money. And by sticking around she could do her best to help the children.

She mustn't walk too fast or it might attract attention. Maria tried to ignore the thumping of her heart. She felt vulnerable in the open as if other people could see inside her and know she was worthless.

After about ten minutes she came to the brightly lit window of the chemist. Her palms started itching and she stopped to scrape them with her fingernails. Then, as she glanced around to see if anyone was watching, she froze. Was she hallucinating? Maria blinked hard and shrank back as far as she could into the shelter of the shop entrance.

The figure across the other side of the road was exactly the same as she remembered – auburn wavy hair, freckles and long legs. Bloody hell, what was Sylvie Delacourt doing in Brighton? Wasn't she supposed to have gone back to Australia?

Sylvie was coming out of a large house. It looked like a doctor's surgery. There was a gold plate on the wall and at the front of the property there was a notice saying 'No Parking Doctor's Clinic'.

Sylvie was heading towards a bus stop.

For one crazy moment Maria had an urge to rush across the road. She wanted to confess to her old friend and tell her everything. Sylvie might be willing to help. The young woman was much more confident than Maria and she had what Maria thought of as a free spirit. What if Sylvie helped her? What if they could escape to Australia together?

Cold reality burst Maria's bubble. Because they'd never really been friends, had they? It had been an elaborate set-up masterminded by him and Maria had used Sylvie and then dumped her.

A red bus pulled up and a few moments later she saw her old friend taking a seat on the bottom deck. It was as the bus drove off that Sylvie lifted her head and she stared straight in the direction of the chemist. Maria clutched the wall so hard she ripped off a nail. She shrank into the shadows. It had been stupid to stand and stare.

The bus was soon out of sight. Whatever Sylvie was doing in Brighton was none of Maria's concern. He must never know and she must never mention it to him. It would throw him into a fit. And if she didn't get back in time he would go berserk so she should forget about it and get on with what she had to do.

Inside the chemist, it smelled clean. A horrible thought occurred to her. What if Sylvie had seen her and she came back to check? Maria's heart began beating extra hard and she wondered if other people could hear it. Anxiety gripped her and sweat broke out on her top lip.

A shop assistant came alongside and asked if she needed help. The assistant was eyeing her so Maria grabbed a basket and walked to the end of the aisle, randomly throwing in a couple of items. She needed a moment to get herself under control and then she needed to get out of here as fast as she could.

She joined a small queue at the counter. It was difficult to think straight and maybe her own imagination was playing tricks. If she was honest with herself, was she really certain it had been Sylvie?

Maria's nose was running. It was the result of snorting and she couldn't risk blowing it or it might turn into a full-scale nosebleed. In the past, when her using was out of control, nose bleeds were common. Maria dabbed it with a handkerchief and after a few moments it was her turn at the counter. She gave the pharmacist a fake smile.

'A friend of mine has a cut which looks red and angry and I think it could be infected.'

'If the mark is slightly red then an antiseptic might be sufficient.' The assistant grabbed an item from the shelf behind her. 'Try this, though if it doesn't get better I'd advise you to consult your doctor. Is it for an adult?'

Maria hesitated. He was always drumming into her the need for secrecy and being ultra-careful except what's the point of buying a product which might not be right?

'It's for a child.'

'Oh that's different. How old are they?'

Bloody hell this was getting complicated.

'Ten,' she lied.

'I highly recommend you see a doctor if the symptoms persist.'

The woman changed the product for another one and Maria paid. When she stepped outside, she scanned the street.

Seeing no sign of Sylvie, she hurried along, her heels tapping on the pavement. She was just being silly and imagining things and it hadn't really been Sylvie. Sometimes the powder made your mind play tricks – that was likely it.

*

When Maria got to the house, he was standing with his phone in his hand and with the electronic stopwatch running. She could see paranoia in his eyes.

'You were a long time.'

'Was I? There was a bit of a queue.'

He twitched with suspicion and of course it wasn't helped by the fact she'd actually got something to hide. If he knew she might have seen Sylvie and Sylvie might have seen her he wouldn't be able to control himself. The whole point of bringing the children down to Brighton was to escape from Himlands Heath.

'I'd better get some of this on her arm.'

He slowly handed her the key. Slipping around him she raced up the stairs.

At the top she was in such a state she almost forgot to put on the mask. Emily was still slumped against the bed and she seemed to be half asleep.

'Do you feel hot?' Maria asked.

The arm looked worse than it had an hour earlier. She fumbled, trying to get the cream onto Emily as quickly as possible. Shit. What if it was serious like it had been with her little brother Billy? Young children could deteriorate quickly. And what about him downstairs? He'd never agree to Emily seeing a doctor. Would she be able to persuade him to dump the child at a hospital Accident and Emergency?

Who was she kidding? She wouldn't have the courage to suggest it. It would leave him with only one bargaining chip – Lisa – which he'd never agree to.

'Happy now?' he asked her when she went down.

'She's worse.' The words slipped out before Maria could stop them.

'Tough shit. Not having second thoughts, are you?' He pushed his face towards hers and there was a nasty look in his eye. It was the paranoia again. From the powder.

She felt her emotions tumble around and there was fear and anxiety and neediness all mixed together. Right from the beginning she'd had zero chance of giving her opinion about his damn plan. There'd been no opportunity to say no because he'd dragged her into it. One day she'd been living her life and trying to build something and then he turned up and ruined it. He forced her. Or had he? Maria wasn't sure anymore because holding it together had been exhausting and when he'd offered her an easier way she'd not put up much resistance, had she?

She bit her lip. 'You know me.'

'Yeah I do, babe, and while you were out, I got Emily to phone her mother.'

It came as a shock. 'Oh, you did it when I wasn't here.'

'Yeah and until this is over, no more little shopping trips for you. You'll be staying where I can see you.'

For a moment she fantasised about calling the police or an ambulance. Though she couldn't, could she, because she was up to her neck in it. She was an accomplice and why would they have any sympathy for her? A druggie? A sad loser who couldn't function without her fixes. She didn't want to go to prison.

As if he could read her mind he reached out and snatched her phone from her back pocket.

'And you won't be needing this.'

He removed the SIM card and the golden square gave a little *crack* as he snapped it in half.

As he tossed it to the carpet he gave her a horrible grin and Maria knew it was far too late for her to get out.

Chapter Twenty

Six months ago – Maria's story

Maria hung the last of the new deliveries onto the rail. These were silky dresses which she would never be able to afford. Her hands were sore from a day unpacking and hanging out new clothes and boxing up returns to send to the warehouse. Where she worked it smelled of the chemicals they sprayed on the clothes to keep them fresh, and it was giving her a headache.

Four years earlier, when Maria first came out of the drug clean-up programme, her probation officer had found her a job in a factory. Maria grew to like it there. Then the factory went bust. They'd written Maria a good reference which helped land her this job at the fashion store. It was a big step up. The boutique owner had taken Maria on against the wishes of the shop manager, and as the shop manager didn't stop telling Maria – Maria was damn lucky.

Maria didn't feel lucky. She felt out of her depth. The shop manager, Mrs Branson, didn't let a day go by without reminding Maria she must never ever show herself on the shop floor. This was a quality fashion boutique and Maria's place, Mrs Branson told her, was in the back room because customers didn't want to see people *like her*. Having Mrs Branson shove her nose in it ate away at Maria's wafer-thin self-confidence.

Mrs Branson suddenly arrived in the back room. It was amazing how the woman could move so stealthily, always trying to catch Maria out.

'You got around to finishing at last?'

Mrs Branson had kept Maria beyond her going home time, which wasn't unusual. Sometimes she forced Maria to miss half her lunch hour too.

Maria nodded.

'See you tomorrow then,' Mrs Branson said. 'Unfortunately.'

Unfortunately for me too, you miserable bitch, Maria thought. Of course, she would never dare to say it out loud.

Stepping into the shopping centre, Maria breathed a sigh of relief. It was well past closing time and the mall was quiet. The metal shutter of the boutique came clattering down behind her.

Maria was dreaming of a hot bath and soaking away the aches and the bullying, when she saw him. He was slouched against the wall with his hands in his pockets. He had the same cocky expression he always had, though she could see the years in prison had given him a kick in the guts.

'Aren't you going to give me a kiss?' he said.

'When did you get out?'

'A while ago. They let me out early for good behaviour.'

He fell into step beside her.

'Long time no see,' she said.

'Yeah. Can I crash at yours? Only for a couple of nights. I've got cash and plenty of it.'

'How come?'

'It was owing to me,' he said.

She knew there'd been a story behind how he got caught and she wondered how the money fitted in.

'Come on Maria, I can pay my way.'

She knew it wasn't a good idea. When she'd first met him she'd been fourteen. He'd taken her in when her mother, and her mother's new boyfriend, had booted her out.

Then he'd gone to prison and she'd spent the last six years trying to put together a life and battling to get clean of the cocaine he'd introduced her to.

When he was convicted she'd been totally reliant on him and had been living at his place, doing the cooking and the cleaning and the sexual favours he asked for, as well as hosting parties for his criminal buddies. It was amazing how, at one time, she'd found him attractive. Now she'd rather not look at his face. He was bad news.

Yet he wasn't the sort of man it was wise to say no to.

When he was convicted, the flat the two of them lived in had been repossessed and Maria had been reduced to begging on the street, stealing and lying and almost ending up working for a pimp to fund her drug habit. Then came a string of arrests and an ongoing tussle with the criminal justice system. She finally accepted the long struggle to get, and stay, clean. Four years ago, and with the help of her probation officer, she landed her first job. It had got her back on the rails.

It had been a long haul. Now Maria had a place of her own – only two shitty rooms with a dirty kitchen but she could scrape together the rent. Every day of the last six years had been hard and she'd kept promising herself one day it would get easier. Unfortunately, the fashion boutique wasn't turning out well thanks to the manager.

And then – bam — this guy from her past turned up again.

'If you've got money then how come you're here?' she said.

'I missed you and besides, I need your help. Won't you do a favour for an old friend?'

He put his hand in his pocket and showed her a small packet of white powder. 'I can make it worth your while.'

And that's when Maria's fight for a new life started draining away.

Chapter Twenty-one

Six months ago – Maria's story

Maria brushed her long dark hair and she stared at herself in the changing room mirror. She could hardly believe how her life had improved. He'd got them a lovely place in Brighton and he'd given her money to buy new clothes and shoes. They had a whole terraced house with three bedrooms and two floors. He certainly had cash and she didn't want to ask how. The house was in a nice area of Brighton called Seven Dials and about thirty minutes' walk from the sea.

He was spending a lot of time out and Maria didn't care. Every day she strolled along the promenade with the wind in her hair. She ate ice cream and paddled in the freezing waves. She'd not bothered to call the boutique to lie about being sick. Likely she'd lost her job, Mrs Branson would have seen to it by now and Maria didn't give a shit.

Besides, he'd told Maria he had big plans for them both, though he hadn't yet told her what.

He'd set Maria a task. He wanted her to befriend a young woman called Sylvie Delacourt. When Maria asked why, he'd told her to wait and see. Sylvie worked as an au pair and she had a membership of a gym in Himlands Heath. For the last few days, Maria had been hanging out at the gym. She needed to bump into Sylvie and engineer a chance to strike up a friendship.

Tying back her hair, Maria shoved her clothes into a locker and slammed it shut. On her way in, she'd spotted Sylvie on the running machine. Now was her chance.

Sylvie was about the same age as Maria, mid-twenties. At the running machine, Maria chatted and made sure Sylvie liked her and the two of them became friends. With her easy-going Australian manner, Sylvie was fun to be around.

Four weeks later and Maria often had to remind herself they'd only met by design. Going out together was a pleasure and it was easy to forget she was doing it for a purpose.

Sylvie had bags of something which Maria never had much of – confidence. When she was around Sylvie, some of it wore off on Maria and Maria found herself looking forward to their meetings. She blotted out the fact he always wanted a report and quizzed her endlessly on everything Sylvie told her. Today, he'd told her to get an invite to the house where Sylvie worked.

'How's it going with the Glovers?' Maria asked.

They were in a café on Himlands Heath high street. Sylvie was biting into a pitta bread stuffed with salad.

'The usual. The kids are great and Alice is demanding. She's taken the children out for the afternoon, some birthday party, so let's hope one of them doesn't come back with bodily injuries they got while their mother was busy knocking back the cocktails.'

Maria got a waft of garlic as her friend laughed. A blob of sauce fell from Sylvie's food and landed with a plop on her jeans. Sylvie scooped it up with a finger and laughed again. Sylvie always seemed to find a lot in life which was funny.

'It's a shame you're not allowed guests. I'd like to see it,' Maria said.

'See what? The house? Of course you can, I never said I couldn't bring back friends. What gave you that idea?'

'I imagined they'd want to keep their home private.'

'I've got my own room and bathroom and I get to use the kitchen. After we've finished lunch I'll take you there and you can gawp all you like. I'll even show you Alice's knickers – they're vile.'

*

An hour later and they were in hysterics after rummaging in Alice's underwear drawer.

'Even my granny doesn't wear giant ones like these,' Sylvie guffawed.

'We'd better get out of here before someone catches us,' Maria said.

'Hey, chill out. There's no one around except maybe Jack and he won't care. He likes me.'

Maria was supposed to be finding out about the Glovers and their routine and the children's routine. She made mental notes because he'd want to write it all down once she got back.

'It's a lovely house,' Maria said. 'And so big.'

'Alice and Jack are rolling in money only don't think it makes them happy because it doesn't. They haven't done it since Lisa was born, can you imagine? And it makes Alice strung out. If you ask me she's desperate for it.'

'How'd you know?'

'I've got my means.'

'Did her husband tell you?'

Sylvie, who usually liked to gossip, wouldn't say more. Which made it even more intriguing when, half an hour later, Jack Glover walked in on them in the kitchen. Maria noticed how Sylvie quickly crossed her legs to show a lot of thigh under her short skirt. She saw too how Jack's eyes lingered on Sylvie and then landed on her.

Jack's gaze had a weird effect on Maria. The lust seemed to ooze out of him, and Maria, who had never once in her life been told she was attractive, had to choke back a nervous giggle. She was glad she'd worn a tight top.

'Good afternoon, ladies, what have you been up to?' Jack had a deep sexy voice.

Sylvie had the gift of a silver tongue and she soon had Jack hanging on her every word and drinking her in with those lascivious eyes of his and Maria couldn't help feeling envious.

Chapter Twenty-two

Grant wanted to interview the Glover's neighbour, Natalie, and he asked Tom to accompany him. When Tom asked why Natalie was the next priority, Grant grunted.

'She's sticking to Jack and Alice like glue, you caught her and Jack intimate in the kitchen, that's more than enough to put her on the radar. There's something about her behaviour which is more than being a good neighbour, isn't there? I want to find out how far it goes.'

Tom enjoyed working alongside the boss. When it was just the two of them, Grant passed on tips and coached Tom how to handle situations. Tom appreciated it and each night he recorded Grant's ideas. Tom wanted to soak it all up before Grant decided to retire.

Knocking on Natalie's door, they waited. When he was first recruited to the team, Tom had been in such awe of Grant he'd sometimes found it difficult to function. These days the feeling had faded, and was replaced by respect.

When Natalie answered, she was wearing a dress with a revealing top line and Tom made sure his gaze didn't dip.

'Oh, Detective Sergeant,' Natalie said. 'I didn't realise you'd be bringing someone with you.'

'I'm sorry if I wasn't clear when I set up the appointment,' Tom said. 'This is Detective Chief Inspector Grant.'

Grant shook Natalie's hand. 'Good morning, ma'am. May we come in?'

'Of course and please tell me there's good news.'

'Nothing so far.'

'Oh god.'

They followed Natalie to a lounge furnished in golden upholstered chairs and giant sofas. There was a gold-themed carpet and pale gold curtains and all the fittings were gold coloured. The room had a pervasive scent of potpourri and two giant glass bowls of what looked like dead petals, and flower heads were displayed on the mantelpiece. The overall effect was over the top.

Natalie hitched herself back on a chair, revealing quite a lot of thigh. Did she do it deliberately? Or was it a mistake? Tom couldn't help feeling she was flirting with him.

'How can I help you?'

While Grant questioned Natalie about her friendship with the Glovers, Tom listened carefully. The woman was impeccably made up, with not a sleek dark hair out of place. Her dress looked expensive and she had a polished air about her.

Natalie told them she and her husband Sanjay had moved in a few months after Alice and Jack, and she and Alice had quickly become friends. At that time, Alice worked at Hardman Construction and she gave up her job several months later once she had Emily. Natalie worked part-time as an interior designer and she ran her business from home, so the two women often saw each other during the day.

'And is your husband working?' Grant asked.

'Sanjay's in banking,' Natalie said.

Grant nodded. 'Could you tell me a little more about the relationship between you and Jack? Is it purely platonic?'

Natalie glanced at Tom and she flicked back her hair. 'I suppose your sergeant told you he caught me and Jack…'

'In a compromising position?' Grant suggested.

'It's complicated.'

'Is it. And does Mrs Glover know about this?'

'I don't know if Alice suspects or not, look, it wasn't something I wanted to happen. You can't decide who you fall for and Jack and I are madly in love.'

Natalie studied her manicured nails and gave the inspector a challenging look.

'And what about your husband?'

'Sanjay and I are finished. If you must know we've been seeing a marriage guidance counsellor, only it made it worse and a few months ago Sanjay told me he wanted out. We've been under a lot of stress the last few years because we desperately wanted to have children and it kept not happening. I got tested. Sanjay got tested. We've tried IVF treatments and they haven't worked. You name it we've tried it, and it's exhausting and depressing.'

Tom wondered what it must have been like to see Alice give birth to Emily and Lisa. Had Natalie struggled seeing her friend with new babies?

'It's been horrible and now we're at the end of a difficult road and Sanjay has filed for divorce. He kept telling me I was ruining everything. He called my desire for children *an obsession*. Sanjay believes I destroyed our marriage.'

Natalie took a deep breath and sighed. 'Sanjay never understood why I couldn't be content. I can't explain and I can't control it. Every waking moment I *yearn* to have a baby. I don't think any man can ever understand.'

'Right.' Grant took out his phone and swiped at the screen. 'Can you tell me if you recognise this?'

He handed it across and Tom watched Natalie's face as she stared at the camisole.

'It's lingerie,' she said.

'I'm trying to find out who it belongs to,' Grant said.

'It's not mine if that's what you're thinking. It's too small and I don't like red, I prefer hot pink.'

Tom ignored the flirtatious look she shot his way. Was Natalie in the frame? Natalie wanted a baby, but wanting a baby was different from wanting someone else's children. She was entangled with Jack and her marriage had failed but did it give her motive or means?

Grant was frowning. 'Do you have an alibi for the night of the children's abduction?'

Natalie tossed her head and she was about to answer when Tom heard rapid footsteps along the front path. Out the window, one of the constables came running. His mind shot back to the pyjama leg and Alice in pieces. Oh no, what now?

He and Grant ran to the door.

'What's happened?' Grant asked.

'DCI Grant, sir,' the constable said, 'the abductor has made contact.'

They sprinted over to the Glover's house. Alice was standing at the back of the lounge by the technicians, clutching at her phone like she might break the plastic. Tom thought she looked terribly vulnerable and Grant guided her to a chair.

Jack was standing so close to the technicians, Tom marvelled at how the techs still worked calmly. Jack looked stricken.

'Someone fill me in,' Grant said crisply.

Ruby was sitting by her lap top. Neither Ruby, the uniformed officers, nor the technicians answered, because Grant had first given each of them a look which made it clear he wanted them to keep quiet. He wanted to hear it from the family. Joan Hardman was the first to pull herself together.

'It was Emily. She called to speak to her mother and she was reading a message. We have to get half a million pounds ready to exchange for the children. It's good news isn't it? It means the children are still…' Joan started crying, '…still alive.'

'You recorded the call?' Grant asked the technicians. 'I need to hear it.'

Joan pulled her daughter into a hug. Jack hadn't moved from a few inches behind the technicians.

'Are you all right, sir?' Tom asked.

One of the technicians tapped at a keyboard and then Emily's voice was coming through the speaker.

Mummy, it's Emily. You're not allowed to interrupt you have to listen. Here are the demands – you have to have half a million pounds in cash ready. The Child Alert must be called off. If you don't comply I will kill both your children. I'll phone again with some in…instructions for the exchange. Then came Alice's voice. *Emily, darling, are you al-* Then the line went dead.

'She was trying to be brave,' Alice said. 'I can hear it in her voice. Oh Jack.'

'We've got the money, Inspector,' Joan said. 'I'll ask my bank manager to get it prepared straightaway.'

The call was much too short to be of any use in tracing it and the abductor had been clever to not allow their own voice to be recorded so they would not be able to use voice recognition software to help with identification.

'He wants to do an exchange. That's a positive thing isn't it, DCI Grant?' Jack said. His voice had a pleading edge to it.

'The abductor making contact is a good sign,' Grant said, 'and we must do all we can to keep communication going. The next time contact is made, I want you to ask for proof of life for Lisa and Emily. You must say you want a video.'

'Wh-what? You mean this might have been a recording? I hadn't thought of that.' Jack gulped and Alice tugged at her hair.

'We don't know if it's a recording or not,' Grant said firmly. 'Like I told you before, you have to keep positive. Do not give in to despair. For the next time, I'll write down what I'd like you to say so you can be prepared.'

When Jack made to speak for his wife, Alice quickly cut in.

'Grant was talking to me not you. Yes, I'll do whatever you ask, Inspector.'

Tom knew Alice was worried Grant would prefer dealing with Jack and leave her out of the loop, especially if there was bad news. She'd spoken to Tom about it and Tom had assured Alice that would not happen. In a way, he was glad the call had been made to the mother because it might help calm her fears about being sidelined.

'Get this straight to the technical team at headquarters,' Grant ordered. 'I want every detail analysed.'

Maybe there would be background sounds to give indication about location and any video footage they received later would undergo the same analysis for clues – it was a long shot but you never knew.

Joan was on her phone, speaking to someone about organising the funds. They listened to Emily's message again and Grant took Tom aside.

'I'm going back to the station to update DCS Fox.'

'What's the next step, boss?'

'You sit tight. I need you and Ruby here for the next call. Jack Glover, Natalie, Zofia Kaminski – the pieces of the puzzle are starting to come together.'

Tom scratched his head. 'Are they?'

'You bet they are,' Grant said, slapping Tom on the shoulder.

*

It took a long while for the family to calm down. Jack didn't seem to be able to function. Eventually he went to his study and Tom noted how Jack always left the door open. He had a similar anxiety to his wife – that news would come through about the children and he might miss it. Both parents looked dreadful yet the phone call had given them a breadcrumb. It was something to hang onto.

Tom tried to coax Alice to eat and he went to the kitchen to make a plate of toast. He carried it through for her.

'It's important to keep your strength up, even if you don't feel like it.'

'You're very kind. Making food isn't your job, you know.'

'That doesn't matter.' Tom pushed the plate towards her.

Alice picked up a piece and stared at it a few moments before taking a tiny bite. 'Last night I dreamed of Lisa calling out for me. And I couldn't reach her.'

Ah, thought Tom, *that was a nightmare not a dream.*

'Why wasn't Lisa on the call?' she whispered.

Tom could see her mind straying to the worst possible scenarios which would not do her any good at all. 'Try not to dwell on it. We must stick with the facts. You heard Emily's voice and you said she was trying to be brave. That means she's in good spirits. And a demand is a positive sign.'

Joan Hardman was sitting on the sofa staring out the window and Tom looked across to include her.

'My Inspector has spoken to Daniel Pearson and Pearson mentioned an ex-employee of Hardman Construction, a woman called Zofia Kaminski. Have either of you heard of her?'

'The name's familiar although I can't give you any details,' Joan said. 'She probably worked in the office.'

Alice had put down the toast and gone back to tugging at her own hair. 'Why is she important?'

'I'm not sure. I think she worked with your husband.'

'Then why don't you ask Jack?' Alice said.

Because we wanted to see your reaction first, Tom thought.

*

Ruby was reading from her screen. They'd received Emily's phone call over an hour ago. It had been terrifying when Alice ran into the room, white in the face. Alice had not been able to express herself, staring at her phone and unable to respond to anyone.

Ruby had felt the emotion of the mother in every sinew of her body.

Had the parents' reactions been genuine, or rehearsed? Grant had asked Ruby the question. Alice had seemed genuinely distraught whereas Jack had jumped straight into overcontrolling mode. They could both be natural responses although there was something terribly strained between the husband and wife and it had been from the beginning. Was it relevant? Was it caused by Sylvie Delacourt? Or by Natalie next door? What was going on with this couple?

Now Ruby had a vantage point to observe Alice talking to Tom. It wasn't the first time she'd seen how Tom's calm manner helped people when they were in distress. He had a way too of being able to slip the questions in with no one noticing. He'd asked about Zofia Kaminski without causing a ripple. No wonder Grant respected Tom.

The lounge went very quiet and Ruby continued working until she was suddenly startled by the constable at the front door arguing with someone.

'No, ma'am, you cannot walk in unannounced.'

Then Ruby heard Natalie's voice raised in protest.

'It's all right, officer,' Alice called out. 'Natalie can come in whenever she wants.'

At the commotion, Jack came out of his study.

'Oh good I'm glad you're both here,' Natalie said, and that was when Ruby started to have a bad feeling. She exchanged a worried glance with Tom.

'This is not the best moment, ma'am,' Tom said. 'Alice and Jack have had upsetting news and I think it might be best if–'

'No you can't shut me up.' Natalie flicked back her hair. 'I've had enough hiding in the shadows. It's time to own it. Tell her, darling.'

Jack stared at her. He opened his mouth but nothing came out.

'Tell me what?' Alice said, and Ruby was sorry to see how Alice seemed genuinely bewildered.

Jack ran his hand threw his hair. 'I think Detective Delaney is right. This isn't the time.'

'I don't understand,' Alice said. 'It isn't the time for what?'

'Oh come on, Alice, don't act the poor victim. Surely even you can't be so dense you haven't realised? Jack and I are in love.' Natalie presented it like a triumphant announcement. She linked one arm with Jack's and placed her other hand on her hip.

Coming after Emily's call it was absolutely horrendous. There was a terrible silence. Everyone was staring at Alice as she tried to grasp what was going on.

'This is nonsense,' Alice said. 'What the hell are you talking about? Have you gone mad?' She turned to her husband. 'Tell her Jack and tell her to get out of my house.'

Jack shook his head. 'This is very awkward and it isn't like it looks…'

Her husband's floundering said it all. Realisation dawned and Alice picked up the plate of toast and hurled it at Jack, missing by miles.

'You bastard!' She rocketed up and in a few strides reached Jack and slapped him across the face. It made good contact and the sound bounced off the walls. Alice rounded on Natalie.

'Get out! Get the hell out of my house.'

Chapter Twenty-three

Grant was in DCS Fox's office. He played Emily's message through twice and Fox took off her glasses and rubbed the bridge of her nose.

'Goddam it.'

'He's making a specific demand which we can respond to and I've instructed Alice to ask for proof of life when the next contact is made. Getting the call has pulled the mother back from the brink of despair.'

Ever since DCS Fox transferred to the Sussex force, she and Grant hadn't seen eye to eye. Grant thought Fox felt threatened by him and for once, since the children were taken, Fox hadn't mentioned his retirement nor his last birthday – two things which were usually on the top of her conversation list because the one thing she could always trump him with was his advancing age.

'Lab reports have come back,' he said. 'Forensics went over the inside of the lockup millimetre by millimetre and they didn't find a thing. Alice has positively identified the hair tie as belonging to Lisa so it places the children there. The pyjama hasn't given us anything so far. And we've got a recent tyre track at the lockup exit – it could belong to the vehicle the perpetrator used to leave.'

'What about saliva on Joan Hardman's arm?'

'Nothing.'

'Damn. That would have been bloody marvellous. Anything from the Child Rescue Alert?'

Grant shook his head. 'Not so far and I've called it off as the abductor requested. We've several reports of blonde children and none of them have yet been flagged as a positive sighting. On phone records and financial details – they're still trickling in for our persons of interest. Then there's the next-door neighbour's bombshell announcement in the Glover lounge. I've no idea how that will pan out, although Delaney and Ruby are on top of it. We need to keep concentrated on the next call.'

'I've got the armed response unit on standby for the exchange.'

'Ms Silver thinks it's someone who knows the family.'

'Does she now. She's always coming up with flashy ideas, isn't she? And what do you think?'

'It fits with the back-door entry. There must be an insider connection.'

'And you're telling me you don't have *anyone* on the radar? I know that look on your face, you've got your suspicions.'

'I'm working on it. Jack keeps getting flagged up and his history with women might be important.'

'Might! I've got Treadgold demanding progress and all you can give me is Jack Glover's sex life!'

The tension was mounting. From experience, he knew Fox could be much worse than this. Grant braced himself for the whiplash.

'What the hell are you playing at! I want results. I want this maniac behind bars. I want those children found.'

'As I said our next move is asking for proof of life.'

'I can see that what do you take me for, an idiot? Don't make me regret putting you on this case and don't imagine Treadgold hasn't dragged up the issue of your age because he has.'

Of course he bloody had.

'The ACC feels a younger DCI would be sharper and have more energy. He's pushing for you to be replaced.'

That was pure madness. Halfway through a critical case a substitution could mean the difference between life and death. Grant felt the heat rush to his face and he jumped to his feet. 'Then he's a goddam idiot.'

'And he's baying for your blood.'

'I'm the one who can solve this case.'

Fox whipped off her glasses and leaned back in her chair. 'For once we're in agreement. Now get the hell out of here.'

The pressure was on and he didn't envy her dealing with demands from the top. She'd kept the media and Treadgold off his back, and for that Grant was grateful.

Fox turned a glacial stare on Grant. 'I hope I don't have to remind you safe return of Emily and Lisa is the priority here not prosecution. If anything happens to those children, everyone is going to be holding you responsible.'

Chapter Twenty-four

It was bad luck for Ruby she was the second to arrive in the incident room and DS Steve McGowan was the first. He was filling the tray with a pile of fresh doughnuts and they smelled sweet and sugary. McGowan helped himself without offering her one.

'I hope we don't have to listen to more of your psycho-bullshit,' McGowan said.

Ruby reached and helped herself. She bit off a huge mouthful. 'Like I said, I'm here to stay. Have you made progress?'

McGowan gave her a scathing look. 'I report to the chief, not to you.'

'Oh grow up, isn't it time you learned how to share.'

He wagged his finger. 'You'll see it's detective work which will find those children, not your fancy theories and mind-bending crap.'

'What is it with you? Why are you so defensive?'

'Are you kidding? You're the one acting like madam-superior as if a few years studying makes you better than us lot.'

'That's crap. Why don't you admit it? You feel threatened.'

McGowan almost choked on his doughnut and she wished he had done. Bits spluttered out.

Grant walked in. 'No time to waste. Are we playing nicely?'

'Always,' McGowan said, and he gave Ruby a death-look which dared her to say otherwise.

She shrugged it off. What an idiot.

Diane and Tom came in together and Grant slung his jacket over the front chair. He looked like he hadn't slept since the beginning of the investigation.

'Right, forensics have found a tyre track in the mud at the lockup. It doesn't match the blue estate so we're assuming it came from the second vehicle. It fits with new information uncovered by DS McGowan.'

McGowan shot Ruby a victory glare. Coming from him, it was like a finger.

Give me a break, Ruby thought.

'Damn well done, Steve. What have you got?' Diane said.

McGowan stroked his moustache. 'It was one of the locals who came up with the info. He's a dog walker. He told me he always goes out at half six and there's hardly anyone about at that time. His route takes him behind the storage units and he noticed a van pulling out the morning of the abduction. It didn't have its headlights on, which was odd because it wasn't daylight. He described it as a white utility van and he took note of where it was heading.'

'Yes!' Delaney said, slamming his hand onto the desk.

Grant gave a rare smile. 'The witness said it went south onto the Brighton road. Brilliant McGowan.'

McGowan cut Ruby a sly glance. *Try not to sink to his level,* she told herself.

'Next,' Grant said. 'Daniel Pearson. He's got motive because he lost his job and he puts it down to Jack although Pearson's health rules him out. Pearson claims he found out Jack was sexually harassing female colleagues and there was an allegation of attempted rape made against Jack by an employee, Zofia Kaminski. Tracking down the women is a priority.'

'Perhaps Pearson is in collusion with the abductor?' Tom said.

'It's a possibility. Anything on Zofia Kaminski yet, Diane?'

'I got a staff shot from Hardman Construction. Here she is.'

It came up on the screen.

'She's got long dark hair,' Delaney said.

'Yup, though I've not been able to locate her yet.'

Grant nodded. 'Keep on it. And check with the retired science teacher and see if Kaminski is the woman seen hanging around the Hardman's street.'

'Our science teacher witness hasn't got as good eyesight as I hoped,' Diane said. 'When I showed her a picture of Natalie, the Glover's next door neighbour, she wasn't sure.'

'It's still worth checking. What else people?'

Ruby felt the tension in the room edge up and she gripped the edge of her desk.

'There's the fallout from Natalie,' Tom said. 'She's caused a rift between Alice and Jack and there's a very difficult situation at the house now because Alice is refusing to speak to her husband.'

'You'll have to work around it. Do everything you can to keep communication going. We can't let tensions jeopardise the response to the second phone call.'

'Right boss.'

Grant rapped the pen on the board. 'Think outside the box people. What about you, Ruby?'

'I've completed my profiling of the family. What's standing out is the difference between Jack's public image versus his private behaviour. There's his suspected infidelity with Sylvie and his infidelity with Natalie. The statement from the woman who alleged rape, Zofia Kaminski, is going to be an important one.'

'It doesn't take a fancy diploma to work that out,' McGowan said. 'I could have told you the same.'

Grant silenced McGowan with a frown.

The message from Emily had been written on a board and Ruby pointed to it.

'I've analysed the abductor's message. Emily said – Mummy, it's Emily. You're not allowed to interrupt you have to listen. Here are the demands – you have to have half a million pounds in cash ready. The Child Alert must be called off. If you don't comply I will kill both your children. I'll phone again with some in...instructions for the exchange.'

She wrote another phrase on the board and tapped her pen on it.

'The structuring of the message doesn't include something like this – if you do as I say they will not be harmed – I think the omission is significant.'

'Why?' Grant asked.

'Kidnappers who demand a ransom purely for financial gain frequently include a phrase in their messages telling loved ones the hostage will come to no harm if their terms are met. On the other hand, abductors who have taken someone for personal reasons tend to omit this phrase. Why? Because in those cases they *want* the family to suffer. Financial gain is not their only aim. They want to inflict torture on the parents. This means the abductor wanted to achieve maximum fear in the Glovers without giving any assurances.'

'It's like I've been thinking all along. You're saying this is personal,' Grant said.

'Yes, it says the abductor has a personal motivation, such as revenge or spite. This isn't only about money.'

McGowan guffawed. 'It's a message sent by a madman. What a load of rubbish.'

'DS McGowan,' Grant warned. 'I won't be telling you a second time. Stop taking cheap shots.'

'This sort of psychological analysis isn't set in stone,' Ruby said. 'There's no hard and fast rule for using it to predict outcome in kidnap scenarios, but my take is, the omission is important. What someone doesn't say is as significant as what they do communicate.'

'Everyone keep the personal angle in mind.'

'We're moving closer, aren't we, sir,' Diane said.

'Stay focused. Ruby and Delaney, I want you back with the family. Collins, keep working on the Kaminski angle. McGowan, continue following up leads, financial records and background checks. Have we made any progress with the phone records?'

'Some but not all,' McGowan said. 'You know what the phone companies are like. They're trickling in and the credit card checks are even slower.'

'Keep pushing. Jack Glover's records are the priority and if this turns out to be an inside job, then somebody in this big mess of a picture might have made a slip up and if they have, we need to notice.'

McGowan leaned close to Ruby's desk. 'Aren't you the little favourite,' he sneered.

*

The escalating tension between Ruby and McGowan was helping to make Grant's choice between the two of them easier.

The team's previous case had dug up skeletons from the past, and unearthed Assistant Chief Constable Treadgold's misjudgements in investigating the murder of two young boys. As far as Grant was concerned, it was Treadgold's mistakes which had allowed a serial murderer to keep on killing.

During their last investigation, Grant had suspected McGowan of being a leak. Had McGowan passed information to Treadgold, behind Grant's back? Information which allowed Treadgold to cover his tracks? Grant's instincts told him – yes. Although he had no proof against McGowan and the bigger fish was Treadgold. Grant intended to nail ACC Treadgold for corruption. All he needed was one scrap of intelligence and he could trigger an investigation of the man.

Patience is a virtue, Grant reminded himself, *keep focused on Emily and Lisa. Bringing down Treadgold is for another day*. And when that day came, Grant would be ready.

Chapter Twenty-five

Ruby stood on a busy London street not far from Regent's Park. Balancing a cake box, with her free hand she pressed the intercom for her friend's flat. The name "Hawk" was written alongside the buzzer.

Hawk was the nickname they had given him in the children's home. Ruby had lived in the home for most of her childhood and she, Hawk and Soraya had formed an unbreakable trio. Hawk and Soraya were still her two best friends and the ones who knew everything about her.

The door opened with a *click*. Ruby stepped inside and the noise from the traffic shut off behind her.

Hawk was a recluse, probably due to the relentless bullying he'd received as a child and because he had a horrible family history. He lived in a massive posh apartment, with his cat, and he'd come a long way since their days together as kids. Hawk made literally piles of money working freelance as a technology and internet mastermind and he did work off-the-grid and off-the-record. Ruby didn't know the details of his CIA contracts and his international networks. What she did know was that Hawk's skills made him the perfect person to help with the Glover case.

The police needed phone records and credit card information on Jack and Alice Glover, and Ruby had asked Hawk to get intel using his own means.

Her friend sat in his living room. Hawk's fat ginger cat

was nearby. Surrounded by computers and screens full of data, Hawk gave a boyish grin and pulled off his headphones. His eyes went straight to the cake.

'Hi, Rube, long time no see. You and Soraya are busy these days.'

She gave him a hug and was pleased he wasn't as thin as he sometimes was.

'You're looking well. And hey, we're never too busy for old friends. I've got my own place in Himlands Heath, you should come and see it.'

'Maybe.'

She'd been asking him for ages and he'd been promising he would and then kept putting it off. It was difficult for him to go out.

'I found some stuff for you on the Glovers.' Hawk took in a deep breath of chocolate. 'Oooh this smells divine.' He dipped his finger into the cake topping. 'And it's de-li-cious.'

'I'll cut it in the kitchen. I hope you dug me up something interesting.'

'You bet.'

When she came back, she carried two plates. One with an average-sized slice for herself and the other with two giant chunks.

'It was the gooiest chocolate extravaganza I could find,' she said.

'Yummy. Well, let me give you the Glover run down. It's a lot of usual stuff – they're a high-income, high-expenditure couple. Alice spends big on treatments – spas, stylists, beautician and the like. Jack spends big on entertainment – nothing smutty but a few subscriptions to clubs, posh restaurants, expensive weekends, golf membership, and boring stuff like that. And then there's this.'

Hawk tapped at the keyboard and then flourished his hand at the screen. 'Ta da.'

Ruby stared. 'What am I looking at?'

'The one on the left is Jack Glover's phone record and this number here is a repeater.' Pressing a key, Hawk highlighted all the instances of a particular phone number. 'Most of these are text messages.'

'I hope that's his wife he's talking to,' Ruby said.

'You're kidding me, right? I said this was interesting. The number he's contacting belongs to a Natalie Karnik.'

On a different screen, Hawk brought up an aerial view of the Glover's street.

'This is the Glover's place and Natalie,' Hawk pointed, 'lives here. Right next door.'

'Natalie gave the impression their fling had only just started.'

'Nope. I'd say it's been going on for at least two years. And then there's this one little entry in Jack's credit card details which I think you'll want to check out.'

The bank statement took up the right-hand side of the screen. Hawk highlighted a line.

'On the twenty-first of January, Jack Glover made a payment to a private clinic in Brighton. It's called PG which stands for Pregnancy Guidance.'

'Pregnancy Guidance, why is that important?'

'Because it's a euphemism. Most of their business is terminations.'

Jack Glover paid for a termination? With Natalie desperate for a baby it seemed unlikely it would be for her. Nor was it likely the candidate was Alice. But hey, it happened in January, shortly after the au pair was booted out, making Sylvie the prime contender.

Hawk was grinning and Ruby gave him a kiss on the cheek and she passed over the bumper plate of cake.

'Hawk, I told you this before and I'm going to say it again. You're a genius.'

Chapter Twenty-six

'You've given me vital intel and my hands are tied. You know I can't use this information, don't you?' Grant said.

He was always amazed how a former university research assistant like Ruby could have such quality sources. She'd helped them out on a previous case and Grant suspected she had contacts from her days in the children's home though he never wanted to pump her for details. All officers had their informants so why shouldn't Ruby?

Ruby bit her lip. 'In January, Jack Glover paid money to Brighton Pregnancy Guidance clinic. It was likely for a termination. It's got to be relevant.'

'Of course it is. It's crucial. The problem is where you got it from. If the source is illegal it will be inadmissible in any future court case. For god's sake don't tell me how you got it because I don't want to know.'

Leaning against the window frame, Grant stared down at the grey tarmac of the car park. Shit. It was exactly what he needed to pin down Glover and yet using unofficial intelligence would prejudice any future conviction. Was there any way around it?

'Goddamit.' Grant yanked open the door of his office and shouted at McGowan. 'Where the hell are Jack Glover's details!'

McGowan almost dropped his coffee mug. 'I'm working on it, guv. They said they'd send them over and that was…' McGowan checked the time, '…two hours ago.'

'Get them on the phone.'

When the call connected, Grant snatched the receiver from McGowan's hand.

'This is Detective Chief Inspector Grant. I'm in charge of the search for Emily and Lisa Glover – you know, the kidnapped little girls who are all over the news? My sergeant requested vital records and we're still waiting! If anything happens to those children I'm holding you responsible.' The person on the other end of the line made faint apologetic sounds. Grant didn't listen. 'We need Jack Glover's banking details. Now!'

Grant glowered at McGowan who had the good sense to keep his attention fixed on his computer screen.

'As soon as they send the email guv,' McGowan said. 'I'll pop it straight through to the printer.' The seconds ticked by. 'Bingo!' McGowan tapped a few keys.

The machine in the corner of the room sprang to life and it had barely finished spitting out the sheets before the DCI grabbed them.

'About bloody time,' Grant said.

*

At Sylvie's coffee bar, Ruby ordered an orange juice and Diane took a cappuccino and Ruby carried them to a table. Grant had sent them down to Brighton to question Sylvie. They cleared the interview with Sylvie's boss and Diane beckoned Sylvie over.

'Hello Sylvie, I'm Detective Sergeant Collins and this is my colleague Ruby Silver. I know you've already spoken to DCI Grant about the Glover children. We need to have another chat.'

Sylvie gave a friendly smile. 'I can't right now, I'm working. I've been watching the news and I didn't see anything. Have you found Lisa and Emily?'

'Not yet,' Diane said, 'and I asked your boss nicely and got you a fifteen-minute break. I want to talk to you about the Pregnancy Guidance clinic.'

'I-I don't know what you mean.'

'Yes you do. I spoke to them myself and they remembered a young Australian woman who fits your description. I think it might be better if you told us what was going on.'

The PG clinic had admitted they recognised Sylvie although they had not been willing to reveal details which would, as they explained, compromise patient confidentiality.

'It's none of your business,' Sylvie said.

Diane patted the seat next to her. 'It is when we're investigating a child abduction. Please don't make me bring you in for questioning.'

Ruby noticed red flush marks on Sylvie's cheekbones. The young woman was either embarrassed or annoyed or both.

'What do you want from me? I haven't done anything wrong.'

'Come on, Sylvie,' Ruby said. 'You told DCI Grant you weren't having a relationship with Jack Glover yet he paid for you to visit the PG clinic.'

Sylvie dropped her gaze to the table top. 'I'm not proud of what I did but it wasn't terrible either. What?' She looked at Ruby and then at Diane. 'Are you going to make me spell it out?'

'If you simply told us it might help,' Diane said.

'Jesus. Okay, I'm pregnant, and Jack is the father. Happy?'

'How did he take the news?' Ruby asked.

'Cliché isn't it? The young au pair who gets seduced by her employer. I never thought I could be so stupid. I was dumb enough to fall for him. Then, when I told Jack I was pregnant, he offered money for a termination. He even made an appointment. I thought he'd be pleased and all he wanted to do was get rid of it.'

Ruby took out a packet of tissues and pushed them across the table. 'It wasn't what you were expecting?'

'What do you think? He went from being all over me to offering me cash. I was stunned. Didn't know what to do. Like I said, he even made the appointment for me though, of course, it didn't occur to him I might want him to come along too. He expected me to go on my own. Did you know they give you a consultation and a counselling session? The termination happens by you taking two pills and if you swallow the first one you have to take the second otherwise your baby can be born with horrible defects. When they told me how it worked I realised I couldn't go through with it.'

'You changed your mind.'

'I never really made up my mind in the first place because I'd been expecting Jack to be pleased. He'd told me plenty about how he liked me and he bought me gifts and made me feel special and all the time he was using me. Jack said he and Alice hadn't done it since Lisa was born and he wanted to leave. I was dumb enough to believe him.'

'You thought he'd make a new life with you,' Ruby said.

Sylvie gave a rueful smile. 'Turns out Alice's money is worth more and Jack is a liar. A baby will spoil my life and ruin my plans – except I couldn't go through with getting rid of it. Now I'm stuck.'

'Does Alice know?' Diane asked.

'Only if Jack told her and I'm pretty certain he didn't. Her jealousy was bad enough – I wouldn't have been able to face her once she found out Jack didn't want me anymore.'

'You fell into a trap,' Ruby said. 'What about your family? Will they help you out?'

'Are you mad? I can't tell them. And you know what? I'm glad you know. Jack Glover doesn't deserve me protecting him. He turned out to be a shit, and right afterwards he allowed his wife to dismiss me. I did leave the children unattended for a few *seconds* and I could see them the whole time. It was Alice's excuse and Jack didn't back me up. How many other au pair's has Jack had sex with? I reported him to the agency. They can't do anything for me but at least they can protect other girls from the same fate.'

'You should have told the DCI,' Diane said. 'It would have saved us a lot of time.'

'It was private and I didn't see how it would make a difference.'

Diane took out her phone. She swiped the screen and brought up a photo of the red camisole. 'Do you recognise this?'

Sylvie sniffed. 'Sorry, I'm so tearful these days it's annoying. Yes, it's one of the gifts Jack gave me.'

'Any idea how it got into Emily's room?'

'I've no idea but I guess she came across it and thought it was pretty or liked the colour or something. Kids are funny like that.' Sylvie gave her nose a loud blow. 'You must think I'm really naïve.'

'That's not at all what I'm thinking,' Diane said. 'So don't put words in my mouth.'

'A married man fooled you and then left you to deal with being pregnant. What are you going to do?' Ruby asked.

'Like I always do – I'll sort it out on my own. Jack doesn't know I didn't go through with it. Once it's born I can prove paternity if I want to. Jack was willing to give money though he hinted how could he be sure it was his, the bastard.'

'You've signed up with a doctor?' Ruby asked.

'Yes and I've found a nice one who doesn't judge. Please don't think badly of me. Jack can be an absolute charmer and he knows how to get women to do what he wants.'

'But he didn't force you?' Ruby said.

'No I wanted it as much as he did.' Sylvie placed a hand on her belly. 'And now I'm going to have to live with the consequences.'

Chapter Twenty-seven

Grant took a good look at Jack Glover. The man wasn't bothering to shave and he slunk around in the same clothes, his expression haggard. Jack's study was littered with uneaten bowls of snacks and half-drunk mugs of coffee. It smelled faintly of Jack's body odour which made Grant want to fling open the window. Grant sat on a sofa and Jack on his comfy desk chair.

'I spoke with Natalie Karnik and she made it clear your relationship with her has been going on for months,' Grant said.

Time to open up Jack like a tin of beans.

Jack tried to straighten his crumpled trousers. 'Did Natalie tell you that? So what?'

'It's obstructive if you withhold information. Every detail has its importance. It doesn't help if you don't tell me the truth.'

'I don't see what difference my personal life makes.'

'The priority here is finding your children and I need your cooperation.'

'And you've got it. Okay, so I cheated on my wife. It's not a bloody crime. And please don't believe my wife's silly accusations about Natalie stealing the children.'

'So Natalie has never mentioned wanting to be in a couple with you?'

'We've never talked that way. It's an affair.'

'And you don't plan to leave your wife.'

'For god's sake, no. I made a mistake.'

'I see. And what about Sylvie Delacourt's pregnancy does your wife know about that?'

It was as if Grant had punched Jack in the face.

'Wh-what,' Jack stuttered.

'Please don't deny it,' Grant said. 'We don't have time to waste.'

'I don't know what Sylvie's said to you.'

Jack was digging except Grant wasn't going to provide. He kept his eyes locked on Jack.

'Okay, okay. Sylvie came to me after Christmas and told me she was pregnant. She said it was mine except I wasn't certain about that.'

'Though you're not denying having sex with your au pair?'

'Once. I had sex with her once. Then she tells me she's pregnant.'

Grant turned the screws. 'And you offered to pay for a termination.'

'Shit, you've been digging. Okay, yes I did. I felt sorry for her. She was in a state. Are you going to shoot me for helping her out?'

Grant remained silent.

Jack shrugged. 'Like I said, I didn't know for sure if I was the father or if she…?'

'You're suggesting Ms Delacourt had sex with another man and he could be the father?'

'Exactly. I don't want to sound judgemental only… she was that type of girl.'

Grant didn't let his dislike of Jack cloud his judgement. He was here for facts which could lead him to the children. Nothing more and nothing less. Jack's sex life and his lack of morals was only relevant if it could relate to Emily and Lisa.

Jack rubbed his hands over his face. 'For god's sake just get my children back. Shouldn't you be out there searching?'

Grant flicked through his notes. 'That's exactly what we're doing, sir, I can assure you. In your banking details there are transactions which relate to the purchase of an apartment on the other side of Himlands Heath. Bought five years ago it's registered in your name. Is your wife aware this apartment exists?'

'No.'

'We've spoken to the concierge and he says you go there occasionally with women. Is this true?'

As soon as Grant discovered the existence of the apartment from Jack's records, Grant and several officers had questioned the doorman and neighbours and they had scanned foyer security camera footage to check for any sign of Emily and Lisa. There had been no trace of the little girls, otherwise Grant would have forced an entry.

'Jesus. Can't a man have any privacy?'

'I need to get inside. Are you willing to show me?'

'Yes! Okay, I use it for sex. So what? You think I've got Emily and Lisa holed up there? Are you mad! Why do I get the feeling you're treating me like a suspect?'

Why, Mr Glover? Because you're a damn liar and people didn't tell the truth for a reason.

'Have your children ever been there?'

A light sweat had broken out on the man's top lip. 'Never.'

'Keeping the apartment secret was a very bad mistake.' Grant stood and felt like dragging Jack up by his collar. 'Get up! You're taking me there immediately. I want it swabbed for their DNA.'

Chapter Twenty-eight

A few months ago

Sylvie tipped a packet of biscuits into a bowl and carried them into the lounge. She had the Glover house to herself and Maria was coming around for the afternoon.

Chatting with Maria was something Sylvie looked forward to. Maria was patient and attentive and she enjoyed listening. She was better than past friends who tired of Sylvie's need to talk.

Maria loved Sylvie's silly stories about the Glovers. She sympathised when Sylvie complained about her family back in Australia and oohed and aahed over the fact Sylvie was expected to return to Australia for her sister's wedding. It was the last thing Sylvie wanted to do and Maria was in complete agreement it was Sylvie's choice. Chloe was the favoured older sister who did everything right whereas Sylvie, in her parents' eyes, did everything wrong. Sylvie had come to England to escape them and do things her own way. Maria got that.

Before breakfast, Sylvie had made an unexpected discovery. It was exciting. That was, until she told Jack. The way he reacted turned Sylvie's world upside down.

And she was going to entrust Maria with the whole wretched story.

The bell rang and Sylvie rushed to the door.

'Hello,' Maria said, giving Sylvie a hug. 'I bought those little cakes you like.'

'Lovely. We can sit in the lounge for a change.'

'I thought you weren't allowed in there.'

'Hey, who's to know cos we've got the place to ourselves.'

Sylvie flounced through with Maria in tow. She installed herself in one of the sumptuous armchairs and Maria perched on the edge of the sofa.

'Go on make yourself at home. I've got something I need to tell you,' Sylvie said. She arranged Maria's cakes on a plate, taking in the scent of fresh cream and icing. Her fingers were trembling. Actually she'd been a wreck all day, ever since she'd done the pregnancy test that morning and got a positive result.

'I'm all ears,' Maria said. 'Don't tell me it's about your sister's wedding.'

'It's nothing to do with boring Chloe though did I tell you Chloe's still sending photos of wedding locations. Hasn't she got the message I'm not interested? The dress she's chosen is ghastly and her fiancé sounds the dullest person you've ever heard of. Of course, Chloe says he dotes on her. Which is totally sickening.'

'Poor you.'

'If I ever get married I want it on a beach and people can dance in the waves and make love in the sand. Here, help yourself.' She pushed cakes and biscuits across the coffee table.

She wouldn't be getting married any time soon, would she, Sylvie thought. Jack had made her angry. She'd expected him to be pleased by the pregnancy news. After all the times he told her he felt trapped by Alice and wanted to get away. Sylvie had expected him to be happy. She thought he'd be ready to take off with her and dump boring Alice. Jack's reaction had been like a kick in the gut. Sylvie swallowed down the bitterness.

'Have a look at the man Chloe's going to marry, doesn't he look awful.' She needed Maria's adoration today. Maria would understand what a shit Jack was. Sylvie could count on Maria to be on her side.

Maria scrolled the pictures and made disdainful noises.

'Wow, look at him. And the dress is hideous.'

'Yeah, ugly as hell.'

Maria passed back the phone and gave Sylvie an expectant look.

Sylvie was about to tell the whole sorry story when a cake crumb went down the wrong way. It lodged, dry and stubborn, in the back of her throat. She coughed so hard tears came to her eyes as Maria slapped her on the back.

'Are you all right? Oh gosh, let me get you a drink.'

'Thanks,' Sylvie said, wiping at her eyes. 'There's juice in the fridge. I forgot to bring it through.'

'I'll fetch it.'

Sylvie leant back. What would Maria say? She was bound to be in awe. Maria was already jealous about Sylvie sleeping with Jack and about the secret apartment Jack kept for their clandestine sex sessions. Sylvie had deliberately taken Maria to the luxurious apartment to show it off.

Her friend was taking a long time. Surely she'd been able to find the drinks by now. Sylvie padded along the hallway towards the kitchen. The kitchen door was ajar and she could see Maria at the side of the fridge. Sylvie stopped herself from calling out because Maria was in front of the little board where the family hung their key fobs and it looked as if Maria had just slipped something into her pocket.

Walking in breezily, Sylvie noticed how Maria scooted away and opened the doors of the cabinet nearest to her looking, presumably, for glasses. Except she wasn't searching for glasses was she? Maria was *pretending* to look for them.

'This place is massive,' Maria said. 'How do you remember where everything is? I can't find the tumblers.'

'They're over here.'

While Maria busied herself organising a tray, Sylvie surreptitiously scanned the little hooks and hanging keys. Alice and Jack were both out so they had their own main sets with them. The ones left were for the garden shed and for Jack's study and spare ones for the offices at Hardman Construction. Was one missing? What on earth had Maria been up to?

Sylvie trailed Maria back to the lounge and all thought of confiding in her friend about the pregnancy was gone. She felt a stab of suspicion. Was Maria one of those weird people who went around collecting other people's belongings? Kleptomaniacs weren't they called? She'd once seen a television programme on it, about a woman who couldn't resist taking items like teaspoons and ornaments from friend's houses. Was Maria one of those? Or was there more to it?

'You've gone quiet,' Maria said. 'Aren't you going to tell me what's on your mind?'

'Oh it's nothing important. It can save for later. What do you think about watching a film with our feet up on Alice's precious coffee table? And they won't notice if we help ourselves to a bottle of wine.'

Maria giggled. 'You're terrible. Sure, whatever you want.'

Sylvie let Maria choose then the two of them settled to watch the film. Once it started, Sylvie couldn't concentrate what with the pregnancy and Jack, and what was she going to do. And the key.

It didn't matter Maria had taken something. Sylvie couldn't care less. What bothered her was *why* had Maria done it? She remembered her friend being curious before about the keys. Should she challenge her? And a little part of Sylvie couldn't help thinking it might make sense of their sudden friendship – Maria's interest in her at the gym, the way they seemed to hit it off right from the beginning, the way Maria hung on her every word and was happy to do whatever Sylvie wanted. The friendship had been too easy and Maria too eager. Sylvie had known it, she simply chose to ignore it because it was difficult to meet people working the hours she did. Or was she being paranoid brought on by Jack's shitty behaviour?

While the film played, Sylvie turned over the possibilities. In the end, she decided a direct challenge wouldn't work and anyway it didn't appeal to her. Maria had been sneaky. Far better would be to go about finding out what was going on in a devious way.

Several hours later, when Maria said goodbye, Sylvie left it a few minutes and then followed her.

The suburban streets of Himlands Heath were full of parked cars and trees which provided convenient cover. If she looked furtive, no one paid any notice, and Sylvie's nerves soon settled as curiosity got the better of her.

It didn't take long for Maria to show her hand. A couple of streets from the Glovers' house, Maria met a man. From a distance, he was ordinary looking, a bit rough perhaps. The two of them had a brief exchange and then Maria handed over a small item from her pocket. It had to be the key. Sylvie watched from the corner of the road peering out from behind a sycamore tree. This was crazy and weird, what was Maria up to? It didn't look like kleptomania to Sylvie. Now she faced a choice – should she follow the man?

He was a few years older than Maria. Dressed in a long dark coat he had a hardened air about him, in the lines of his face and the intense way he spoke to Maria. The daring part of Sylvie said yes, follow him, though she realised he wasn't the sort of man she was used to. He was a more dangerous type.

Sylvie shuffled her feet. *Come on girl,* she said to herself, *what's life without a bit of risk.* Hadn't she come to England to escape the suffocation of her family? And now she was in the shit with a baby on the way, so what the hell? How could it get any worse?

When Maria went one way and the stranger went another, Sylvie made a quick decision and followed the man.

Chapter Twenty-nine

Tom received a call from Grant.

'Nothing at Jack's apartment,' Grant snapped. 'No trace of the children, and no bloodstains showed up after luminol testing.'

DNA results would take a while to come in but it didn't sound promising. When Tom told Ruby she was as disappointed as he was.

'We wait,' Tom said. 'Our focus is next contact from the abductor.'

An unexpected visitor came ringing at the door a while later. It was Uncle Philip.

'My poor Alice,' Philip said. 'I've been worrying about you day and night.' He put his arms around his niece.

'Joan, I know we've had our fallouts but let's forget about all that rubbish. I want to be here for Alice.'

Joan Hardman gave a small nod.

Philip took Tom's hand. 'Good to see you again. Has there been any news?'

Tom shook his head. 'This is my colleague Ms Silver. I'm sorry we can't divulge any sensitive information.'

Tom was interrupted by Jack storming into the house, back from his visit with Grant. 'What the hell are you doing here?' Jack demanded.

'I'm supporting my niece.' Philip's voice was tight. 'Which is a hell of a lot more than you're doing.'

'You mean you're here to wheedle more funds out of her,' Jack sneered. 'I know your game.'

The two men took a step closer – Jack with a superior smirk and Phil with his arms rigid with rage.

'This isn't helping Alice,' Ruby said.

'Ms Silver is right,' Tom said sternly.

The last thing they wanted was more tension.

'There's no room for men like you in this family,' Phil shouted. He took another step until he was nose to nose with Jack.

Jack didn't back down. 'Shut the fuck up. How dare you talk to me like that. You're not welcome here.'

'Yes he is,' Alice said.

'You're the one who's betrayed my niece, you worthless piece of shit. When Alice told me what you'd been up to, my wife had to stop me coming straight over here to wring your neck.'

Tom took a hold of Philip Hardman's arm. 'Sir, I need to ask you to accompany me to another room.'

Philip shook Tom off. 'Course. I need a change of air. There's a stink around here.'

'Fuck off. You've been sniffing around my wife for money from the day she was born.'

'He has not! Phil has always been there for me. You're the one screwing Natalie. She can't have babies and now she wants mine!'

'Darling, that's ridiculous,' Jack said.

'Don't you dare call me that.' Alice looked like she wanted to rake her nails down Jack's face. She turned to Ruby. 'Natalie wanted to adopt and Sanjay didn't. That's why Sanjay's leaving. Only why should Natalie bother to adopt when she can steal mine!'

'Alice, you need to sit down,' Joan said to her daughter.

'Shut up! Everyone shut up telling me what to do!'

Her nervous habit of tugging at her hair had got a lot worse. She did it now, digging in her fingers, making it look as if she'd just crawled out of a hedge.

'It's my babies who are gone not yours! When the hell is he going to call?'

It was the million-dollar question.

'Why don't you and I go to the kitchen,' Ruby suggested.

Tom turned to Philip Hardman. 'And I think it might be best if you leave.'

*

'Our priority is the next call,' Ruby said to Alice. 'Do you feel prepared for it?'

'I know what DCI Grant wants me to say. Don't worry I'm not cracking up.'

Ruby thought Alice was changing. She was stronger than she had been before – answering Jack back and her mother.

'You're very kind and so is Tom. It's horrible you hearing Jack's dirty secrets about Natalie and his shitty accusations about Uncle Phil. I knew Jack wasn't an ideal husband and I turned a blind eye. I thought it was temporary and he'd get back on track and he never did.'

Ruby was making some food. She cracked eggs and they sizzled in the pan. 'The affair with Natalie wasn't a complete surprise then?' she asked carefully.

'A part of me suspected and I ignored the warning signs. At least with the au pairs, when I got suspicious I could get rid of them.'

Ruby buttered the toast and kept a diplomatic silence.

'Last night I finally realised – I loved Jack far more than he ever loved me. It's a horrible thought only I couldn't help wondering if Jack married me to get in with Dad.'

'You're both under an incredible amount of stress. It doesn't mean your marriage won't survive,' Ruby said.

'Yes it does. My babies are all that matters and I don't care about Jack. I feel a fool to have made so many allowances.'

Jack walked in, bringing the smell of body odour with him.

'Alice we need to talk,' Jack said.

'No Ruby please don't leave. Tell my husband I don't want to talk to him now or ever. The only communication we will have is through my lawyer when I file for divorce. Tell him he disgusts me. I want him out of my sight.'

Ruby gave Jack an apologetic look. 'Perhaps it's best if discussions between you and your wife are left until later.'

'There aren't going to be any discussions,' Alice said. 'It's over.'

'Please, Alice, I'm sorry. I didn't mean for it to happen.'

'Like you didn't mean for it to happen with Sylvie and the other girls? You are such a damn liar.' Alice picked up a plate full of scrambled eggs and hurled it at the wall.

*

At the sound of breaking crockery, Tom rushed in.

Alice continued. 'You make me sick. *Our children are missing* and all you're interested in is getting it off with my best friend. I hate your guts.'

Tom stood between them. 'Ma'am please, this won't help.'

Alice's phone suddenly rang and everyone froze. Eggs slithered down the wall.

'It's an unknown number,' the technician shouted from the other room. 'Likely this is it.'

Ruby turned off the cooking gas and she and Tom moved close to Alice.

'It's all right,' Ruby said. 'Remember what you need to say. Take a breath and answer the call.'

Tom held out a piece of card. On it were the words asking for a proof of life video.

Alice's green eyes were large and scared and fixed on Ruby. Ruby nodded. 'You can do it.'

'Answer the call and please say only what we have agreed,' Tom said. 'If it's Emily, remember you are not speaking to Emily you're speaking to the abductor. He is controlling what she can say.'

She was shaking so hard, wisps of hair around her face were trembling. Slowly she lifted the phone and pressed the speaker button. Ruby could see Alice's lips quivering.

'Hello this is Alice.'

'Mummy, it's Emily. Here are the instructions -- you will bring half a million pounds in unmarked notes. You'll receive the drop-off coordinates beforehand. You must come alone.'

'I will only give you the money in exchange for my children. Please do not harm them. I want proof of life,' Alice read from the card.

There was a long pause during which Tom took Alice's arm to support her.

'You'll get it. Don't be late,' Emily said, and the line went dead.

Chapter Thirty

When Maria followed him into the children's room, it was obvious Emily had deteriorated. He didn't notice, or if he did, he ignored it. He had been back on a high ever since the phone call to Emily's mother.

Maria wondered if he had taken a snort that morning. It was pretty likely because he wasn't worried they needed to send a video, when on a video it would be difficult to hide the state Emily was in.

'This is going just like I want it to,' he said.

Maria wiped her hand over Emily's forehead. The child was sweating and yet she was cold and the two together were a bad sign. A purple line snaked from the child's elbow to her armpit. Maria almost fainted.

'If they want proof of life they can have it,' he said. 'Sort that kid out and get her ready for the recording.'

Maria dabbed Emily's forehead with a damp towel and brushed the child's hair. Emily was floppy the same as Maria's little brother had been when he had blood poisoning. Poor Billy, she remembered the doctors saying if it had been left longer it might have been too late.

He was flicking the button on and off, on and off, for the recording. 'Stop fussing and get on with it. I don't like waiting.'

Emily had to be propped against the bed.

He'd bought a copy of that day's newspaper and Lisa was instructed to hold it up. This time Lisa would say a short message as well as her sister. Since she couldn't read very well Lisa had to learn her part by heart.

He tapped his foot, impatient to get it over with, but the first time they tried it, when they watched the playback, it was obvious Emily was slurring her words.

'Is she doing it on purpose?' he said.

'She's going downhill fast. I think she needs a doctor.'

'What are you now, a nurse? There's no fucking way I'm taking her to a goddam doctor.'

'Can't you see how bad it is? If we don't she might die.'

'You're always one for the melodramatic, aren't you.'

He placed pillows on either side of Emily to stop her keeling over. When he started Emily's recording again he had his knife out and this time Lisa was wedged under his arm.

'Speak clearly, kid, or I swear I'll hurt your sister and I know you don't want that to happen. And she's already done her recording so it won't matter what I do to her, will it?'

Poor Emily did her best. It was an improvement on her first try and though he wasn't pleased, he decided it was the best they were going to get.

Back downstairs, he sent the files over to the mother's phone.

'This'll give her something to think about and just so long as the bitch comes up with the cash. What are you looking so gloomy about?'

It was hard for Maria to drag up a placating smile. The kid was dying, she felt sure of it.

'My little brother had an infection when he cut his finger. He went like the kid is and he almost died.'

'I told you to shut up with the dying shit. She's fine.'

For once, her concern for Emily pushed her beyond her own fears. 'You're wrong. We need to take her to a hospital.' In all the years she'd known him it was the first time she had ever stood up to him.

Rage and paranoia flashed across his face. Maria backed up against the wall.

'Well, well, you've got mighty big for your boots all of a sudden.'

Her nose started bleeding. Muttering an excuse, she escaped, scuttling to the bathroom. She locked the door though she knew he could get in from the outside if he wanted. Leaning over the sink, she tried to stem the flow with a wad of tissue.

He hated talkback. She hoped he would forget about it enough to not take it out on her later, because she knew the story of how he once beat up one of his girlfriends so badly she needed thirty stitches in her face. He had always been volatile, and prison had made him worse.

The nosebleed took an age to stop and she had plenty of time to stare in the mirror. Sores were starting to break out at the base of her nose. Snorting coke had that effect. She'd known users who'd disintegrated the septum of their own damn nostrils.

Blood dripped into the basin and she could not hold in the tears. She despised herself – for getting together with him, for falling into using. *You've slid to the bottom,* she whispered to herself. It was horrible being back where she'd been when he went to prison. She was a useless junkie again, craving her fixes and unable to break away.

And this time it was worse because of the children and what happened with Billy kept playing in her mind. If Emily died she would never forgive herself.

Chapter Thirty-one

Maria felt relieved because he hadn't mentioned her outburst again. Him needing her for the plan seemed to be stopping him flying into a foul temper. She was the one who had visited the apartment Jack Glover kept for his mistresses. Sylvie had taken her there which meant Maria should be able to get in the building without arousing suspicion – and that was their next move.

Taking her time, Maria made herself look nice, putting on a blue flowery dress and her favourite jacket and carefully applying make-up. The cosmetics helped to cover the signs of her deteriorating health and the ravages of the drug. Even he thought she looked nice, and his eyes followed her as she crossed the room.

'Do you think I'll do?' she asked.

'Not bad and remember you drop the package and you come straight back here.'

He handed her the envelope containing the pay-as-you-go phone and Maria nodded. A few minutes later and she was out the door and feeling the fresh air on her face. She was glad to be away from him. If only she could get rid of him forever.

Taking the train to Himlands Heath, she sat by the window chewing viciously at her nails. He wouldn't tolerate any deviancy from his plan and he'd made it clear he had no intention of taking Emily to the hospital. At the start of this, he had promised he wouldn't harm the children. He always had been a liar.

The train sped along and the Sussex countryside whizzed by. Maria barely registered the green fields. Her life, which was already grim, had been closed down by the powder and by him. Should she make a run for it? This was her chance. Yet she knew she'd need another fix by nightfall or she would suffer and she could not bear the cravings.

He had been clever hooking her back into the habit. It took strength to de-tox in some clinic full of junkies. Strength Maria knew she lacked. The terror and pain she endured going through withdrawal the first time made her want to piss herself.

What about going to the authorities? Maria wanted to but she couldn't because she wasn't an ordinary person, she was a druggie and the police had no sympathy for people like her. She'd be condemned alongside him and thrown into some dirty cell to go cold turkey on her own. Then they'd lock her up for several years.

And if she crossed him, he would punish her. He'd chase her down and make her pay and where could she go? There was nowhere she'd be safe. Even if he went to prison, one day he'd get out and he'd come after her. She knew she was trapped.

The train arrived at Himlands Heath and she followed her instructions and walked to Jack Glover's secret apartment. Her mind was churning trying to find a way out. What about Sylvie? Could she find her friend in Brighton? But where would she start looking and what if Sylvie wouldn't help?

The foyer was quiet, and going to the gold-fronted mail boxes she popped the package in the one with Jack's name on the front. The concierge smiled at her. The man was used to being discrete about the women Jack saw there. If what Sylvie told Maria was right, the concierge would notify Jack about the delivery, which was essential because the plan hinged on it.

The next train back to Brighton was due in half an hour. He would be expecting her on the dot, which meant she was running out of time to make a decision.

Waiting on the platform, Maria's palms itched. When the arrival time of her train flicked up on the display board, her heart beat faster. Should she go back to him? Should she try to run?

By the time it pulled into the station she was sweating and shivering from head to foot. The electric doors opened with a *hiss*. She stood in front of the doorway. A man pushed past to board the train. There were people inside the carriage, one was reading a book and another jiggled a baby on her knee. Maria shuffled forward until she could smell the inside of the carriage and someone's sandwich. The next step would take her into the train. Squeezing her eyes closed, Maria willed herself to be brave.

She had a sudden vision of her brother, not as a child but as an adult, when she'd last seen him and he screamed at her he never wanted to see her again and he'd never, ever give her more money to feed her habit.

Do it for Emily, do it for Billy.

The doors beeped, warning her they were about to close.

As the doors hissed, she took one tiny step. Then the air swept past her face and the train pulled away, leaving Maria on the platform.

Chapter Thirty-two

Alice received a video recording showing Emily and Lisa. Tom and Ruby were at the Glover house when it arrived and they stayed with Alice and Jack long enough to make sure the couple were able to cope. Then they left the Glovers in the capable hands of support officers and headed to the police station because Grant wanted to give instructions about their next steps.

In the incident room, Tom pressed the play button on a remote control and the video came up on the big screen. The team were gathered round. The recording started and they saw Lisa sitting with her back against a bunk bed. Lisa was holding up a copy of the day's newspaper.

'Hello Mummy,' Lisa said. 'Hand over the half a million and you'll get your kids in exchange. You must approach the meeting point alone.'

Lisa looked terribly serious and scared. It made Tom feel sick. Her young voice didn't fit the stark words she read out. 'No cops,' Lisa said.

The film cut and then Emily came on screen. 'Look out for further instructions.'

That was the end of the message. They watched it through several times.

'The technicians are analysing it,' Grant said. 'What are your observations? Throw them out.'

McGowan had started pacing which he always did when he was stressed. Tom rewound the recording and froze it on a shot of Emily's face. 'At least it shows the children are both still alive.'

'Emily's ill,' Diane said.

Ruby nodded. 'That's what Alice said.'

'She's sweating and her eyes don't seem focused. And her part was ultra short. She was the main player in the other message. What did her mother say?' Diane asked.

'Alice was relieved because she was desperate to see them both. But Emily's appearance frightened her, actually she got a bit hysterical afterwards. She said what you said – that there's something terribly wrong.'

'Oh no, I knew it,' Diane said. 'Can we get a doctor to look at this?'

Grant nodded. 'I've contacted a paediatrician at Himlands General. What else?'

'The abductor tried to hide the problem by putting less emphasis on Emily and making Lisa speak for longer. Did you see how there were pillows on either side of Emily,' Ruby said.

'Yes,' Grant said. 'Like she was being propped up. I'd like to know Jack's reaction.'

Tom put the remote on a nearby table. 'He was less certain than his wife about Emily not being well. He said she could simply be tired though I got the impression he said it to calm his wife.'

'I doubt if that worked,' Diane said wryly.

Tom shook his head. 'It didn't, and Alice is still not speaking to her husband. Also, Jack's not happy about Alice doing the drop-off. He wants to be the one to handle it. He told me he doesn't want to put Alice at risk.'

McGowan made a snorting noise. 'Isn't it a bit late for him to be worried about his wife? I think Mr Glover's burned his bridges.'

'Jack Glover has no say in this,' Grant said. 'I'm sticking with the abductor's demands for the wife to deal with the handover. As for the phone calls, the constables have identified the SIMs from them and we've traced them through to a network provider. They're still trying to trace a retail outlet where they were purchased.'

'That's going to take ages, guv,' McGowan said.

'Yes, thank you, McGowan,' Grant said sharply.

Tom thought the strain was starting to show.

'The techies have used azimuths to locate where the calls were made from and I don't see any correlation with the addresses of any of our persons of interest.'

'Damn it,' Tom said.

'Exactly and we've no choice about the drop-off. We go along with the abductor's demands or we risk the children's lives. Alice will wear a microphone and we'll set up a perimeter so we can control who goes in and out. How efficiently we can protect her will depend on the location. The force helicopter will be on standby to give air support and we'll have dog patrol units at the perimeter in case.'

'The best scenario will be if we can ring the abductor in. Let's hope we get lucky on that one,' McGowan said.

'DCS Fox has the armed unit on stand-by. We'll have sniper support for Alice but it will have to be from a distance. Again, we can't risk alarming the abductor. The uniformed division are ready to give us full support to have the area locked down. Delaney and Ruby, do you think Alice is up to it?'

Tom answered first. 'It's an odd thing. The marital rift seems to have given her more strength than I gave her credit for.'

'I agree and Alice told me she's determined to carry out the demands to the letter,' Ruby said. 'I think she can do it.'

'Good because it's going to be tough and I can't risk her cracking at the last minute. Keep talking to her and prepare her as best you can,' Grant said. 'Jack called me to request he take his wife's place. I refused. I'll give Jack permission to attend the exchange on the condition he remains in the background which means putting him inside a squad car on the perimeter.'

'He won't like that,' Tom said.

'Too bad. All we're waiting for are the coordinates of the drop-off.'

McGowan stroked his moustache. 'We know the perp's going to choose a location which works for him and not for us, guv. And whoever he is, he's a smart bastard.'

'Of course he is except that doesn't mean he'll have the upper hand. I want everyone's absolute best. I'll be in command of the operation and we are going to get those children back.'

'Yes, guv.'

'And be ready to move at a second's notice.'

Waiting was always the worst part. Grant shut himself in his office. Would they get a visual on the abductor during the exchange? What sort of instructions was Alice going to receive? Likely it would be to drop off the money and she would be told the location of the children because the abductor would want to get away, not walk into a trap.

Grant was too wired. The results of the DNA swabs at Jack's apartment had come in and there was no trace of the children. Diane had tracked down the whereabouts of Zofia Kaminski, the woman who had made a rape allegation against Jack. She worked in a florist in London and Grant badly wanted to interview her. Travelling was out of the question with the drop-off likely to happen at any moment and Grant couldn't spare anyone from his team. How long would the abductor keep them waiting?

The team were holding up under the pressure. Delaney and Ruby were on top of it with the family, Collins and McGowan had carried out some great detective work and everyone was giving it all they'd got.

Grant took the call from his paediatrician friend.

'Hello, David. I got your message and I examined the video.'

He could tell by her voice she hadn't liked what she'd seen. 'And?'

'The older child is ill. Emily's six? It's not looking good. She has limp body tone and she's slurring. What's more worrying are the red patches on her forearm.'

'I didn't see them.'

'They're barely visible but I caught a glimpse at the edge of her sleeve.'

'How bad is it?' Grant asked.

'You said her blood was at the scene and you suspect the abductor used a blade, well, if Emily had a dirty wound or one which got infected, I think the infection may have become systemic. This isn't a hard and fast diagnosis but those red patches tell me there's a strong chance she has sepsis.'

'Blood poisoning?'

'It's known as that although it's much worse. Sepsis is life threatening. Untreated, it can take an adult's life within twelve hours. Emily requires urgent treatment. Even with hospital intervention, if she enters the last stage of sepsis, which is septic shock, we might not be able to save her. Her vital organs will shut down.'

'Jesus.'

'If it's sepsis Emily's fever will turn to chills. Then the red patches will spread and become purple which is the first sign of organ failure. At that stage, her heart will struggle. You must find her, David. It might be a matter of hours.'

Grant hung up and shouted to the team in the cubbyhole.

'Diane, I want the constables to phone every GP surgery in the area and hospitals in adjacent counties. Check if Emily's been seen by a medical professional.'

He muttered, 'And let's hope to God she has.'

*

Hours later when they had not yet received the drop-off information, Grant was sweating.

Every kidnap case was different. Yet such a long time between a proof of life call and the final demands felt plain wrong. They were dealing with someone who planned carefully. For certain, the abductor had already chosen a location for the drop-off. They'd have carried out surveillance to make sure it met their needs while giving as few advantages as possible to the police team.

Did the delay mean there was an issue with the drop-off point? Grant was afraid Emily might be the problem.

McGowan clenched his left hand over his right fist. It was a habit of his when he was extremely stressed. 'The delay doesn't make sense. Something's gone wrong.'

Grant rubbed his eyes. 'We can't make assumptions. We have to keep going forward.'

The kidnapper had a sick child on their hands. Wouldn't it make them want to get rid of the children sooner? It wasn't a reason for them to prolong it unless the kidnapper meant to kill the children.

Grant didn't want to face that possibility, nor the other worst-case scenario; perhaps Emily was already dead.

Chapter Thirty-three

Air rushed past Maria's face as the train sped out of the station. She was perilously close to the edge and she stepped back. She'd done it. She had defied him. As soon as he realised she'd not stuck to the plan he would be furious. She must hide.

Pulling up the collar of her jacket, Maria hurried away. Where could she go? It was then she realised she had no money. He'd given her only enough to buy the return ticket. Wait -- she had money at her apartment which would be the first place he'd look for her, though surely he'd be occupied with Emily and Lisa, and be focused on collecting his half a million. Wouldn't that be more important to him than coming after her? And if she went to her place quickly he wouldn't have time to make it to Himlands Heath from Brighton, would he. She could grab money and clothes and get the hell away – far, far away where he'd never find her. Thailand, she decided on a whim, where it was sunny and people were nice. It was supposed to be cheaper there too. She'd sleep rough until something turned up. The idea of escape made her giddy.

It was a long walk to her old place and a little voice in Maria's head kept saying the same thing over and over – *what about the children*? She tried to squeeze out the voice which kept telling her to help them. She was involved which meant she couldn't go to the police. *I don't want to go to prison. It's too late. No it isn't, think about Emily. You've got to help them. Shut up,* she argued with herself, *shut up, shut up.*

She promised herself if she made it to the airport she'd leave a note somewhere telling where to find Emily and Lisa – and then she'd be away flying across the skies to a new life.

The trade-off for the money would be happening soon and then Emily would be out of danger. She must put Emily out of her mind and concentrate on her own safety. *As soon as he realises you've not stuck to the plan you know what will happen don't you? He'll lose control.*

When a passer-by gave Maria a strange look she realised she was whispering and arguing with herself out loud. Damn it, she needed a fix. There would be the chemical demons to face soon.

Arriving at her old street, she made herself wait out of sight. The paranoia was ramping up and she half expected him to spring out from behind a parked car and grab her, having made it up from Brighton in supersonic time.

Don't be stupid, she told herself. *He can't have got here. Get in and take what you need and get out.*

She ran to her front door. Yes, she'd change into trainers and jeans and pack a small bag. He'd searched her pockets though he'd not searched her bra. Reaching in, she pulled out her front door key and felt like kissing it.

It was musty smelling inside. Ripping off her shoes and tights, she ran into the bedroom. Her hands were shaking as she pulled on jeans and a top. Rifling in the bottom of her wardrobe she found a holdall and stuffed in a few essentials. Her small stash of emergency money was hidden in one of the drawers in the bathroom and she rushed there and grabbed it. It wasn't much yet it was her ticket to freedom.

As she zippered up the bag, she had the idea of getting herself a small supply to keep her going. That way she'd be able to cope for the next few days until she found her way and was safe in hiding.

Maria hesitated. It was a risk. It would be much safer to get away now not lingering for anything. She could be at

London Heathrow airport within a couple of hours. Yet, the craving was already kicking in. When it got worse she wouldn't be able to think straight, she'd be a physical wreck. No, she must get some to take with her. She pulled her jacket back on. She had time.

*

Maria's old dealer hung out in the centre of town by the bus station. He'd likely still be there and if he wasn't there'd be someone else who had taken his place. She persuaded herself it was a good omen because she could take a coach direct to London afterwards. Once in the capital, it would be easy to find public transport to the airport.

She was out of the flat within minutes, checking up and down the road for anyone watching and then running full pelt for the centre of town. Several times she checked over her shoulder and the shadows seemed to jump out at her.

When she got to the bus station, Maria walked around the block and had a momentary panic because Joey wasn't there. Of course, Joey wasn't his real name and she had no idea what was. Then she spotted her old dealer in one of his habitual hang outs, lounging outside an off-licence with a roll-up dangling from his lips. With his lazy stride and slouched shoulders, Joey spotted her quickly, though he gave no sign of recognition.

'Hi,' she said.

'Long time no see.'

'I need some.'

'Is that right? I heard you got clean.'

He was eyeing the street behind her and then to either side, taking his time and sizing her up. Did he think she was working for the cops now? It wasn't her style.

'That was then and this is now. Well?' she said. 'I've got money.'

'Come back at five.'

Shit. It was what he said to his new customers and it was Joey's way of sussing people out and reducing the risks for himself. It told him if people were genuine. It told him if they were being tailed or if they had no money. It told him too, how desperate they were and how much he could charge and whether they'd be good repeat customers. Glancing at the station clock, Maria saw it was just after three. Two more hours to wait! No way.

'Come on, you know me. I need it now. It's important.'

Reaching into her bag, she gave him a view of some money. 'I've got the cash.'

'Yeah but I've not got the merchandise. So see you at five.' Joey then sauntered away.

Shit. Were the cops onto him was that why he wanted to delay? Had he had trouble earlier that day? Had he been forced to stash his stock in case he got frisked? In a daze, she went to the bus station and queued to buy her ticket to London.

'The next bus leaves at three thirty,' the man at the ticket counter told her.

'And the one after that?'

'Five thirty.'

She should get the three thirty and get the hell out of there. Sitting in Brighton waiting for her to return, he would already have realised she'd deviated from his plan. If she took the bus leaving in half an hour he'd never catch her. The problem was if she travelled without a supply would she be able to hold out? Would she be able to get some in London?

'Which one would you like, miss?'

'The three thirty please.'

'A return?'

'No, definitely a single.'

With half an hour to kill, she decided to get something quick to eat. At a kiosk, she paid for a sandwich and spotted Joey down the street speaking to a man with a scar down the side of his face. A jolt of fear shot up her back. She tried to slink out of sight just as the man with the scarred face looked down the street and spotted her.

Of course, she should have realised. He'd sent his friends to find her. It had been a mistake to speak to Joey.

Dropping the sandwich, Maria ran.

Chapter Thirty-four

Maria had been born in Himlands Heath. She'd gone to school there, spent her teenage years hanging around the streets and whenever her mother took in a worthless boyfriend, Maria got used to spending the night in the shelter of doorways or under the bridge. It was better than hearing her mother at it, or finding a naked stranger in the kitchen often throwing lecherous glances in her direction.

Maria knew paths dog walkers took and the cycle tracks and the cut-throughs, which was how she got away from the man with the scar. Shit. He'd sent instructions up from Brighton and ordered his spies to find her. How stupid she'd been.

As she was hiding at the back of the supermarket, she spotted the second of his spies searching for her. This one was a lanky young man with a long stride and dirty matted hair hanging halfway down his back. He looked like a rough sleeper and the type to know the alleyways of Himlands Heath as well as Maria did. She tried to slink out of sight but he saw her.

She sprinted through a maze of streets trying to shake him off until she came out at her old primary school. She had lost Lanky, she was sure of it. The school was deserted and, scaling the wall, she dropped down into the playground. Daylight was fading and she crept along in the shelter of the wall until she came to a niche. Maria hunkered down. She would have to hide until dark and then go across country. She would hitchhike down to the coast and get a train to London from there.

Her skin was itching like hell from needing a fix and she knew it would get worse. If her muscles started cramping and she needed to run, what would she do? *Don't think about it,* she told herself. *Lanky didn't follow you so you should be safe. Just wait a little longer and then work your way to the main road and get a ride.*

On the far side of the playground, the iron grille of the gate gave her a view onto the street. The occasional car passed and a few pedestrians. It wasn't until cold from the ground started to seep up her legs that she realised withdrawal had her in its grip. The lack of coke started messing with her mind.

In the gloom, shadows jumped out at her. Someone was calling her name. She screwed herself as small as she could, hugging her body to stop the shivers. *It's not real. It's made up.* Then she made out a shape by the gate – a tall form with dreadlocks.

The withdrawal symptoms brought a terrible fatigue. Her body's cravings sucked the energy from her and muddled her thoughts. Was it real? Should she run? Could she bargain with Lanky? If she offered him money would he let her go?

'I can see you,' he said.

Maria eased out from the recess. She had to run. Her muscles were so weak she couldn't get up and instead she crawled.

'You can't hide from me. He's coming for you.'

Oh god. 'I've got money. If you let me go I can pay you.'

Lanky was peering through the bars of the gate. 'Sorry I can't do that. You know what he's like.'

A car's headlights shone outside. She heard the engine cut out and then Lanky turned and spoke to someone. Using the wall, Maria pulled herself up. She wept with fear and she tried again to run but couldn't.

'Hello Maria.'

Her left leg went into spasm and she fell.

'You shouldn't have left me,' he called out.

Maria tried to drag herself away. A trickle of urine ran down her leg as they climbed over the gate and walked towards her.

'I'm s-s-sorry. I got scared.'

Kneeling beside her he stroked her hair. 'I know, babe. Don't worry, I'm going to make it right.'

He snapped his fingers and Lanky picked her up and carried her to the car.

Chapter Thirty-five

When Alice was finally sent details of the handover, Tom's adrenalin spiked. The abductor had given them very little time to prepare. Worse, the location was outside their area, in the middle of the countryside at a South Downs beauty spot, a few miles north of Brighton.

Tom hurried to the team briefing. Grant had put in an emergency request and the team were to be joined via online linkup by two officers from Brighton.

By the time Tom got there, a uniformed chief inspector and a younger woman, presumably a detective, were present on screen. It looked as if everyone had been waiting for Tom.

'If your DS is here at last, can we get started?' The Chief Inspector on the screen said. 'The seconds are ticking away.'

The barb stung and Tom shrugged it off. DCI Grant knew Tom had come straight from the Glovers, so he didn't need to give excuses.

'I'd like to introduce Chief Inspector Billingham and Detective Inspector Sarah Hunter and thank you both for joining us at such short notice,' Grant said. 'Chief Inspector Billingham will be coordinating the uniformed division operation. The location falls within the north Brighton patch and his officers are best placed to know the ins and outs of the area. DI Hunter will be our link to their CID.'

There were murmurs of greetings and Tom noticed how Chief Inspector Billingham was courteous to no one except Grant, whereas Sarah Hunter was friendly all around.

'Chief Inspector Billingham and I will be jointly coordinating this operation. I'll be Gold Commander and the Chief Inspector will be the second in command,' Grant said. 'Let's see what we're working with.'

Diane tapped at her keyboard and sent a map and a photographic image to the second screen.

McGowan groaned. 'It's in the middle of bloody nowhere, guv. How the hell are we going to make it safe for Alice?'

'It's going to be a challenge,' Grant said. 'And we've no time for a site visit. Chief Inspector Billingham, can you fill us in on the local details?'

Billingham cleared his throat. 'The spot he's chosen is an area of natural beauty and it forms a basin at the foot of the South Downs. It's a popular area for ramblers.' Billingham used a red pointer to show them. 'This here is the South Downs – they're a line of low hills stretching across the Sussex countryside. The spot for the handover is on the side of the Downs furthest from Brighton. It's a basin about a mile across and remote, accessed by a network of footpaths and cycle tracks. There are two car parks and neither are close. This one is the nearest and I'd estimate it to be about ten minutes' walk away. The other parking area is more than twenty.'

'What about visibility?' Grant asked.

'They'll be some from the nearest car park because it's at the same elevation and there's nothing in between except heather and gorse. We'd have visibility from the top of the Downs, except that's a real hike, so by binoculars only. Our best bet is this little wooded area and this line of trees straggling along the bottom of the Downs.' Billingham wiggled the pointer. 'It provides cover and it's about as close as the car park.'

'Basically you're saying the perimeter must be back behind this line of trees, if we're to stay out of sight of the abductor.'

'Correct.'

'Bloody hell we'll be miles away. That's not giving us much advantage,' McGowan said.

'That's one way of putting it,' Billingham said stiffly.

Billingham had a sour tone. He was a man with a chip on his shoulder, Tom thought, though he had good knowledge which was what they needed.

'How do you think he's going to bring in the children then, sir? By car? And how will the abductor leave the area? They must know we'd set up road blocks,' Collins said.

'Yes, I was wondering about that,' Sarah Hunter said. 'I'm not convinced the children will be brought here. It seems a highly unlikely place for an exchange, don't you think so, sir?'

Sarah Hunter was much more friendly than Billingham and she was doing her best to make up for Billingham's lack of rapport.

Billingham puffed out his cheeks. 'It's impossible to say.'

Ah, thought Tom, a man who didn't like to risk being wrong.

'We've been told to bring half a million in exchange for the children,' Grant said. 'That's what we're putting Alice at risk for. The abductor must have a plan to get in and out. Is it possible to land a light plane?'

'The basin could be a landing spot,' Hunter said.

'Collins, check with local airfields and see what flights have been logged. We're running out of time to stop him if that's what he's planning. Another scenario is he'll head across country and have a getaway vehicle waiting somewhere we can't anticipate. What do you say, Billingham?'

'Like I said, it's a natural bowl with no cover until the wood. Outside of the basin, your guess is as good as mine. There are plenty of paths and small patches where you could conceal a vehicle and it would have to be a four-wheel drive to cope with the terrain. There are two roads which we can cut off. However, this whole place is covered with footpaths and cycle tracks which go for miles. It makes it impossible to cover all exit points.'

Grant nodded. 'If I were him, at the same time Alice leaves the money, I'd give coordinates for where to find the children. Then our search for Emily and Lisa will take priority especially if he's put them in danger. The abductor would bargain on it giving him time to grab the money and get away.'

'It's all very odd,' Tom said. 'What makes him think he's going to have a window to get the cash? Surely he knows we'll be waiting to nab him even if we're scrambling for the children.'

'I agree,' Sarah Hunter said. 'It's difficult to see how he's going to get away with it.'

'I think it's all hinging on him making further demands,' Grant said. He's got a plan we haven't thought of and there's always the possibility he has an accomplice.'

Tom shook his head. 'I don't like it.'

'Whether you like it or not, son, it's what we've got to deal with,' Billingham snapped.

Tom felt so stressed his stomach was in a knot, and everyone was on edge.

'We won't get anywhere if we're not on the same page. I need everyone focused.' Grant stamped out the rising tensions.

'Have you got uniformed officers with bikes?' Grant said. 'If he tries to get away across country then we can pursue him.'

'Yes,' Hunter said. 'What do you think, Chief Inspector? Officers use bikes on Brighton seafront and we have a couple of officers on scrambler bikes we can bring in too.'

'We can try, though is there enough time to organise it?' Billingham said.

McGowan stroked his moustache. 'I could bring my mountain bike as well, guv.'

Grant nodded. 'Great.'

'Alice is going to be very exposed walking into the middle of that open area,' Ruby said.

'I've asked for sniper support. It's the best we can do.' Grant looked at his watch. 'We've very little time to be in position. At the scene, Delaney and Ruby, I want you with Alice when she sets off from the car park. You'll observe her from there and I'll watch her from the trees. It means you and I must be in different places. We'll keep contact with Alice via her earpiece. McGowan and Collins, you'll be with the uniformed officers who'll be spread out along the line of the woods. Communication has got to be slick. Everyone stay on their toes. Let's get to it.'

Chapter Thirty-six

Forty-five minutes before the exchange, Tom was in the car park near to the drop-off point. The area was teeming with officers. Brighton division had put together a team of six on bikes and McGowan joined them. They pedalled off towards the woods where they would hide amongst the trees, ready to give chase should the abductor flee the area by track or footpath.

The paramedics and an ambulance were on standby and the technical team were equipping Alice with her microphone and earpiece. Tom found himself alongside Chief Inspector Billingham who was giving final orders to his uniformed officers.

'Spread out and keep your eyes open,' Billingham said. 'I'll keep you updated as the situation evolves. Meanwhile, anyone and anything is to be treated as suspicious even if it's a little old lady walking her dog.'

Billingham's officers dispersed and he turned to Tom. 'I'm guessing you've not been involved in a hostage exchange before.'

'No, sir.'

'I thought not. Grant speaks highly of you, though in my experience, young officers tend to fuck it up. Frankly, I'm astonished you've been given the lead with the mother.'

Tom didn't know what to say. Apart from something rude and that wasn't an option.

'I follow DCI Grant's orders, sir. I do my best and I've been working with the Glovers since the beginning.'

'I think the best thing will be if you keep out of my way,' Billingham said.

'If it doesn't conflict with our mission then I'll try to.'

'Perhaps I'm not making myself clear. I said I don't want you near me and I don't want your lack of judgement making a mess of this operation. Are we clear?'

'Crystal.'

'That's Chief Inspector to you. I'm glad to hear it, *Detective Sergeant.*'

The tone of Billingham's voice grated but Tom swallowed it down. There was no point retaliating against a senior officer besides, he had every intention of focusing one hundred percent on Alice. He'd leave getting twisted up by petty rivalries to Billingham. It simply wasn't Tom's bag.

Tom went to check in with Ruby.

'Was Billingham giving you a hard time?' she asked.

'How did you know? Don't tell me you can lipread.'

'Oh. No I can't and I was too far away to hear. I could see it in his body posture and the way you reacted.'

'Right. Yeah, Billingham's behaving like an idiot. I hope it isn't going to get in the way.'

'It won't if you don't let it.'

Alice was talking to Grant and Tom could tell Grant was worried she might not be able to handle it. Once Grant moved away, Tom and Ruby took Alice aside.

'My boss is having doubts,' Tom said. 'If you want to pull this off you've got to dig deep.'

'Oh Tom, I want to do it but I can hardly function. It's like my mind has turned off.'

Tom took a light hold of her elbow and her green eyes fixed on him.

'It doesn't matter. Let me and the chief do the thinking for you – that's what we're here for. All you need to do is follow our instructions. We'll guide you every step of the way.'

Ruby nodded. 'You can do this. You're tougher than you think.'

'Am I?'

'Yes! You've changed, you've found strength you didn't know you had,' Ruby said.

'Thank you. I couldn't do it without you and I don't want to let Jack take my place. He's bursting to and I won't let him. You're right -- I can do this as well as him. They're my babies and I'm going to get them back.'

'Good,' Tom said. 'You'll hear my voice playing in your ear the whole time. I'm going to talk you through it. If for any reason you go out of my sightline DCI Grant will be the one who'll be talking to you.'

'Thank you. Oh god, please let me get through this.'

'I know you will,' Ruby said. 'Believe in yourself.'

Grant came back. 'Everyone is in position. This is a very difficult task, Alice, and whatever happens please do as we say. Are you ready?'

Alice lifted her chin. 'Yes, Inspector. Is it time for me to start walking?'

*

Grant was staked out, hidden with the other officers amongst the trees. He didn't like this one little bit. With everyone separated all it would take was an unexpected move on the part of the abductor, or a blip in the police communications, and the whole thing could become a disaster. He cracked his knuckles and cleared his mind, breathing steadily. ACC Treadgold was right, he might not have as much endurance as a younger DCI but one thing he did have was experience. And that's what they were all relying on.

Diane had drawn a blank with local airfields and Grant didn't know whether to feel relieved or not. It was always a possibility the abductor owned his own damn plane, but a flight schedule had not been registered.

Grant had chosen a spot at the far end of the woods because it gave the best visibility of the mother. McGowan and Diane were close by. The abductor had sent instructions for Alice to walk due west on a footpath crossing the middle of the grassy basin. She was to start walking from the car park at two o'clock precisely.

'Send Alice Glover out, Delaney,' Grant ordered.

Alice was wearing dark trousers and a red jumper. The jumper was so she would be easy to spot in the landscape and it was bulky to hide her bulletproof vest.

She had tied her blonde hair into a ponytail and Grant couldn't help thinking Alice was very brave, stepping out alone from the shelter of the cars, leaving the activity and the security and walking across the heather and the gorse into the open and the unknown. They would be far away from her.

In a black bag, she carried the money, and hidden inside was a transponder to track the bag's location. The load was heavy and Grant could hear Delaney encouraging her to take it steady.

Grant could hear Alice's quick breaths in his earpiece and soon she was a good distance from the cars. With the woman exposed like that anything could happen. To Grant's right, a sniper and their spotter tracked Alice's progress.

Like Grant, Diane trained binoculars onto the basin. McGowan was in full cycle gear and he waited astride his bike, listening to her commentary.

'No movement from any side so far,' Diane said. 'Not even a rabbit.'

The only non-natural feature in the basin was an abandoned water trough. At one time it had been used for cattle farming and Billingham's crew had checked it out and found a rusting metal trough with no potential for being a hazard and nor did it hide one. As Alice came alongside the trough, she paused and put down the bag. Her hand went inside her pocket.

There's a message come through on her mobile phone, the technical team texted through to Grant. *Sending a copy to you now.*

The message read, 'Put the money in the trough and climb to the top of the hill. Wait there.'

'Shit,' McGowan said. 'What the hell is he playing at?'

'Tell her to follow the instructions, Delaney,' Grant said.

Billingham was standing beside Grant. 'There's nothing at the top except rolling countryside. Where are the children? And how does he expect to retrieve the cash and get away?'

Grant pursed his lips. 'We've no option but to play along.'

Grant was liking this less and less. He watched as Alice hefted the bag into the trough then she turned and began the long climb to the top of the hill. It was a steep path, full of stones and dotted with chalk deposits. Right at the bottom, as Alice set off, she slipped and almost fell.

'Where are my children?' Alice asked Delaney. 'He promised they'd be here.'

Grant was listening in. 'She's got to hold it together, Delaney. Keep the pep talk going.'

He heard Delaney's calm voice reassuring Alice and encouraging her to put one foot in front of the other for the climb.

Grant turned to McGowan. 'See if you can sneak around the other side of that damn hill and find out if anything is coming. This is getting hairy. Chief Inspector, what's the access like from the other side? Can we move officers into position?'

'It's miles and miles of countryside. There's one road coming in from the east. I can send a car the long way if I pull officers from one of the car parks but it's half an hour's drive to get around.'

Half a damn hour by road? Bloody hell. 'Okay. Go ahead.'

It was painful watching Alice. She kept slipping and she clearly wasn't a sportswoman. When she had climbed halfway up, Grant got a text message from Ruby.

Jack Glover just left the car park.

What do you mean? Grant messaged back.

He was in a patrol car, and one minute he was there and then I turned around and he was gone. I think he took his own car.

Shit. Jack was a wild card. The reason Grant had put him in a patrol car was because he didn't trust him. Where the hell was the father going at such a critical time? Grant could not spare Delaney, and he, Diane and McGowan were too far away to help.

Take DI Hunter and go after him, Grant texted.

*

Several minutes later and Alice had reached the summit of the hill. There had been no reports from the road-blocks apart from ordinary people being turned away. Nothing had moved in the area. Where the hell was the call with the next step? When were they going to get the vital information on the children?

'If she goes down the other side we'll have no one in position to see her,' Diane said. 'Wait, she's taking out her phone. It looks like she's got another message.'

Seconds after, the techies forwarded Grant the text received by Alice.

If you want to see your children again walk down the hill until you're halfway and then wait.

'Stay in position, Delaney,' Grant said. 'Ask her to keep talking to you and tell you what's happening and what she can see and hear. Tell her to not stop speaking.'

'And then?' Delaney asked.

'Now is not the time to get the wobbles, DS Delaney. Do as I say! No one has yet come to pick up the money so stay focused on your task.'

Diane was gesticulating. 'McGowan contacted me. He has sight of Alice. He's on the other side of the hill.'

Grant thanked his lucky stars. 'Tell him to stay out of view. Billingham, send around half your other bikers.'

The Chief Inspector seemed about to object but Grant cut him off.

'Do it. He's moving us around like damn pawns on a chess board but it takes two to play a game and we're not finished yet.'

*

DI Sarah Hunter did the driving. Ruby could see the firm set of the Detective Inspector's jaw, her hair short and styled to suit her face, hazel eyes calm. The woman was unruffled and determined, and there was something solid about her which Ruby liked. A bit of a rebel underneath, Ruby thought.

'What the hell is he up to?' Hunter said.

'Jack can't have been gone long,' Ruby said. 'I saw him when Alice was about halfway up the hill.'

They could see a small dust cloud some way ahead.

'That's thrown up by Jack's tyres. Looks like he's turned off the road and is taking a dirt track. Can you find it on the sat nav?' Hunter asked.

'Got it. It's two hundred metres ahead on the right.'

'Where's he going? Why would the father cut and run leaving half a million sitting in the middle of nowhere and while we're waiting for news on his children?'

'Good question,' Ruby said. 'It makes it sound like Jack knows something we don't.'

'Please call me Sarah, and I know Chief Inspector Billingham isn't good at diplomacy so I'm sorry if he's rubbed any of you the wrong way.'

'Don't worry about it and oh, call me Ruby. I don't see any more dust. I think he's stopped.'

They took the turn for the track. It was two lines of dirt with a band of weeds down the middle. They followed as fast as they could, the car bouncing and tussocks of grass scraping against the front bumper. Sarah swore now and again as the steering jerked in her hands. As they rounded a corner, they found Jack's car abandoned at the side.

'He must have continued on foot,' Ruby said. 'This is getting strange.'

She got out as quickly as Sarah.

'Take a good look around, Ruby. Let's see if we can pick up his trail.'

They tramped through the undergrowth, scanning in all directions. It was a pretty flat landscape with scrubby bushes and rocks and a few trees.

'There he is,' Ruby said. 'It looks like he's moving fast.'

'He hasn't seen us which is good. I'm going after him. You stay here.'

Sarah started jogging after Jack Glover and Ruby went with her.

'You're kidding me, right? Of course I'm not staying put.'

'I thought you were a criminal psychologist,' Sarah said, her breathing steady as she ran. 'I didn't imagine you'd be up for action.'

'Then you thought wrong. I'm in training for a fun run so I should be able to keep up and I'm a climber, and us climbers are feistier than you think.'

Sarah cut her a quick grin. 'Aren't you a dark horse. Okay, we follow him and we need to be careful because we don't know what we're walking into.'

Jack seemed to know where he was going. He was heading along a path which followed a stream.

'Do you see that bag he's carrying?' Sarah said.

They exchanged a glance. It was a black holdall and very like the bag Alice had packed half a million pounds in.

'Someone examined the bag Alice took with her, right?' Sarah asked. 'It hasn't been swapped at the last minute has it?'

'It can't have been. Tom checked it.'

They jogged after Jack, keeping out of sight as well as they could. Jack's attention was focused ahead and he never once glanced behind. A cluster of buildings came into view. It looked like an abandoned farm and Jack made straight for it.

When they reached the first barn they crouched at the corner.

Ruby caught her breath. 'Do you know this place?' she whispered.

'No and it's in the middle of goddam nowhere. Looks disused. Must have been a farm at one time.'

'What do we do?'

'We call for back-up.' But when Sarah tried to send a message, her radio wasn't working. Neither was there phone signal.

'Damn we're out of range. The South Downs has that effect because sometimes the signal gets cut off.' Sarah peeked around the corner. 'I can't see a thing. I'm going to find out what's going on. You stay here.'

'I'm coming too,' Ruby said.

Sarah's hand landed on Ruby's arm. 'Wait – you're a civilian and this isn't safe. Whatever Jack Glover is up to it doesn't look good.'

'If you think I'm letting you go on your own, think again.'

Sarah was stern. 'You could get back to the car and drive until you get a signal. That would be prudent.'

'Prudent, my arse. No way am I leaving you here.'

'Okay then, on the condition you stay behind me.'

Scooting around the barn, they dashed to the next building. Ruby was so close to Sarah that when the DI stopped abruptly Ruby banged into her. Sarah signalled for them to get low. Not twenty metres away, Jack was standing in the middle of a courtyard amidst the buildings. He was talking to another man.

Jack was angry. He dropped the bag and the other man opened it and checked inside.

'It's a drop-off,' Sarah whispered in Ruby's ear. 'And I'm betting it's the real one.'

Ruby's heart was hammering and she was sweating. If Jack Glover was handing over money did it mean the children were close?

'Lisa and Emily,' she whispered. 'They could be here.'

The other man gripped the holdall and made to move off. Jack grabbed him and they heard Jack shouting.

'You bastard. You promised! Where are my children!'

The other man sneered and in a lightning quick move he took out a knife and stabbed Jack in the belly. 'You think you're better than me, but you're not.'

Sarah shouted and ran out. The stranger fled.

Jack staggered into Sarah's arms. With a look of surprise, he stared at the red stain spreading across his shirt. Sarah lowered him to the ground and Ruby ripped open Jack's shirt.

'Oh shit. Ruby, put your hands right here and apply as much pressure as you can.'

'What are we going to do? He might die.'

Then Sarah was gone leaving Ruby trying desperately to stem the blood flow. Within seconds, Jack Glover was having problems breathing. He stared up at her.

'Who was that man? Where are Emily and Lisa?' Ruby demanded.

Jack's eyes were losing focus.

'Answer me!'

'My children,' he whispered.

'Where are they? Who was that man?'

From the way Jack approached the man and the way they spoke together, Ruby felt sure they knew each other.

Sarah came running back and she was covered in dirt and her trousers were ripped. 'The bastard got away. Press harder, Ruby, it's not working.'

Sarah took hold of Jack's shoulders. 'Sir, listen to me, you've been seriously injured. You must tell me what you know before it's too late.'

'Emily,' Jack whispered.

'Who was that man? Give me a name.'

'Lisa...'

'Give me a name.'

Jack Glover's eyes rolled into the back of his head and he lost consciousness.

Sarah checked his pulse. 'He's still hanging on. The priority is searching this place. Maybe they are here.'

Ruby nodded. 'You go.' And she watched as Sarah sprinted for the first building.

Chapter Thirty-seven

Grant and Tom stared down at Jack Glover. There had been no sign of the children at the farm. Glover lay on a hospital trolley and he was ready to be wheeled into an operating theatre.

'Can you wake him up?' Grant asked.

'Impossible. He's been prepped for emergency surgery,' the doctor said.

'Lisa and Emily Glover are missing and their father has vital information. Couldn't you administer a stimulant?'

The surgeon wasn't amused. 'Out of the question. A man's life is in the balance. Please get out of my way.'

The surgical team left, taking Jack Glover with them.

Grant was fuming. 'Jack has been talking directly with the abductor. The idiot kept us in the dark. That pay-as-you-go-phone we found on him? Well, the techies have recovered messages setting up the hand over. The *real* hand over. And when I checked with the damn concierge at Jack's apartment, he told me a package had been dropped off there yesterday. It must have been the phone. We were there earlier asking questions and searching Jack's apartment, why the hell didn't the concierge call me?'

'I'm sorry, sir,' Delaney said. 'I don't know how a second phone slipped past me. I thought I had good lines of communication with both Jack and Alice.'

'Don't beat yourself up. If people want to be underhand they find ways to do it. Jack Glover had his own agenda and now we're in a bloody mess.'

The doctors would be saving Jack's life and Grant wasn't sure the man deserved it.

It had gone horribly wrong. Half a million pounds stayed in the middle of a field while Alice climbed to the top of a hill, clambered halfway down the other side, and then waited desperately for news of her children. Grant had left her there for ten minutes, knowing each moment was torture for her.

He'd paced and Billingham had chewed his nails and they'd stared at the landscape willing the abductor to appear until their eyeballs practically dropped out. And nothing happened. By the time Grant heard from DI Hunter and he called it to a close, Alice had been a wreck and McGowan had to carry her to the bottom while she screamed for her children.

Grant now knew events had been unfolding at the barn between Jack and the person Grant assumed was the abductor. By the time DI Hunter had managed to contact Grant it was all too late.

Alice had been set up. Hers was the dummy drop-off to keep attention from the real one and they'd since found out Jack had withdrawn one million pounds from his private account.

'Now we know why the abductor left half a million sitting in the middle of nowhere,' Grant said grimly. 'Because Jack was going to hand over twice that amount. What a fool Glover is.'

Grant slammed his hand into the wall. ACC Treadgold had labelled the handover a fiasco.

'Right boss, except now we have a lead on the abductor,' Delaney said. 'That's got to be good news.'

It was the one bright point of the whole mess.

*

They rushed back to the station and Tom closed the door of the incident room.

'It was a damn set-up.' Grant wasn't trying to hide his fury. 'And Jack bloody Glover will probably live.'

'Stupid bastard,' McGowan said.

They had thoroughly searched the farm and the surrounding countryside and they found no trace of Emily and Lisa. Since the drop-off, neither Alice's mobile nor Jack's secret pay-as-you-go-phone had received any further messages from the abductor.

'Well done to DI Hunter and to you too, Ruby. You overhearing the exchange gives us a lead.' Grant slapped his palm on the board. 'The perp said, "You think you're better than me, but you're not." I've heard this exact phrase before.'

Everyone's attention was riveted on Grant.

'It links straight to the man who broke into Daniel Pearson's house six years ago. Pearson told me the person who knifed him said exactly the same thing.'

'You're talking about Ronnie Hardman's accountant? The one who was accused of embezzling funds?' McGowan asked.

'That's the one. Pearson's house was broken into and he was knifed. His assailant, Nick Riley, said exactly this phrase as he stabbed Pearson. Riley is a known local criminal and he got a sentence of nine years. On the way here I checked his records and he got out three years early for good behaviour. The time of his release was a few months ago.'

Grant wrote Nick Riley's name on the board.

'It's one tiny detail and it's all we need. Plus I checked with the prison and he was known as a biter. When Riley was inside, he bit off another prisoner's earlobe during a fight.'

'The same as with Joan Hardman,' Diane said. 'When she fought him, he bit her.'

'We've damn well got him,' McGowan said.

Grant had already circulated Riley as wanted missing on the national computer. Officers were looking to track him via his usage of money, phone and financial records. If research threw up a car and that car passed a camera, using automatic number plate recognition it would trigger an alert. The net would be closing in on Nick Riley.

'I'm sure Riley and Jack knew each other,' Ruby said. 'From the way they spoke it was obvious they weren't strangers.'

'Think about the Pearson break-in. Pearson was a threat to Jack. Perhaps Jack believed Pearson already had evidence or was going to find evidence from those young women Jack assaulted. Jack risked losing everything if Ronnie Hardman turned against him. I'm betting Jack Glover wanted someone to shake Pearson up. And the person he found to do the job was this known local villain.'

'I wonder how Glover hired him?' Diane said.

'I'll be asking as soon as he's conscious. Like I said, Riley was released several months ago. Previous to the Pearson case, Riley had been connected to petty crimes in the area. The worst of them was a heist at a local jewellers where Riley was one of a gang. He was a minor player in the hold-up not the mastermind.'

Grant pinned up a picture of Riley. 'I found out too late a package was put into the mailbox at Jack's apartment. A woman dropped it off. It must have been the pay-as-you-go phone passed to Jack by Riley.'

'So you were right, guv, he's got an accomplice,' McGowan said.

'We've got information about Riley's girlfriend. At the time of his arrest for the Pearson break-in, Riley was living with a young woman called Maria Fernandez.' Grant nodded to Diane.

'This picture was taken a few years ago,' Diane said.

It flashed up.

'She's got long dark hair. Like the woman seen in Joan Hardman's street,' Delaney said.

Grant cracked his knuckles. 'The concierge had positively identified her as the woman in the foyer. DCS Fox has sent out a nationwide alert to apprehend Maria Fernandez.'

'The abductor has the money so it's likely he'll abandon the children,' Ruby said. 'They're no use to him now.'

'Agreed and if it's sepsis, the paediatrician didn't give Emily long. We've two priorities -- we find this bastard Riley and we locate his girlfriend. They're our best bet of tracking down the children. The whole country will be looking for them by the time we walk out of this room. Delaney, I want you to lead on Maria Fernandez. Collins, McGowan and I will be on the trail of Riley.'

Chapter Thirty-eight

Everyone was going full out. They now had two key suspects to track.

Ruby had an idea niggling at the back of her mind. She wasn't a police officer, which meant she couldn't take a lead on the action, but she wanted to follow up on what didn't make sense.

What if Nick Riley had an accomplice they had not yet identified? Ruby wanted to go through the case notes again to see if she could work out what felt wrong.

Grant's team had left the station and Ruby was on her way to her office when she noticed McGowan slipping into the cubbyhole. Why hadn't he gone with the others? Finding Riley and Fernandez was a priority.

McGowan's body posture was off. He was usually cocky and strutting and he stomped in and out of rooms as if he owned them. Why was he slinking about? What was he up to?

The cubbyhole was partitioned from the corridor by a semi-transparent panel and she could make out McGowan's movements. He was making a phone call.

It was brief. Then, McGowan turned and strode out, giving Ruby just enough time to slip into the photocopying room. The last thing she wanted was for him to spot her spying. Likely he'd blow a gasket.

This is stupid, she told herself. *You don't like him, only it's no reason to be suspicious.*

He was heading for the emergency stairwell. Ruby didn't give herself time to think. She slunk after him, keeping her back close to the wall while trying to maintain an appearance of normality. If someone else saw her she didn't want them to think she'd turned into a nutter.

McGowan disappeared up the stairs. The fire door had a habit of banging shut so Ruby made sure she closed it soundlessly behind her.

His footsteps were gritty against the stairs as he ran several flights above her. Then there came voices. He'd bumped into another man, or was it a pre-planned meeting? Ruby strained to hear though she couldn't catch the words. Who was McGowan talking to? Could she risk peering up the middle of the stairwell to see? What if they spotted her? *So what if they do,* she told herself. *The worst is if McGowan shouts at you and he does that anyway.*

Little by little, she leant out. If she looked down, she could see the long drop to the ground floor minus one. Looking up, she caught sight of the arm of the man McGowan was talking to. It was dressed in a dark jacket. She leaned out as far as she dared and caught a glimpse of the insignia on the man's shoulder.

It was Assistant Chief Constable Treadgold. The man Grant believed to be corrupt.

The two men suddenly stopped talking. McGowan's head jerked over the railing and she found herself staring him in the face. Shit.

'What the fuck do you think you're doing?' McGowan yelled.

Her heart raced as she yanked open the door to the corridor. Ruby wanted to run and she told herself to walk normally and not act as if she'd done anything wrong. McGowan caught up with her when she was outside her office. He pushed her into the wall. Damn, she should have gone the other way because there were always less people down this end. The corridor was deserted.

'Have you been eavesdropping, Silver?'

'Get away from me.'

'Answer my question.'

'I don't have to. Aren't you supposed to be out catching the kidnapper?'

'You're not the one who gives orders around here, darling. And if I find out you've been spying–'

'Detective Sergeant McGowan what the hell is going on?' snapped DCS Fox.

McGowan jumped and a sound came from his trousers which sounded like a fart.

Fox did not look amused. 'The case has reached a critical stage. What the hell are you still doing at the station?'

'I'm on my way out, ma'am.'

'Too bloody well right. Get moving.'

Once McGowan had gone, Fox turned to Ruby. 'Whatever it was I saw there, Ms Silver, I didn't like it. Once this case is over I think you and I and DCI Grant need to have a proper talk.'

Chapter Thirty-nine

In the morning, the woman who'd brought the eggs didn't come.

'Will there be something to eat?' Lisa asked her sister.

'Maybe later.'

Lisa whimpered with hunger and Emily had nothing to give her except a drink from their water bottle. It was half-full from the day before and Emily only realised too late perhaps they should save some for later. By then, Lisa had gulped most of it down. Emily screwed back the top and shook it. About a quarter remained.

'Aren't you going to have any, Em?'

Emily shook her head. She didn't feel thirsty and she vaguely wondered, why not? Although it didn't matter because this way she could keep it for Lisa.

Despite Emily's best efforts, Lisa had noticed the red splodges on Emily's tummy and she'd been scared. It was a good job Lisa hadn't seen the patches on Emily's arm where the skin was turning purple. If she saw those, Emily felt sure her little sister would panic. The dark blotches were weird. They looked like spilled paint and they didn't rub away.

Emily closed her eyes.

'Are you cold?' Lisa said. 'Shall I give you a hug to get you warm?'

'Yes please. I'm not feeling well.'

Lisa snuggled up. 'I hope Mummy comes soon and then she can make you better, just like she always does.'

Chapter Forty

When Grant received Ruby's call, he was on his way to Brighton. They'd uncovered intelligence about Nick Riley's mother owning an apartment. With a search warrant already secured, Grant and Chief Inspector Billingham would be raiding the property as soon as equipment and personnel were in place.

'You have a lead on Riley, sir?' Ruby asked.

'Going there now. Riley's mother died while he was in prison and she left her apartment to him. I don't know the situation on the ground yet. Billingham and I are on our way. Has something happened at your end?'

'It's McGowan.' Ruby hesitated. Was she being silly and wasting Grant's time at a crucial moment?

'If you've got something to say then spit it out.'

'He was hanging around in the cubbyhole after you left and I thought it odd.'

'McGowan is joining me. He left after with Diane. What of it?'

'I saw him talking to Assistant Chief Constable Treadgold.' Ruby blurted it out. 'It was a private chat on the stairwell and then McGowan realised I was listening. I got the impression it was clandestine, the way they were talking and where they were talking.'

There was a small silence down the line.

'Have you mentioned this to anyone else?'

'No.'

'McGowan knows you saw him?'

'Yes.'

'And he realises you know who he was talking to?'

'I'm not sure. He can't know for certain. He came after me except he was interrupted by DCS Fox. Do you think there's anything in it?'

'I don't know, and you're right to flag it up. I'll have to get back to you on this.'

'Everything all right, sir?' The uniformed driver asked Grant.

'Fine. Let's get there as quick as we can.'

Grant stared out the window. Maybe the choice between Ruby and McGowan had been made for him. Grant already suspected McGowan as the source of the leak within his team. Leaking information had caused a problem on their previous case in which ACC Treadgold had come under suspicion.

Though why would McGowan be speaking to Treadgold now? Grant quickly pulled up the police files on Riley. He scanned the information. Before being arrested for the Pearson case, Nick Riley did a term in prison in connection with the heist on the jewellery shop. In the heist, the shop assistant had been killed and Riley had been outside the premises acting as lookout which meant he got a lighter sentence than the rest of the gang. Some items of jewellery had never been recovered. And the officer in charge of the investigation? As he was then, DCI Treadgold. Very interesting.

It was possible McGowan was keeping Treadgold informed about the Glover case. It was also possible that if McGowan leaked information to Treadgold in the past to help Treadgold cover his tracks he was doing it again. Did this mean there was a link between Riley and Treadgold? Had the jewellery heist been another case in which Treadgold had been corrupt? It was possible.

Keep your eye on the ball, Grant told himself. *Emily and Lisa are the priority.* But if he got a shot at Treadgold afterwards, he'd definitely be taking it.

Chapter Forty-one

Waiting for Nick to come back after the handover was torture for her. They had taken the precaution of moving across town, leaving the children to their fate. When he finally came in with the money, he swaggered like a gunslinger from a Western movie. He thumped the bag on the floor and stood with his legs astride.

She ran into Nick's arms and kissed him. She was relieved to see him. Thing were going okay between them but there had always been a chance Nick would scarper with the loot and leave her behind. He swung her off her feet and they both whooped.

She recovered her breath. 'Can I see it?'

'Sure, get an eye full.'

Unzipping the bag, she thrust in her hands. 'Oh. My. God.'

This was what one million looked and felt like. Holding a bunch of notes to her face, she smelled them. 'You're a genius.'

He strutted with pride and she kept her grin to the maximum. It wasn't all fake. The money made her genuinely delirious. Nick she felt much less enthusiastic about. Still, she wouldn't need to be with him for much longer.

Taking a handful, she threw it in the air and it rained down like confetti. She could tell Nick still liked her and it was her job to make sure he stayed liking her. Her share in the million was her reward.

*

Nick was on a high. The look on Jack Glover's face as he pushed in the knife had been worth the wait. Jack was too arrogant for his own good. At last, Nick had the payoff he deserved because Jack Glover had been a stingy bastard in the past. He'd paid Nick a measly five thousand for the break-in at Pearson's and that break-in had cost Nick six years of his life.

But there was more to the story.

While Nick was in prison he'd done a lot of asking around. He was the type of man others avoided. The sort to go from cold to red hot in an instant which other offenders recognised and didn't want to get on the wrong side of.

He had worn gloves when he'd broken into Daniel Pearson's cottage and he'd not taken them off the entire time he'd been there. So how the hell had one of his thumbprints turned up at the scene? The prosecution used it to put him away. In prison he found out he'd been set up. By who, that's what he wanted to know. And by the end of years of questioning his fellow inmates, Nick had his answer. By Jack fucking high and mighty Glover. Glover had paid him to break in and he'd made sure Nick was caught by the police.

For the rest of his time inside, Nick plotted his revenge. He wanted his just pay for being put away and not only that – he wanted Jack Glover to suffer. He wanted him to suffer and suffer and suffer. The one million was recompense for time wasted in a brick cell. But the agony inflicted on Jack by the taking of his children, that was the real reward.

'This place is nice,' she said. 'Your mum had good taste. Will you sell it?'

'Not sure. Don't need to, do I? Not now I'm rolling in it.'

She giggled. 'When do we leave?'

'The boat sails in two hours. It's safe here and we can hole up until then.'

'Shouldn't we get moving in case the police are onto us?'

‘They haven’t got a clue. Not about this place nor the rented house. There’s no need to sweat, besides, the boat hasn’t arrived yet and we can’t hang around at the marina.’

That was one of the advantages of his inside contacts. Nick had commissioned a ride over to France without too much hassle and on a luxury motor yacht, no less.

‘If you say so,’ she said.

‘I know so.’ Nick pulled her on top of him and groped her breasts. ‘This time tomorrow we’ll be halfway to sunny Spain and our new champagne lifestyle.’

‘I’ll drink to that.’

‘Get some glasses then and be quick about it.’

He’d been wondering if she might protest when he told her the plan was to leave the kids locked up to die. She hadn’t twitched. Which was good, because if she had, he would have had to deal with her.

Taking the kids had been the beginning of the revenge on Jack Glover. Leaving the kids to die a lingering death with no water or food – this was going to be Nick Riley’s triumph. And then, high and mighty Jack fucking Glover, who was going to be the loser?

Once the kids were eventually found dead in the rented house, with any luck it would drive Jack insane. Nick took a slug from his glass. It wouldn’t take long for those brats to die. By the time he was sunning himself on a beach most likely. After all, one of them was half gone already.

Chapter Forty-two

They had been left for so long it seemed like forever. Emily had almost given up hope.

The last time she had heard footsteps on the stairs, her first thought had been, please can they bring water. And food for Lisa.

When the door had opened, Emily wondered if it was the woman who brought the eggs though this time the woman's hair smelled faintly of oranges. There was something familiar about the scent, though Emily hadn't been able to work out what. Her thoughts were messed up. She wondered if she might be imagining things.

'Can we have food?' Lisa asked.

The woman said nothing and her hands were empty. She hadn't brought a tray or a drink. Emily glanced at the water bottle lying by her side. Lisa had drunk the last drops a long time ago.

'Some water please?' Emily asked, and her voice came out as a whisper.

The woman stayed silent. She crouched and reached towards Emily's face but then she hesitated, quickly pulling her arm back. Emily caught another waft of the woman's orangey scent.

'What are you doing up there?' The man's voice boomed from downstairs. 'We've got to go.'

The woman stood and made for the door.

'Wait,' Emily pleaded. 'Don't leave us. Please. We want to go home.'

The woman ignored them both and left, locking the door behind her.

Since then there had been no more visits. Lisa cried on and off. The tears flowed freely because Lisa was no longer afraid of the man shouting at her. There were no sounds filtering upstairs from below and they both felt sure the woman and the man had abandoned them. Now, hours, or was it days later, when Lisa cried it was a horrible sound, as if her tears had all dried up.

Chapter Forty-three

Grant had a search warrant for Nick Riley's place in Brighton. Billingham met Grant there, together with a battering ram for gaining entry, commonly known as an enforcer.

'Do you think he's holding the children inside?' Diane asked.

'We'll soon find out,' Grant said.

Riley's apartment was on the second floor of a five-storey block. Billingham's officers were already stationed at the front, on the stairwell and on the fire escape. The elevators were also covered. An ambulance waited below ready to receive the children.

'Did you get any information from the neighbours?' Grant asked.

'Most are elderly and spend a lot of time inside. They say Riley's place has been unused for months though one neighbour told us his son saw a younger man go in there a few weeks ago. No one mentioned any children.'

'Any sign of a white van in the vicinity?'

'Not so far. I've got personnel checking adjacent streets.'

'Ready when you are, Chief Inspector Billingham.'

Riley's apartment lay at the end of an outside walkway. The other residents had been told to stay locked inside. As Billingham gave the order, officers brought the enforcer to Riley's door.

It was a familiar sound to Grant as the steel ram breached the door hinges. Within seconds Grant, Billingham and the six-person uniformed team were inside. Grant let Billingham's team do what they were good at, while he waited inside the entrance, listening as they systematically checked each room and called out the results to Billingham. McGowan raced down the hallway to the furthest rooms.

'Clear.'

'Clear.'

'In here, sir,' an officer shouted. 'She's chained to the bed.'

Grant's heart thumped double time. Was it Emily and Lisa? He ran to the third room along. An officer was on his knees, checking the metal cuffs chaining someone to the bed. But it wasn't one of the children. Grant stared at the tear-stained face of Sylvie Delacourt. What the hell was she doing here?

'H-he tied me up. He kept me p-prisoner,' she sobbed.

'I can't get the cuffs undone, sir. We'll have to cut through them,' the officer said.

'Do it,' Grant snapped.

Grant got in close to the young woman. She wouldn't look at him. 'Sylvie. Sylvie look at me. I need your help. Have you seen the children?'

'He forced me to…'

Sylvie broke down. She had a wild look about her. Jesus. How long had Riley kept her here?

Grant paused and inspected her wrists more closely. Then shouting came from one of the other rooms, followed by furniture breaking.

'Weapon! Get down,' McGowan yelled.

Grant threw himself to the floor, pulling Sylvie with him. He pushed her as far as he could underneath the bed and crawled to the door just in time to see Riley run past, with McGowan on his heels.

'He's heading for the fire exit,' one of Billingham's officers called out.

'Seal it off,' Billingham ordered.

With no way down Riley had no choice, he went up. They heard his steps ringing out on the metal rungs of the emergency escape with McGowan right behind him.

'There's no way out from the roof,' Billingham said.

Grant was at the doorway. 'Then we've got him. Do you have the children?'

'No sign of the children in the apartment, sir,' one of Billingham's officers reported.

'Shit. You're certain?'

'Positive, sir. We've checked thoroughly.'

Grant had been hoping against hope. An apartment in a quiet neighbourhood. Recently left to Riley. The chances had been high. Damn it.

'Then check again,' Billingham snapped. 'And get forensics out here. I want this place gone over with a toothcomb.'

Grant needed answers. 'I'm going up. I'm a trained negotiator and I'll try to talk sense into Riley. See if I can form a link with him. Billingham, get any information you can out of the young woman. Her name's Sylvie Delacourt and she was the Glover's au pair. Ask DS Collins to speak to her.'

Billingham got on his radio and when he turned back to Grant, he looked alarmed.

'What's wrong?' Grant asked.

'I can't locate DS Collins. The last intel we've got is she was stationed at the entrance to the fire exit. I think Riley may have taken her to the roof.'

Chapter Forty-four

Nick put the blade back in his pocket. The woman copper had put up a fight, though one stab to her stomach had soon put an end to it. He leant against the elevator shaft and caught his breath. He didn't have much time. It wouldn't be long before they came after him.

The wind whipped across the rooftop and he searched for a place to hide. As he hunkered down in a space between two ventilator outlets, he felt the urge to take a last hit. It was strange because he had never cared that much for her, but Nick couldn't stop his mind going back to Maria and the way Maria had stared up at him. Not much gave him nightmares but Maria's eyes still haunted him. She'd been terrified. Snot and blood had been running down her face.

Nick Riley wiped his nose on his sleeve. He waited to hear footsteps on the fire exit. This was it. Now it was his turn.

*

When Maria had been found in the school playground, she had been picked up and dumped in Nick's van. She slumped in the back footwell while Nick drove. Her nose had bled and she had cried with mucus and blood running down. He was a monster and he would make her suffer. The withdrawal had got so bad she hadn't had the energy to lift her own head.

'I'm s-sorry,' she'd kept saying. Her nose was pressed into the carpet. He had ignored her and carried on driving.

It seemed like they drove for an eternity. When they stopped, Nick got in the back and took out his kit of tourniquet and syringe.

'I don't want it,' she said, her teeth chattering.

'You know you do and anyway it's too late to back out now.'

He took off her jacket and gripped her arm, twisting on the tourniquet. She saw a vein pop up and then he was filling a syringe and injecting her. She didn't look at his face. The dose sent her mind spinning and her heart into a canter and as he dragged her out of the car, Maria felt her heart go into arrythmia. She was dumped on the pavement, and the car drove away.

The ground was gritty under her cheek. It was quiet. She could see a sliver of moon out of one eye though she could not turn her head to see the whole of it.

Deep inside, she despised herself. For being dirty and worthless. And what about the children? What about Emily? She should have gone to the police. She should have been better. Strong enough. Brave enough.

She was so cold. He'd given her an overdose, she knew it and her heart was racing its way to a crisis. Soon she would lose consciousness. There was nobody in this world who cared for her apart from her brother Billy, and Billy had written her off. Maria felt an aching loneliness. Her vision faded.

Then she heard a soft voice.

'Maria.'

It was Billy. He was a short distance away. Digging in her nails, she tried to drag herself towards him.

'I'm sorry, Billy,' she whispered. 'I tried. It was too hard.'

Billy came to kneel by her side. She remembered the good times they'd had together as children and the way he had felt in her arms when he was small and she rocked him to sleep.

'I know you're sorry. Why don't you write a message,' he whispered.

In her dying moments Maria tried to move her fingers, and as the light went out of her eyes, the last thing she knew was Billy gently stroking the side of her face.

Chapter Forty-five

Emily couldn't think straight. The purple blotches had spread to her legs and she felt so cold not even Lisa's cuddles made her warm. The chills were bad. Emily's body shook and her mind drifted. Sometimes she was at home drinking hot chocolate in the kitchen, another time her mother was putting her into a warm bath and she could smell the flowery bubbles of the bubble bath.

Emily could hear her mother singing a nursery rhyme and then she realised it was Lisa, humming the tune and mixing up the words.

'Do it again, Lise. It's nice.'

Lisa hummed and stroked Emily's hair, just like Mummy liked to do. And Emily's heart beat faster and faster -- t*a-dum, ta-dum, ta-dum* -- it raced along as if it was galloping and might any moment burst from the effort.

Chapter Forty-six

Maria Fernandez's photograph had been circulated to patrol officers so when a young woman matching her description was found dead, a message came straight through to Tom.

The body was hidden behind a row of dumpsters not far from Himlands Heath high street.

'It looks like an overdose, sir,' the uniformed officer told Tom. 'She was found by the refuse collection guy, he's waiting over by his van.'

'I'll view the body first and then I'll speak to him,' Tom said.

The crime scene manager was already on site, directing two SOCOs who were photographing the area.

'Hello Delaney,' the CSM said. 'It looks like it's your woman and since it's so important I'll make an exception and let you in quickly, but you'll have to suit up into full gear.' The CSM jerked her head towards her car. 'Grab what you need from my boot.'

Tom jogged across the road and rummaged for a coverall and shoe protections. The pathologist, Luke Sanderson, arrived. Luke was a personal friend of Grant's.

'I know this one is a priority,' Luke said. 'Shall we see what we've got?'

The woman was lying on her stomach in a film of grime spreading out from the base of the dumpsters. Judging by the tracks in the sludge, she'd dragged herself for three or four metres. There was no syringe in sight but the injection marks on her arm were obvious. Most were old, with one more fresh.

Tom didn't think this was a hangout for druggies. 'Officer, do you often get people shooting up here?'

'The more frequent trouble spots are in the park or under the bypass. This used to be a problem area until the council installed CCTV cameras and new lighting.'

'That's what I thought.'

Luke was crouching. 'These marks on her arm are healed except this one.' He pointed. 'This is a recent injection site and by the looks of the sores at the base of her nose, she's been snorting cocaine on a regular basis.'

'Can you tell what's been injected?' Tom asked.

'Not unless I've got a crystal ball.'

'Right. What about time of death?'

'Give me a chance. I need to take her body temperature first.'

'It looks like Maria Fernandez to me,' Tom said.

'We've got her fingerprints on file so it will be easy to check and I don't see any other wounds, though it's curious how she dragged herself.'

'Almost as if she was trying to get away. Or go towards something. Could she have been hallucinating?'

'If it was a cocaine overdose then hallucinations are highly likely. And if it was a bad trip then she could have died trying to escape her nightmares.'

'Bloody hell. Any signs of foul play?'

'Not as far as I can see.' Luke rolled the victim gently onto her back. 'Oh hello, what's this?'

Maria's arm had been covering some scratchings marked in the sludge.

'Did she do that with her finger?' Tom asked. 'Or was it there already?'

'It's fresh and it's like she wrote it herself and then her arm fell on top of it,' Luke said. He waved a SOCO over to take photographic evidence. 'It says "nine", spelled out as a word and then maybe the start of another word which has been smudged away.'

Tom was taking a picture with his own phone when one of the SOCOs called out. 'There's something over here.'

It was a jacket with a flowery lining lying by one of the dumpsters. It looked as if it had been tossed there amongst the garbage spills.

'Anything in the pockets?' Tom asked.

The SOCO checked. 'Fraid not.'

A purse lay near the dumpster wheel. It could have fallen from a pocket. Or not. The SOCO reached out a gloved hand.

Small and with a zippered opening, the purse didn't contain money. What it did hold was a train ticket, Brighton to Himlands Heath. Tom had to stop himself from shouting. And there was something else.

'What is it?'

'Looks like a receipt.'

He held his breath as the SOCO unfolded the paper.

'It's from a chemist in Brighton dated two days ago.'

'Bloody fantastic,' Tom yelled.

Chapter Forty-seven

Tom contacted DI Sarah Hunter. Brighton was her patch and he needed her knowledge. Sarah met Tom outside the chemist and it didn't take long for them to locate the pharmacist Maria had spoken to.

'Oh yes,' the young woman said. 'She was acting sort of spaced out. I remember she wanted an antiseptic and if I look up our records for that day… yes, see here, she bought antiseptic. She told me it was for a child.'

'Emily is likely suffering from sepsis. I think Maria bought treatment,' Tom said.

Sarah checked her phone. 'Chief Inspector Billingham is over with your boss at Riley's apartment. Billingham just told me there's a potential hostage situation so he can't leave. He'll mobilise officers from the station to start a house-to-house. They'll be arriving any minute to help us.'

'If Maria walked here there's a big chance the children are being held close by.'

'We'll start the search with the chemist as the central point,' Sarah said.

'At the scene of her death Maria scrawled the word nine. Does it mean anything to you? Anything connected with the local area?'

'You think she left a clue? I thought she overdosed.'

'It's likely she did but I can't help thinking it's odd.'

'Junkies do all sorts of weird things. The number nine doesn't have any significance I can think of. There's an area of town known as Nine Elms only that's over half an hour's walk away up by the hospital and it's difficult to get to on public transport.'

The personnel in the chemist drew a blank on it too.

'Let's have a look at a map,' Tom said. 'Perhaps she meant a house number?'

Bringing up a satellite view, Tom drew circles radiating out from the chemist. 'This is the five minute walk radius and this is ten minutes.'

'There are plenty of streets but there aren't many houses which are number nines,' Sarah said. 'I used to patrol here when I was in uniform.'

'Let's start with them. The uniformed officers can do the rest systematically. How many are we talking about?'

'If we go out to the ten-minute radius then we've got less than a dozen. Come on, it'll be quicker on foot.'

They covered fourteen number nines. There were five with no one home and for those they spoke to neighbours. For the rest, when they knew it was in connection to the missing children, all the residents allowed Tom and Sarah to search inside.

'Nothing.' Tom wiped the sweat from his face. 'Shit. I was so sure they'd be nearby. Emily might not have long left.' He checked his phone again. Still no news from Grant.

He'd already got rid of his jacket and rolled up his shirt sleeves and Sarah was down to a shirt and suit trousers.

'What about the uniformed officers? Anything so far from the systematic search?' Tom asked.

'Not yet. The uniforms are already well into the search pattern around the chemist. Do you want to join them?'

Think, man, think. If Maria bought a treatment for Emily it meant Maria must have known where Riley was keeping the children.

'I can't get over the idea Maria was trying to help us.'

He half expected DI Hunter to laugh.

'You know the case better than I do,' she said. 'If Maria wasn't a willing accomplice, it's not a ludicrous idea.'

'I don't have anything concrete to support my theory. Look, I know it doesn't sound logical. You do what you think is best. I'm going to check the number nineties to ninety-nine. There was a second smudge, like she'd started to write something else. Only time is running out and I don't want to drag you down with me.'

'You're not dragging me anywhere. Come on, there are less streets which go up to the higher numbers. It won't take long to check.'

Chapter Forty-eight

Slowly and deliberately, Grant walked up the fire exit. He wanted Riley to know he was coming because it was important to signal this wasn't an aggressive move. The last thing Grant wanted was to scare Riley into taking rash action.

Riley had manoeuvred himself into a corner, and like cornered animals, cornered criminals were extremely dangerous. The children were still the priority and Grant needed to find the whereabouts and status of his officer. And he needed to find a way to talk Riley down.

As he pushed open the door leading to the rooftop, Grant called out.

'My name is Detective Chief Inspector Grant. It's important we talk.'

He stepped onto a flat concrete roof the size of twenty two-bed apartments. Grant scanned the area. It was rectangular and dotted with obstacles -- ventilator shafts, metal housings and brick towers which presumably stored the heating and elevator apparatus. There was a strong wind and hanging cables whipped like something alive.

The door clanged shut behind him. No sign of Riley or Diane.

'Mr Riley?'

Grant walked slowly forward, his hands held in sight, searching to left and right. Riley was hiding. What he must avoid was giving Riley the opportunity to jump out from behind.

'The stairwells have been blocked off,' Grant said. 'We need to talk.'

'Got nothin' to talk about.'

The wind skimmed through Grant's hair as he carefully pivoted towards the voice. Riley came into view and Grant's heart went cold. Riley was leaning against a ventilator shaft. One of his arms was crooked around Diane's neck and he held her against him like a human shield. A horrible red stain had seeped across Diane's shirt. She was wounded. And it looked serious.

Grant's gaze flicked to Diane's eyes and she was looking straight at him. Part of him registered how calm she seemed as his mind raced to work through the permutations and come out with a strategy to save her life. In Riley's other hand, a blade glinted silver. The bastard had stabbed her.

Grant couldn't help thinking of Daniel Pearson and his ostomy bag and of Jack Glover fighting for his life in a white bed. Grant blinked hard and concentrated, squeezing all his experience into his next moves.

'Stay where you are,' Riley said.

'Whatever you say.'

Riley sounded strung out. Grant reminded himself this man could be cold or he could be hot. *Play for time,* was what his hostage negotiation training said, *build a link with the perpetrator and get them talking*. Yet Grant knew Diane didn't have much time.

Grant stood still. 'Please let my officer go.'

Riley wanted a bargaining chip, Grant understood that.

'Please let her go and I will willingly take her place.' Grant had to shout against the wind.

'I don't think so.'

'Tell me what you want and I can help you.'

Riley shook his head.

'What do you want? Where are Emily and Lisa?'

'Ah. I thought you'd be asking me about those kids sooner rather than later.' Riley shuffled towards the edge of the roof, dragging Diane with him.

Sweat ran down Grant's back. 'Please tell me where to find Emily and Lisa.'

'You can't do anything for me.'

'If you tell me where to find the children it will be in your favour.'

'I've been inside for six years and I'm not going back there. It's enough to make a man lose his mind.'

If Riley didn't value his own life then Grant risked losing the children and Diane. They were five floors up and falling to the ground below would be lethal. And there was no way Billingham would have had time to get a sniper on scene. He must try another tactic.

'Did Jack Glover pay you to scare off Daniel Pearson? Did he give you money and ask you to break into Pearson's house? Is that the reason you abducted Jack's children?'

'The bastard set me up. I wore gloves the whole time. There's no way my thumbprint could have shown up at Pearson's except if Glover planted it there. I was sentenced to nine fucking years for it. And six almost killed me.'

'So abducting Jack's children is revenge.'

'Glover used me then he set me up. And he paid me a pittance for the job. One million doesn't even start to pay back for the lost time. Although taking his kids, well, that might do the trick.'

'Emily and Lisa didn't do anything wrong.'

'Who gives a fuck about those brats.'

'Please tell me where to find them.'

'If I tell you then he's won.'

Grant could not see a way around Riley's twisted logic.

Riley took a few more steps until he was right at the lip of the edge. 'Why don't I set you a little test? Which do you want most, your officer or the children?'

With Riley's arm choking her windpipe, Diane couldn't speak. Grant could see her mouthing something at him. He couldn't make it out except he knew what she was probably saying – 'the children.'

'I asked you a question. Answer or I'll decide for you,' Riley said.

'Both. And if that's not possible, then the children are my priority.'

'Oh, so this one is disposable?'

Riley was teetering on the edge and there was no way Grant would be able to overpower him without endangering everyone's life.

'God, I could do with a final snort.'

'Then why don't you have one? You're not in a rush, are you?' Grant said. He caught a movement and forced himself not to look. Could it be McGowan scuttling out from behind the elevator shaft, running towards the cover of the ventilator?

Riley laughed. 'You're a smart one aren't you, Inspector? Don't think you can trick me because it won't work.'

'There's no trick. I'll sit down if you like and then you can have a snort in peace. And my name's David Grant.'

'Okay. Grant. Keep your hands where I can see them.'

With the amount of blood which had pumped out of Diane it was a miracle she was still conscious. Grant could see she was going limp. Reaching into his pocket, Riley pulled out a small plastic bag.

'At least you've got balls,' Riley said. 'Unlike some police fucking officers I could mention.

Grant immediately picked up on Riley's tone. 'What do you mean?'

'Since we're having a nice chat and I'm not going to tell you where to find the brats, I might as well pass on something before I go.'

Riley stuck his finger into the bag and scrubbed powder around his gums. Breathing in deeply, he half closed his eyes. Grant saw McGowan crawling towards the nearest cover to Riley. Any closer and McGowan would be within Riley's eyeline. What was the distance between McGowan and Diane? More than ten metres by Grant's judgement. It was too far. By the time Riley saw McGowan coming, he'd have launched himself off the roof taking Diane with him.

'I'm all ears,' Grant said.

'I bet you are. Well get a load of this. I heard a lot of stuff when I was inside. Last person I shared a cell with was Parks. Poor bastard is dead now. Pancreatic cancer.'

Grant knew the name. Parks had been the mastermind behind the jewellery heist Riley had been involved in, though he was much higher up the criminal food chain than Riley.

'Parks was pissed off with one of your lot and I promised I'd do something about it if I could. Looks like this might be the moment.'

Riley's eyes were bulging from the cocaine hit. His legs started jittering. 'Parks hated this bloke called Treadgold who's some big job at your place. Seems like Parks and Treadgold used to get on, and then Treadgold turned and he made sure Parks got put away.'

Parks and Treadgold used to get on? It could only mean one thing. Treadgold had some deal with Parks in exchange for turning a blind eye to criminal activities. This was proof of Treadgold's corruption. Proof Grant had not been able to find before. He suddenly felt wary McGowan was overhearing this. Ruby had said McGowan met Treadgold on the stairwell and it happened just after Nick Riley's name came up in this case.

'If you want to fulfil your promise to Parks you've got to give me something concrete against Treadgold,' Grant said.

Riley was rubbing a second dose around his mouth. 'The jewels from the heist,' he said. 'They were fenced by a guy called Hector Mason. Treadgold got a cut and Mason will be able to confirm it.'

Bingo. Hector was a known fence, selling on stolen goods and sometimes turning informant if the police leaned on him hard. This would be enough to put Treadgold away. All Grant needed was to get to Mason first.

At that moment, McGowan charged out from his hiding place.

'No!' Grant shouted. 'Stand down, McGowan!'

Riley was taken by surprise but he was close enough to the edge to get there first. Riley took one glance back at Grant and grinned. Then he plummeted from the roof, his arms spread out as if he was flying.

Chapter Forty-nine

Lisa was too tired to cry and she was so thirsty her head and tongue hurt. Her arms and legs felt heavy and she couldn't lift them. She lay on the floor beside her sister. Emily was cold and she seemed to have fallen asleep and Lisa was not able to wake her.

'Shall I sing your favourite song again?' Lisa whispered in Emily's ear.

When Emily didn't answer, Lisa pretended she had.

'Yes all right, Em, I will.'

And she started humming the tune, though by now she'd forgotten all the words.

Chapter Fifty

Tom's phone pinged at the same time as Sarah's. He read the message from Grant.

Riley dead. No intel on the children.

Tom felt like his chest might explode. It was all down to him and Sarah. Nine? What could it mean? What did it mean?

Within their search area, there were four streets with houses numbered ninety and above and they'd already covered two of them. Tom met Sarah's hazel eyes.

'Oh shit, it's down to us,' he said.

Sarah was calm. 'We check the last two and then we regroup,' she said. 'Follow me.'

Tom was glad to be working with her. She knew how to keep her head when the pressure was on. She'd made no errors navigating around the back streets, dodging easily from one residential road to the next. It had saved them masses of time. She was fit too so they'd been able to keep a fast pace.

As they rounded the corner and jogged along the next row of houses, Tom's eyes drifted to a car parked halfway down. It had a logo of a blue cat painted on the side and a slogan – Nine Lives Insurance.

'Nine Lives! Sarah, look!'

It was parked outside number seventy-five which was in the middle of a long terrace. When Tom banged on the front door, he could feel his heart hammering. The woman who answered had hair dyed bright pink and gelled up in spikes.

'Can I help you?' she said.

Tom showed his identification. 'Is this your car?'

'It is. Why are you interested?'

'We need to question you in connection with the missing Glover children,' Tom said. 'May we come in please.'

Olwen Vickers, with the spiked hair, was very cooperative. They searched the two floors of her house and found nothing. Then they quizzed her about the name of her business.

'I'm a financial consultant,' Olwen said. 'I work a lot from home and I interview most of my clients via the internet. The car is part of my advertising.'

Tom showed a picture of Emily and Lisa. 'Have you seen these children? Or any suspicious activity in the street recently? Any strangers coming and going?'

'I've seen those two little ones all over the news and if I'd spotted them I'd have contacted the police straight away. I'm sorry, I don't think I can help you. As for strangers, well, in this area there's a pretty high turnover. A lot of these places are let out and people come and go all the time.'

Sarah brought up a picture of Riley and of Maria Fernandez. 'What about these two? Do they look familiar?'

Olwen hesitated. 'The girl definitely not and he looks like any ordinary bloke doesn't he, though with those ears… I dunno, I suppose it could be the tosser who took my parking space. He had the cheek to plonk his bloody van right outside my house. I had to ask him to move and he had a hoodie on and his ears were hidden but I kinda got the idea they stuck out.'

'I saw the disabled parking bay. You've got a dedicated space,' Sarah said.

'The council gave it and it's legit.'

'What colour was this van?' Tom asked.

'White.'

A common colour, yet the same as the van seen leaving the lockups in Himlands Heath. Could it be the same one? Tom found it hard not to spring to his feet. 'And do you know where the owner lives?'

'Oh yes he moved in two doors down earlier this year. I remember because that's when he took my spot. Number seventy-one.'

They didn't have a positive identification on Riley. They had the number nine and a white van. It was sufficient. It gave them power of entry to save life and limb.

Tom was covered in sweat. He banged on the door of number seventy-one. There was no answer.

'We're going in,' Tom said.

Sarah nodded.

They checked the windows and there was no sign of movement inside. Tom didn't have time to go around the back. Emily was dying. She might already be dead. He found a brick by the neighbour's wall and used it to break the front window.

It took seconds to clear away the dangerous shards. Sarah was right behind him as he climbed in.

They quickly searched the downstairs where it smelled of stale takeaways and manky carpets.

'Look at this,' Sarah said. 'Drug paraphernalia. And plenty of booze.'

Tom was already on his way up the stairs. He found the room with new locks outside. 'They're here,' he shouted, 'Stand back. And call an ambulance.'

A few solid kicks and the door was down. Inside, Lisa lay on the floor and she blinked as Tom knelt by her side though she was not able to speak. Emily was on her back with her eyes closed. Her body was covered with purple splotches and Tom couldn't find a pulse.

Chapter Fifty-one

Grant and McGowan reached Diane at the same time.

'Get a paramedic up here,' Grant shouted. He placed his hands over the wound.

Riley had jumped from the roof, which Grant was pretty sure had been Riley's intention in the first place.

By rushing forward, McGowan had endangered Diane's life. It would have been easy for Riley to take her down with him and McGowan had deliberately disobeyed a direct order. The question was, why? Grant wasn't ready to face the answer.

Two paramedics came running. Down below, officers were attending to Riley and it wasn't long before Billingham sent Grant a confirmation.

Riley is stone cold dead.

Diane was placed on a stretcher.

'We're taking her now, sir,' one of the paramedics said.

Grant bent to Diane's ear. 'I'll be checking on you,' he said. 'Hang on in there.'

He hated the helplessness. She was out of his hands now and he had to trust the medics.

'Take care of her,' he called after them.

She was carried to the stairs and Grant waited until Billingham was on the roof before he tackled McGowan. It was always good practice to have a reliable witness.

'Detective Sergeant McGowan you will go straight to the station and report to Detective Chief Superintendent Fox.'

'What's wrong, guv?'

It took huge willpower for Grant to rein back his fury. 'You endangered the abductor's life and your fellow officer's. You ignored my command – I told you to stay where you were.'

'I didn't hear you because of the wind. I saw a chance with Riley and took it.'

McGowan was a damn liar and now Grant knew it. His phone pinged. Whipping it out of his pocket, Grant read the message from Delaney.

We have Emily and Lisa.

The wave of relief was physical.

A second message came through. *Emily in a critical state.*

'They've found the children.'

'Jesus, I thought we'd blown it with Riley out of the picture,' Billingham said.

'Me too,' Grant said, his tone dark.

'Brilliant work. The chemist tip-off was the right one then?' Billingham asked.

'I don't have details. Lisa and Emily have been taken to hospital and Delaney says Emily is critical.'

'At least she's alive, sir. Sounds like Delaney got there just in time,' McGowan said.

Grant gritted his teeth. And it was lucky for McGowan Delaney had made it because with Riley splattered below there was no chance to squeeze him for information, was there? Without Delaney, those children would have been dead.

'Like I told you,' Grant said, 'Go straight to the station and report to DCS Fox.' Grant's tone was deadly dark and he turned and walked away. He sent a message to DCS Fox – *Urgent. DS McGowan is to be relieved of duty. Bring Hector Mason into protective custody. I'll explain later.*

Chapter Fifty-two

In the back of the ambulance, Sylvie overheard people talking about Nick Riley jumping from the roof. It meant she had a chance. Now there was nothing to connect her to Riley. Maria, the only other loose end, was also taken care of. It had been useful Maria was the one to risk dropping off the phone and after that Maria was disposable. Sylvie congratulated herself on her idea of giving Maria an overdose.

It seemed ages ago that Sylvie had seen Nick Riley meet with Maria in Himlands Heath. After Maria had handed him the key from the Glover house, Sylvie had followed him and spotted him entering a pub. It had been dark inside with the usual British pub smell of beer and old carpeting. She had got to the bar just as he was handed a pint.

Sweeping back her hair, Sylvie smiled at him and then at the barman.

'A white wine please.'

Apart from a pockmarked face, the most notable thing about him was the way his ears stuck out. He stared at Sylvie like she was an alien. When she went to pay, she deliberately dropped her purse. He retrieved it for her.

'Gosh that's kind of you. There aren't many gentlemen around these days.'

It had been funny to watch confusion spread across his face. That's when she realised he wasn't used to attention from women. Which meant he would be easier to manipulate. Sylvie had cut him another smile.

'Looks as if I've been stood up.'

'A nice girl like you. I can't believe it.'

She raised her glass. 'Cheers.'

When he introduced himself he fumbled his drink and beer slopped over.

'Pleased to meet you too,' Sylvie said. 'I suppose it's my bad luck you're probably meeting someone special.'

As her chat-up line met him head on, he froze, a band of froth clinging to his upper lip as he stared at her.

'I'm not meeting anyone. I only popped in for a quick pint.'

He had a rasp to his voice and his eyes were cold and hard yet she sensed a weakness in him. She guessed he didn't get many offers like hers.

She shimmied up onto a bar stool and crossed one leg over the other. 'Oh, really? At least something's turning in my favour.'

Chapter Fifty-three

Ruby got to Brighton as quickly as she could. She waited while Sylvie Delacourt was treated by paramedics. They had Sylvie in the back of an ambulance, checking her over.

'Ruby,' Grant called, as he jogged towards her.

'I heard what happened to Riley,' Ruby said.

'Listen,' Grant said. 'We found them. We've got Emily and Lisa.' Grant led her away from the ambulance.

'Thank goodness,' Ruby said.

'Yes, though...'

'What is it, sir?'

'Emily might not make it.'

Ruby watched as Grant wiped at the corner of his eye.

'Delaney got there just in time,' Grant said. 'Emily was in a critical state and I'm waiting on news.' Grant glanced at his phone as if willing it to ring.

'Oh no.' She clutched his arm. 'What happened on the roof, sir?'

'It's complicated. Diane lost a lot of blood and I've sent McGowan back to the station – I'll explain later. How is Sylvie?'

'Sylvie's in a state of shock,' Ruby said. 'She told me she's been kept prisoner. It seems Riley ambushed her. He kept her handcuffed to the bed and Sylvie says he drugged her.'

'Does she need to go to hospital?'

'I don't think so. The paramedics told me she doesn't have any physical injuries.' Ruby scrunched her nose. 'I'm not certain Sylvie's story is as straightforward as it seems.'

Grant raised an eyebrow. He thought back to when he was in the bedroom with Sylvie. Her wrists had not been sore from the cuffs. It had struck him as odd.

'I've not got time for nuances right now. Care to elaborate?'

'Why would Riley keep Sylvie locked up? The man already had Emily and Lisa so what did he want with the au pair?'

'I agree her story doesn't make sense. That's why I wanted you here.' Grant ran his hand through his hair. 'Sylvie is saying she's the victim in this but maybe it's not as straightforward as it seems. Give me a minute.'

Lack of a red mark on her wrists. Was it enough? Did he have grounds to arrest Sylvie Delacourt? Was there more to the au pair's story? Grant was finding it difficult to concentrate because he *needed* to know about Emily. And Diane.

'Sir?' Ruby asked.

Grant watched as Billingham's officers wound the operation down. Emily had been flown to the hospital by air ambulance. Grant paced. It was only minutes, though it seemed like an eternity before Grant received a message from his paediatrician friend.

I have Emily. She's in intensive care and it will be touch and go until the antibiotics have a chance to act. She's slightly conscious which is a good sign, though she is not yet out of danger.

Grant sent his silent thanks skyward.

He tapped a quick 'thank you' reply then turned back to Ruby. He trusted her judgement and his own take on the au pair. There was more here. He needed to search for one final piece of evidence concerning the identity of Nick Riley's true accomplice.

Chapter Fifty-four

Sylvie pushed her hair back from her face. She closed her eyes and listened to the paramedics talking as they went about checking her over.

A lot had happened since she'd followed Nick to the pub and chatted him up. That day, he'd been practically drooling over her by the time she delivered her ultimatum.

'I know you're up to something with Maria,' she'd told him. 'If that's even her name. I know she got friendly with me to wheedle her way close to the Glovers. Tell me what you're up to or I'm going to the police.'

It had been a huge gamble. If they hadn't been in a public place maybe Nick would have hurt her. As it was, Sylvie had already given him a hard-on by stroking his leg and he had seemed stunned by her mouth and by the threat which came out of it.

'How do you know? Did Maria tell you?' he asked.

'She's too stupid for that. It was pure chance -- I saw Maria take a key. Then I followed her and that's how I met sweet little you.'

Nick had a mean, pinched face. 'What do you want?'

'I want an in.'

It had been a brazen request and Sylvie knew it. The bitter kick in the gut she'd received from Jack Glover spurred her on.

Nick sized her up. She watched him trying to get a handle on her and failing. To give him a bit more persuasion, she slid her hand back towards his dick.

'How do I know you're not a cop?' Nick asked.

'Give me a break, do I look like one? Besides, I hate the Glovers. So any plans you've got to screw them, I'm interested. And I don't want Maria to know. You and me get to be partners in whatever scam you're pulling off and we'll do it behind her back.'

Nick had shaken his head in incomprehension. Of course, he had no idea Sylvie had been on the verge of telling Maria the biggest and most important secret of her whole life only to discover Maria wasn't a friend at all. She'd been stringing Sylvie along and Sylvie didn't like feeling a fool, nor being screwed with.

Nick had been cautious and cynical, of course he had, until, a while later, he started to appreciate her.

The paramedic took the blood pressure cuff off Sylvie's arm. 'We'll take you to the hospital for some quick blood tests and then you'll be able to go, miss,' he said. 'You have no physical injuries from your incarceration though you may suffer from the mental stress.'

'It was horrible,' Sylvie said. 'He was a mad man. I won't ever feel the same again.'

'Hmm. If you experience worrying symptoms in the next few days, I recommend you make an appointment with your doctor.'

She leant her head back. 'I still feel so shaky.'

The paramedic tucked the blanket around her. 'After the ordeal you've had, you'll need to take things slowly.'

'Thank you, I will,' Sylvie said.

The detectives were hanging around the back of the ambulance and she needed to get her story straight for when they questioned her. Sylvie hoped she'd be able to shake them off and then get to the money before they did.

Chapter Fifty-five

Blood had been taken from Sylvie to find out what substances Riley had forced into her. Sylvie complained of memory blanks and overwhelming anxiety and the paramedics said she might be suffering from Post-Traumatic Stress Disorder.

Grant went to Himlands Heath high street. He wanted to question business owners and then he needed to get to the hospital and talk to the children and bring in forensics to check their clothing. Dealing with McGowan's suspension was in Fox's hands.

An hour later Grant was sitting at his desk impatient for the lab to contact him when they finally did.

No intoxicants in Sylvie Delacourt's blood.

Bingo.

*

Grant's expression was grim as he read Sylvie her rights. 'Sylvie Delacourt, I am placing you under arrest for conspiracy to commit abduction, false imprisonment and demanding money with menaces…'

The young woman refused to have a lawyer present. Grant took her to an interview room where Ruby was waiting.

'I'm going to be recording this,' Grant said. 'Let's start with everyone saying their name for the record and then I want you to tell me how you came to be at Riley's house.'

'Why have you brought me here? Why have you arrested me?' Sylvie asked. 'I'm the victim here and you're treating me like a criminal! I have rights. He took me by force. Riley was a mad man.'

'And now he's dead and I can't get his side of the story. I need to piece together what happened.'

'The stuff he pushed down my throat messed with my mind. It's all a jumble.'

Grant flipped open the lab report. 'There were no intoxicants in your blood.'

Sylvie didn't miss a beat and she started to cry.

'Perhaps you could begin with how you got to be with Nick Riley?' Grant asked.

Ruby passed over a box of tissues. 'Take your time, Ms Delacourt.'

'All I remember is coming out of work late.' *Sniff.*

'Are you talking about your job as a waitress at the seafront coffee bar?' Grant asked.

'That's right.' *Sniff.* 'It was dark. He must have been waiting because he pounced on me and put a hood over my head.'

'And this was when?'

'I'm not sure. It's all mixed up in my head.'

'My colleague and I questioned you at the coffee bar,' Ruby said. 'Was it the same day?'

'Maybe. I don't know.'

'And around what time?' Grant asked.

'About ten thirty.'

The Inspector nodded. 'Was there anyone around? Did you shout for help?'

'It was stupid of me when I think about it because I went out the back entrance. It gives out onto an alleyway and it's shorter to walk home. I didn't see anyone. When he forced the hood over my head I panicked. I couldn't breathe. I thought I was going to die.'

'I see. And then?'

'The next thing I remember I was chained to a bed and that's where I stayed until you found me.'

*

Ruby was watching Sylvie very carefully. 'Did Riley speak to you?' she asked.

'I don't remember.'

Ruby made encouraging noises. 'Hmm. What about food and drink?'

'I had water, and he let me use the bathroom. Of course, I thought about escaping and it was impossible. Why are you asking me these things? He attacked me. He kept me chained up.'

'We're trying to understand why Nick Riley would snatch you *after* he took Emily and Lisa. You said you don't know him,' Ruby said.

'I've never met him before, no.'

'Except it seems he knew you and he knew enough to know where you worked. Is it possible he met you while you were working for the Glovers?' Grant asked.

Sylvie was screwing a tissue up and ripping it to pieces. She kept shifting around and glancing at the uniformed constable in the corner. It was as if she felt her captor was still there, though Ruby was not fooled. Sylvie Delacourt had been a brilliant actress from the beginning. For a moment, Sylvie stopped and considered Grant's idea.

'If he was following Emily and Lisa then I suppose it's possible he saw me from a distance. I mean, you hear about people who get obsessed, on the news and stuff. Do you think he might have been the type to get fixated on me?'

'When he had you tied up, did he touch you?' Ruby asked.

'I d-don't think so.' Sylvie started crying again. 'How can I be sure? Maybe he d-did something and I can't remember it!'

'And he never mentioned Emily and Lisa? He never spoke about them?' Grant asked.

'He liked to sit on the end of the bed and stare at me. It was creepy. I was freaked out and who knows what the hell was going on inside his head. I just wanted him to get away. And no, he didn't talk about the children.'

*

Grant glanced at Ruby and he gave a small nod. Grant had a brown envelope in front of him and he slid out a photograph. 'Do you recognise this person?' he asked.

Sylvie peered at it. 'I don't think so.'

'A yes or no answer please,' Grant said.

'No. I've no idea who it is.'

'You've told a very convincing story,' Grant said. 'Now I'd like to tell you what I think. You told my officers you are pregnant and Jack Glover is the father. This is what I believe happened -- you and Maria Fernandez became friends. Then at some point, you realised you were being played and you found out Riley and Maria's aim which was to kidnap Emily and Lisa and demand a ransom. At that point you could have come to the police and you didn't. Instead, you recognised a wonderful opportunity for getting back at Jack and for cashing in at the same time. I think you teamed up with Nick Riley. Likely that was your real reason for moving down to Brighton.'

'That's crazy. You're making it up.'

'Was it you who copied the key to the Hardman's house and then slipped it back where it should be? Or Maria?'

'I don't know what you're talking about. This Maria woman, I've never met her.'

'Untrue. I have video footage of the two of you together at a gym in Himlands Heath. You seem to be quite friendly with Maria Fernandez, in fact, the staff there told me you trained together frequently during the time you worked for the Glovers.'

It hadn't taken much for Grant to find out Maria frequented the gym. The staff confirmed his suspicion the two young women knew each other. What he couldn't work out was how exactly Sylvie got in on the kidnapping plan.

'Wait. Oh yes now I remember. Yeah sure, I met up with her once or twice on the treadmills though I don't remember her name. So what? I've no idea what she might have been up to. If you think she's involved in abducting the children why don't you ask her yourself? Instead of trying to drag me into it.'

Grant took out a second photograph. It was a crime scene shot of Maria's body. 'Because Maria Fernandez is dead. But I think you knew that already, didn't you.'

'Riley abducted me! He kept me against my will. You're not allowed to talk to me like that.'

'You colluded with Riley in the abduction of Emily and Lisa. You knew the location of the children all along. When officers arrived at Riley's residence you chained yourself to the bed to make it look as if you were innocent, and you concocted your whole story. That's why there were no marks on your wrists from the cuffs, because you'd just put them on.'

'Did you have handcuffs with you the whole time?' Ruby asked. 'Just in case we came after Riley and you needed an escape story?'

Grant placed his hands flat on the table. 'That was quite clever. You might be interested to know we've located the one million. Will we find your prints on the notes? I think so.'

Billingham's team had recovered the money stashed in Riley's van, in a garage several streets from the apartment block.

'You kept the location of the children secret even though you met with me and with my officers. At Riley's house, you also declined to pass vital information on about their whereabouts, even when you had another chance to save them.'

'You're making this up. I'm innocent. You don't have a shred of evidence–'

'That's where you're wrong,' Grant said. 'It seems you have a favourite shampoo with an orange scent and Lisa Glover recognised it from your hair. You left them for dead. Lisa told us the last person who visited them in the locked room was a new woman. You wore a mask but Lisa realised it was you.'

'From the scent of my hair? For god's sake, Lisa is a child! She's mistaken. I never went there. You can't take the word of a four-year-old...'

Grant fixed Sylvie with his grey eyes. He'd met despicable criminals in his time and Sylvie Delacourt was one of the worst – a young woman willing to throw away the lives of two children. He savoured his final words.

'There's also the fact a long hair was found on the front of Emily's clothing. It's the same colour as yours. It will be tested for DNA and I'm sure it will be a match. The only explanation is – you visited them in the locked room. On at least one occasion. Which means you were Nick Riley's accomplice.'

*

With Sylvie Delacourt in custody, Grant finally allowed himself to relax. *To hell with the paperwork,* he thought, and he drove straight back to the hospital.

Lisa had been dangerously dehydrated but she was slowly gaining strength. Emily's situation was more serious. The paediatrician met him outside Emily's room.

'How's she doing?' Grant asked.

'Emily came very close to dying but she's a strong little girl. As I suspected, she had sepsis. By the time your officers found her, she'd gone into septic shock. It will take forty-eight hours for the antibiotics to do their job.'

'It was pretty close then.'

'The child was near death. Even a few moments more and it might have been too late.' She placed her hand on Grant's arm. 'Seems like you did a fantastic job finding them.'

'Not me. It was everyone.'

She laughed. 'Yeah, you always say that.'

*

Grant's next stop was checking on Diane. The nurse told him she was out of the operating theatre and the doctors had been able to repair the damage. *Thank goodness, no ostomy bag for Diane.* Diane was asleep, surrounded by her husband and three sons. Grant scribbled a get well soon note and left it by her bedside.

Emily and Lisa were safe. Riley was dead and Sylvie Delacourt would be sentenced. For the first time in days, he could have a proper night's sleep.

Chapter Fifty-six

It wasn't until the following day that Tom and Ruby met Alice at the hospital. Tom had never seen Alice so happy and she definitely had a new confidence about her.

When Alice saw Tom she rushed towards him and flung her arms around his neck. 'I've so wanted to see you. Thank you. Thank you so much for saving my children.'

'My pleasure,' Tom mumbled.

They walked towards Lisa's room and every time Alice looked at him, she smiled. It was sort of nice and it was kind of embarrassing too.

'Not used to being the hero?' Ruby teased.

Tom went red. 'DI Hunter had her part to play in it.'

'Except I know hers was a minor one,' Alice said. 'Come and see Lisa. She wants to give you a hug.'

After a night in hospital Lisa was able to walk and the doctors said she could go home soon. Emily's situation was now stable though she was still only permitted to see her mother. Not even her grandmother had been allowed beyond the glass window of Emily's room.

'My mother insisted I tell you again how grateful she is, Tom,' Alice said. 'And guess what? Emily wants to be a police officer when she grows up and she'd like to see you as soon as she can.'

Tom smiled. 'Oh don't you worry about that, she won't be able to keep me away.'

When Lisa saw Tom she clung onto him like a koala, with both arms and both legs. 'You save me and you saved Emmy.'

When Alice eventually persuaded Lisa to let Tom go, Lisa proudly handed over a drawing. 'This is you.'

It was a picture of Tom carrying her and Emily from the house, with one child tucked under each arm. She had drawn him with sticking up hair and big boots. One child was crying and the other had their eyes closed.

Tom stared at it and felt a big lump in his throat.

'What a lovely picture. How is Emily doing?' Ruby asked.

'The doctors are happy with her progress. She's talking which is a very good sign and they don't think she has any permanent organ damage. She's still fragile, and it might take a couple of weeks, but they expect her to make a full recovery. A few minutes later, and well, you know…' Alice dabbed at her eyes. 'But this isn't a day for being tearful. What you did was wonderful and I'll never forget it.'

When they left, Ruby linked her arm in Tom's.

'Are you going to put Lisa's picture on your wall?' she asked.

'If I do, are you going to come see it?'

Ruby smiled and tipped her head on one side in that nice way she had. 'Maybe.'

And Tom really hoped she meant it.

*

On another hospital ward, Jack Glover had regained consciousness. They knew the first thing his wife had said to him was, she was going ahead with the divorce.

Zofia Kaminski had reported that Jack raped her at the Christmas party. She had decided to press charges. Once she knew of Jack's part in Daniel Pearson's break-in, it made her change her mind about keeping silent. Zofia said she owed it to the other women Jack had assaulted and to Pearson. All those years ago, she had gone to the police after the rape and they had photographic and biological evidence on file, which was enough for a prosecution to go ahead.

Chapter Fifty-seven

Assistant Chief Constable Treadgold was suspended.

Grant knew they had enough to convict him. Hector Mason, the fence, was willing to testify that jewellery from the heist had been given to Treadgold as a payoff for his silence. Treadgold's trail of corruption had finally caught up with him. Once the investigation completed, Treadgold would be facing a custodial sentence.

As Grant found out on their previous case, Treadgold had turned a blind eye to murders in the past and it looked as if Treadgold had been accepting payments from criminals for years. Hector Mason, the middle man, would be placed in a safe house until Treadgold's enquiry was complete.

Grant was in Fox's office. Fox had her back to Grant and she was staring out the window.

'It looks as if we'll get enough to charge Treadgold. When it hits the media, the hacks will have a field day. Dishonest officers tarnish all of us.'

'True, and then the storm will blow over, and for the moment we're basking in the Glover story,' Grant said. 'Enjoy it. The press can't get enough of those two blonde lovelies.'

'The video of DS Delaney pushing Emily on the swings was the clincher. It's all over the television,' Fox said.

'It's her smile I like.'

'I didn't know you were such a softie. You never cease to amaze me, Grant. How on earth did you pull this case off?'

'By having the best team in the business.'

'No, by being the best boss in the business which is why…' Fox sat down and gave him a level stare. '… why I'm recommending you for a promotion. They're looking for someone to head up the South East Major Incident Team.'

The MIT? *Goodness,* Grant thought, *that would be a real challenge.*

'Ma'am, I'm not sure.'

She wafted her hand. 'Think about it and keep it to yourself for the moment, until you've made your decision.' She sniffed and placed one finger on the top of McGowan's file. 'If there's one thing I can't stand it's rotten apples in the barrel. An officer like McGowan could have gone on to be as dirty as Treadgold. It turns out McGowan has a gambling habit. I guess Treadgold paying him for information was too much of a temptation.'

Grant would never forgive McGowan for the betrayal nor for endangering Diane's life. You could never underestimate the power of money. McGowan had sold out for the lure of easy backhanders from Treadgold. And for it, Steve McGowan was also suspended pending an investigation and he would be losing his badge.

Fox sighed. 'It's been exhausting. Well done, David, and I mean it.'

'Thank you, ma'am. And thank you for putting my name forward for the MIT.'

She snorted. 'Don't let it go to your head, and if you don't mind, I've got a mountain of administration to get through.'

He got the hint. As he was about to step out of the room, Fox looked up from her keyboard and called after him. 'Oh yes I almost forgot, will you be doing a drinks thing for your birthday?'

Fox had the nerve to pretend innocence. He almost laughed out loud as he waited for the punchline.

'Fifty-eight it'll be this year, won't it?' Fox said, the triumph in her voice unmistakable.

'That's right.' Grant said. Fox never could resist getting the knife in about his age, could she. And he laughed all the way back to the cubbyhole.

Chapter Fifty-eight

Ruby was glad to attend the funeral service for Maria Fernandez. She and Tom were there representing Sussex Police because Grant was still caught up dealing with Treadgold and McGowan. It was sad how few people attended – only six in all. One of them was Maria's brother, Billy.

Afterwards, Ruby laid flowers by Maria's resting place and Billy came to speak to her.

'Thank you. My sister always liked flowers,' he said. 'Where we grew up, there were tennis courts down the road and she used to like going there. Not to watch the tennis but because they grew flowers alongside the courts.'

'My condolences,' Ruby said. 'I'm sorry you lost your sister.'

'Listen, I want you to know Maria wasn't a bad girl, it was Riley who ruined her with drugs. She tried so hard to break the habit. In the end, it was ruining my life as well as hers because she kept asking for money until one day I snapped. I told her I never wanted to see her again. Of course, I bitterly regret that now. I wish I'd been there to help her.'

'Maria helped us to find Emily and Lisa,' Tom said. 'When she died, she left a message which led us to the right place.'

'Did she?'

'Yes,' Ruby said. 'Without it, the children would never have been found in time.'

Billy was fighting back the tears and he gripped Ruby's arm. 'She always was kind at heart. Thank you for telling me Maria did good in the end.'

Chapter Fifty-nine

With thirty stitches needed in her abdomen, Diane had been lucky. She was expected to make a full recovery, though it would take time. Tom emptied a bag of grapes into the bowl and pulled up a chair.

'How're you feeling?' Ruby asked.

'I move a centimetre and it's agony,' Diane said. 'And for goodness sake don't make me laugh because that's the worst. Have you heard any more about McGowan?'

'He's been suspended pending an investigation,' Tom said. 'And so has Assistant Chief Constable Treadgold. The word is Treadgold will be going down, and McGowan will be dismissed. Grant is knee-deep in it at the moment.'

'To think Steve was passing on information behind our backs,' Diane said. 'After all we've been through together.'

'I didn't like him from the beginning but running at Riley like he did,' Ruby said. 'Wow. It was complete lunacy.'

No one mentioned how McGowan had risked Diane's life.

'Steve was as corrupt as Treadgold. I would never have believed it,' Tom said. 'It makes me feel sad he did it for money. I heard they've found gambling debts and cash transferred to Steve's accounts. It looks like Treadgold was paying him for information on our previous case.'

'How's Grant taking it?' Diane said.

'He's satisfied he can finally nail Treadgold for corruption though the part about McGowan, well, I think it's been a horrible kick in the gut.' Ruby helped herself to some of Diane's grapes. 'Grant doesn't want to talk about it.'

'Uh-oh that's not a good sign. I guess I should wait to tell Grant my news then,' Diane said.

Tom had a horrible sinking feeling. Being betrayed by McGowan was the worst. They'd been colleagues, friends even, and Tom had always felt McGowan had his back. Now what? Don't tell him Diane had decided to quit?

Diane patted his hand. 'Don't look so glum. I've got a long recuperation ahead of me and I'm not going to leave the police force although… I think it's time for a change of direction. When I was following up on Zofia Kaminski it reminded me how I've always wanted to work with the Sexual Assault Unit. I put it on the back burner except now I feel the time's right. I'm going to ask for a transfer to SAU.'

Tom tried to take it on the chin. 'The SAU. Right. They're pretty neat, so I've heard. I'm going to miss you. Wow, it'll be cosy, just Grant and me.'

'I'll still be around. No need to act like I'm going to another planet. Oh, and I heard on the grapevine there are big changes coming up for everyone,' Diane said. 'No, no I can't say more or I'll be in trouble. Oh gosh.' She frowned. 'Sorry, I'm getting a splitting headache.'

Diane refused to be pumped for more information and Ruby ushered Tom out the door. 'Diane needs to rest. Hey, don't be upset about her news. Emily and Lisa are safe. Revel in the successes for a while.'

'And what about the future? We've lost McGowan, and Diane wants to leave and it sounds like there's a shake-up on the horizon. Grant asked you to dinner tomorrow, right?'

'Yes. You too then?'

'I thought it was to celebrate the Glover case only what if it isn't? What if he's got something more serious to tell us?'

'Don't worry about it, if he's got news I don't think it will be bad. Sarah Hunter told me she's invited as well.'

Ruby looked into Tom's dark eyes and he caught the change in her expression. They'd been friends for a while now. Don't say Ruby was ready for a new direction too? He didn't think he could stand losing her.

'What?' he asked.

Ruby put her hand to Tom's cheek. 'This,' she said softly. And she brought her lips to Tom's and gave him a long sensual kiss.

Epilogue

Sometimes Grant felt sorry for his wife, Lily. She wanted him to take early retirement and the two of them go on some goddam cruise. He couldn't think of anything worse though his daughter had laughingly told him if he ever did go on that sort of vacation, there was likely to be one mammoth Agatha Christie case for him to solve, stuck in the middle of some ocean.

Heading up the Major Incident Team would be a big step up and bring him the most difficult cases in the business. He loved a challenge but was that what he really wanted at his age? Did he have a few more years left to give? Or was it time for retirement and a quieter life. Maybe settle down as a private investigator somewhere?

Opening up the letter he'd just written on the matter, Grant checked it again. It was definitely time for a change. He signed the letter with a flourish, and with a small smile, sealed the envelope closed.

*****

A message from Ann Girdharry –

Hello,

Thank you so much for choosing Deadly Lies.

One of the things I love about being an author is hearing direct from readers.

So if you'd like to get in touch, please do. You might have a question about one of my books, or maybe you have a general question about publishing. Or maybe you've spotted a typo or an error.

Whatever it is, feel free to send me an email. I'd be delighted to hear from you.

If you're an avid reader and you'd like to receive news and updates, I'd love you to join my Reader's Group. Don't worry, no spam. I'll only get in touch when I have something I think you might genuinely be interested in, like the release of a new book. I offer a free gift to new members and you can find details on my webpage – www.girdharry.com.

Happy Reading,
Ann Girdharry
Email – ann@girdharry.com

Good Girl Bad Girl (Kal and Marty book 1)

The darkest crimes can't stay hidden forever…

A young body washed up by the river in London, and a matron murdered at a children's home thousands of miles away…could there be a link?

Only one person wants to find out – Kal. Why does she want to know? Because Kal's journalist mother was researching the story and now she's missing.

Kal's father was a criminal, which is why she trusts no one and least of all Detective Inspector Spinks. Kal takes on the investigation herself. She's going to need all the skills she learnt from her father, especially when she discovers a link between her own family and the crimes that are being committed.

Trafficking, deception and dark family secrets - she'll be forced to confront her own worst nightmares, and form an alliance with the police, if they're going to nail a twisted killer.

What readers are saying –

'A stunning read'

'On the edge of my seat'

''Loved the characters and the writing!'

'Great to have female leads who were strong but realistically vulnerable at times too. Can't wait to read about these characters again!'

Good Girl Bad Girl is an Eric Hoffer Book Award Finalist.

Grab your copy today!

London Noir (Kal and Marty book 2)

A predator who tracks prostitutes…

When a woman is murdered in her own bed, Kal and Marty suspect the killer is a predator who tracks former prostitutes.

Kal befriends Sophie, a troubled young woman. Sophie suffers from nightmares and memory loss.
Her mother was murdered when she was a child. Sophie was there and she can't remember a thing about it.

But the deeper Kal digs, the more she unearths disturbing secrets.
Working with Marty and Detective Spinks, she realises they're dealing with a twisted mind, more clever than anyone could imagine.

There's a predator hiding in plain sight, moving ever closer. And it's time to kill the one who got away…

Praise for *London Noir*-

'A five-star thriller which keeps you guessing until the end'

'Highly recommended'

'Had me hooked from the beginning'

'Well that was a twist I didn't see coming'

Grab your copy today!

Acknowledgements

A huge thank you to my wonderful beta readers - Greta, Kat, Kate, Kiltie and Shalini.

Special thanks to Mark Romain for checking through the police procedural elements. Mark was a Metropolitan Police officer for thirty years. He spent two stints on homicide, the last one spanning ten years, and worked on a number of high-profile cases.

Avid crime readers can be assured any mistakes in the storyline are entirely my own or included for dramatic effect!

Titles by this Author

Deadly Motives
Deadly Secrets
Deadly Lies

Good Girl Bad Girl
London Noir
The Beauty Killers

The Couple Upstairs
The Woman in Room 19

Printed in Great Britain
by Amazon

34437791R00159